# ARTiSTiC

## *differences*

# ARTiStiC

## *differences*

## *Charlie Hauck*

*William Morrow and Company, Inc. • New York*

◆ ◆ ◆

HAU

Library of Congress Cataloging-in-Publication Data

Hauck, Charlie.
    Artistic differences / by Charlie Hauck.
       p.      cm.
    ISBN 0-688-12152-7
    I. Title.
    PS3558.A7562A89   1993
    813'.54—dc20            92-43759
                         CIP

Printed in the United States of America

First Edition

1  2  3  4  5  6  7  8  9  10

BOOK DESIGN BY LINEY LI

JUN 1 4 1993

*For Flannery, Maurice, Seth, and Perry*

# *Acknowledgments*

I'd like to thank the following for contributing anecdotes to this book:

Eric Cohen, Bob Ellison, Cliff Fagin, Rod Parker, Jerry Perzigian, Bob Schiller, Don Siegel, Ed. Weinberger, Bob Weiskopf, Tom Whedon and, particularly, Arthur Julian.

This is a work of fiction. These characters are imaginary. Any impulse on the reader's part to perceive them as actual, while flattering to the author, is misguided.

■ *Phil Silvers won acclaim on Broadway in* Top Banana, *portraying the egomaniacal star of a television variety show who went so far as to wear a whistle around his neck at rehearsals and blow it in everybody's ear. The character was based on Milton Berle, which was widely known and added to most theatergoers' enjoyment of Silvers's performance.*

*One night after the show, Silvers was told, "Milton Berle was in the audience. He wants to come back and see you." Silvers waited in his dressing room, anxious about Milton Berle's reaction to this rather cruel portrayal. But Berle entered in a good mood, all smiles and appreciation. "Phil, you were beautiful," he said. "I plotzed. Hilarious. What a fantastic thing you did out there. You nailed it."*

*And then, leaning in confidentially, Berle added, "You know something? I know pricks like that."*

◆ ◆ ◆

# ARTiStiC
## *differences*

# *C h a p t e r*

# *1*

■ At a wrap party for *The Mary Tyler Moore* series, one of
the producers was attracted to a striking young woman who
stood unattended. He chatted with her briefly, then offered to get
her something from the bar. Over the drinks he asked, "Are you
with anybody?"

"Yes," she said.

"Oh," he said. "Who are you with?"

"International Creative Management," she said.

◆ ◆ ◆

I met Geneva Holloway at a memorial service for Milo Lally's dog.
In fact, I drove her home. In fact, it was that night, inspired by
her beauty and proximity, that I first articulated my now widely
appreciated theory that producing a half-hour television comedy is
exactly like Chapter Thirty-seven of *Moby Dick*.

Milo Lally was what's known in the television industry as a
"hyphenate." A writer-producer is a hyphenate, or a producer-
director. Milo was an actor-masseur. We were in the same therapy
group. I'd recently been through a divorce. Milo's main issue in
group was his difficulty in relating to women. He was quite wrench-
ing when he talked about his hunger for intimacy. Of course, he
could also bring you to tears when he talked about the berries
from his neighbor's mulberry tree splotching all over his driveway,
which is one reason I'm against having actors in group.

Milo was not incapable of intimacy. It was just that he denied it to the young women who streamed through his home and life and invested it instead in Larry, a thirteen-year-old smokey-yellow Labrador whose passing we gathered to observe that warm October evening six years ago. Milo and Larry transcended the bonds of owner and pet; they were a couple. They were consistently referred to as a unit; a hostess might be asked, for example, "Are Milo and Larry here yet?" People who hadn't met them assumed them to be a gay twosome. They were featured equally on Milo's Christmas cards. The last one had shown them sailing down the Pacific Coast Highway in Milo's open-topped Jeep, both wearing Santa hats: "Merry Christmas from Milo and Larry." When our therapist's mother died, I noticed a wreath at the foot of the coffin that came "with deepest sympathy from Milo and Larry."

Milo lived on a dangerous curve in Beverly Glen. I shot by his house—a tiny box with high fencing, suggesting a compound—and pulled into a narrow canyon street around the corner from the Four Oaks Café. I parked, illegally but judiciously, several houses up, and slipped my radio out of its housing. I had already donated three sophisticated Blaupunkts to third world countries, which I considered sufficient. As I walked toward my trunk, a stunning array of blond hair drove by in a vintage Jaguar XKE convertible, pulled in and out of a driveway with an undignified grinding of gears, and angled up behind me to park. My instinct was to hide the radio with my hip. I didn't want to seem like some jerk who was worried about his eighteen-hundred-dollar Blaupunkt.

The young woman came out of the Jaguar hair first. It was pre-Raphaelite hair, blond and ringy, about two and a half pounds of it, and it framed a freckled Nordic face of precise beauty. She was in her late twenties, I suppose. I recognized her from a commercial for a light beer—a smoldering blonde at a desert truck stop who gets the local boys all excited. She was dressed in a great deal of white, all layered and lacy with long sleeves, as if she were on her way to the vicar's lawn party. She walked by me and gave me the tentative glance of acknowledgment people use on other people when they don't know each other but seem to be headed to the same party. I returned her attention with the shy smile I reserve for women who are intimidatingly sexy and beautiful.

"You're parked illegally," she said, very pleasantly, as she passed.

To give her a fair head start on me, I fussed over my trunk as if it were the kind of thing that required a great degree of skill and planning to close correctly. As she walked down the narrow canyon, her chaos of hair was enriched with gold, benefitting from the last of the sun. She looked like a French countess balancing a hay rick on her head.

In the little courtyard just off his front entrance, Milo had composed a shrine to Larry on a piece of wallboard: favorite snapshots, pedigree papers, Larry's dog license, the red bandana he often wore around his neck, a rawhide chew. The focal point of the display was an eight-by-ten glossy of the deceased taken by Harry Langdon, photographer to the stars, which Milo had commissioned when he was trying to find commercial work for his pet. Larry was backlit and gleaming, forever young. In front of the photograph stood a votive candle the height of an iced tea glass featuring a portrait of Pope John Paul XXIII, a souvenir of the pontiff's then-recent visit to Los Angeles. The legend beneath the portrait read, "Vive il Pape." This was an error that had apparently never impinged on the consciousness of the concessionaire. The slogan, correctly translated from the Italian, read, "Long Live the Potato."

When I came to Milo, who was receiving guests at the far end of the wallboard, he was scolding a young woman in short-shorts and over-the-knee boots.

"Put it back," he said, taking one of his trademark baseball caps off her head. "And I don't want you in that bedroom unless I'm there with you." When he noticed me, he ratcheted his face down into an appropriate comingling of sadness and courage.

"Hey, man . . . thanks for coming."

He took my hand. This was my first memorial service for a dog and I had nothing to fall back on except the words I had heard as a child at dozens of Irish Catholic wakes on the Near West Side of Cleveland.

"I'm sorry for your troubles," I said.

"I wanted it to be a happy time," said Milo. And then, following his own instructions, he brightened. "Hey, you know who's here? Marshall Katz."

"Who's that?"

Milo seemed hurt. "He was supervising producer of *The Iron Man.*"

"Well, we comedy writers don't overlap much with those hour-long guys."

The young woman in the very short shorts and very high boots reappeared, without a Denver Broncos cap.

"Hey, Ashley, come here," said Milo. "You know who this is?" And then, overlooking a mention of my name: "He produces *Awful Nancy*," citing my current but not particularly distinguished credit.

Milo stood at Ashley's side beaming at this trophy he had just presented to her.

"Hi" I said. "I'm Jimmy Hoy."

"Hi" said the girl.

She had lovely almond eyes and a pretty, open face, but it was flat in a way that sometimes betrays a lack of intelligence. The tails of her blouse were tied in a knot across her tawny belly. She seemed to need a sword to complete her outfit.

"Ashley's an actress," said Milo, without actually introducing us.

"Ah," I said.

"I'm just studying now. With Franklin Fraser. Do you know him?"

"No, I don't."

Her face collapsed into a pout. "See?" she said to Milo. "Nobody's ever heard of him."

But Milo had turned to greet new arrivals. A lanky black man in a cowboy hat pushed forward a wheelchair. The young man in the wheelchair was a dwarf and a paraplegic and, as if to spread irony over misfortune, he carried his right arm in a sling. When Milo greeted him, the young man broke into a wail of tears, and Milo crouched at the wheelchair to comfort him.

I excused myself from Ashley, who smiled shyly, and went into the house. This memorial for Larry caught pretty much the same flavor as Milo's annual Halloween fete; it was far too crowded, and there was even one person in costume. I saw the blonde— my blonde, as I had come to think of her—down at the end of a hallway, talking conspiratorially to two young women who shared her idea of how hair should be worn. I overheard the phrase "a hundred and twenty-five thousand dollars." I pressed on into the kitchen, where I was presented with a college sophomore's idea of a spread. All the food was in Tupperware bowls on the Formica tabletop. Two kinds of potato chips, ridged and not ridged, Cheez Doodles, pretzels, popcorn, dry roasted peanuts, and a bowl of guacamole already scraped clean. The only item of interest was a sheet cake dedicated to the memory of the late dog. Within a fluted white border, the frosting inscription read:

> "O FOR THE TOUCH OF A VANISHED HAND,
> AND THE SOUND OF A VOICE THAT IS STILL."
> —LARRY

Which left the impression that the Labrador himself had composed the sentiment.

I had thought to bring along two miniatures of Johnnie Walker Black Label, one in each pocket, like sidearms. The ice supply was already exhausted and the only club soda came with artificial lime flavoring mixed into it, so I settled for a generous splash of tap water.

The kitchen door opened onto a concrete patio around a small swimming pool. Across the pool, a plastic awning bellied inward between supporting beams from the weight of accumulated rain-water. Beneath it, a band was tuning up; the reverberations from the amplifiers caused the awning to judder. The young dwarf in

the wheelchair was offering his left hand, one of his few body parts
that remained functional, to members of the band.

Milo approached me. "I'm thinking of changing my name," he
said. "Jack Lally, Mike Lally, something more serious? I'd like to
get an *L.A. Law.*"

"Maybe you should bring it up in group," I said. "What's wrong
with that kid? He's awfully upset." The young man in the wheelchair was sobbing again.

"Oh, well, he usually plays the guitar at these parties, but his
arm is broken. Don't feel sorry for him. The little fucker killed
my dog."

"What do you mean, he killed your dog?"

"He killed my dog. Did you ever see Larry's trick? Larry had
this one trick. You hold your arms in a circle, out to the side of
your body—you make a hoop—and Larry jumps through. He associated it with Mallomars. I always gave him a Mallomar when
he did that. So, apparently, Denny—that's his name over there,
Denny—he tries this, without any appreciation of what's involved.
He doesn't even have access to the Mallomars, for Christ sake,
he's in a wheelchair."

"Where was this? Here?"

"Yeah, here. He hangs out sometimes, answers the phone. He
hopes he'll get a look at a naked girl, if I have a massage client
over."

"So Denny makes a hoop with his arms."

"He makes a hoop with his arms. But the thing is, he doesn't
make it to the side of his body. He forms it *in front* of his body.
Because of his physical limitations, he wants to get his arms in a
circle first, and then move them to the side. But poor Larry, he
doesn't know that. He sees a hoop, he thinks 'Mallomars.' He
bounds across the patio—they were right out here. . . ." Milo made
a terse sweep of the concrete with his leg. His face was suddenly
shrouded with remorse.

"So, what happened?" I asked.

"Actually, it's largely conjecture. Larry nose-dives into Denny's sternum, and the wheelchair falls over backward. Larry ends up in the swimming pool. He must have been going like Apollo Six. Denny doesn't remember anything. He got knocked out for a little while. Then he wakes up in pain and starts making noises. But I'm in there with a client—it was Lucy Ditlow, you know her?"

"I don't think so."

"She was a semiregular on *Newhart* last season?"

"Maybe."

"So, anyhow, I play these Windham Hill tapes when I'm working. So I didn't hear anything. When I come out, little Denny's lying on his back, flopping around like a turtle . . . and there's my dog, facedown in the pool."

"The dog drowned?"

"Never learned to swim. He was terrified of water. Lucy Ditlow. She played the girl who would come in and try to sell flowers in the restaurant?"

"I rarely see *Newhart*. That's our taping night."

"Excuse me . . ." It was my blonde. She gave me a lightning-stroke smile, and then turned to Milo very purposefully. "Milo, my love, I'm going. It's a wonderful party, and you're being very brave . . . but I'm the biggest name in the room and it doesn't do me any good to be seen here."

"Fuck you," said Milo. "Come on, stay, we're going to have dancing."

"I caaaan't."

She held herself as if her beauty were an accessory, one she could emphasize at will. Suddenly, Milo grabbed my arm.

"Hey, this is a name, here's a name."

"What's the name of this name?" asked my blonde.

"Jimmy Hoy," I said.

"He produces *Awful Nancy*," said Milo.

She raised her eyebrows as if she had just been presented to a Nobel laureate. "Hello," she said, and she concentrated her charm so it came at me like a flying wedge. "I'm Geneva Holloway."

"I recognize you from the light beer commercial," I said.

"She's in my scene study class with Darryl Hickman," said Milo. "You should see her. Major. Two national commercials already. She gave up a career in retailing."

"Career. I was a buyer for Fabric Farm," said Geneva. "Milo, really, I have to go." She kissed him on the cheek. "Sorry about your dog." She gave me a little smile of good-bye, then made her way between the few couples who were now dancing on the patio.

"One night with her," said Milo as he followed her with his eyes. "Just one night. That's all I want. I can't believe she came. Why do you suppose she did?"

"Maybe she thought you were more important than you are," I suggested, and Milo nodded his head soberly, accepting this wisdom.

A horrible electronic shriek went up from the band into the sides of the glen and came back down over us like the voice of an angry god. Young Denny, with his one able arm, was darting his wheel-chair into an amplifier repeatedly, like a sewing machine needle. The tall black cowboy and some others hurried over to restrain him.

"He shouldn't drink," said Milo.

"That's pretty quick to get hammered."

"No, he was tanked up when he got here. I guess there was a lot of pressure in him showing up tonight."

Denny was wheeled by us.

"Do you believe in karma?" asked Milo. "Because that's what I think is going on. Two years ago, on his birthday, I hired a hooker to go down on him. And the little fucker got so excited he fell out of his chair. He fractured his left elbow. And now here it is two years later, and my dog is dead, and Denny's other arm is broken."

"What goes around comes around," I said.

"There you go."

Milo mingled, and I tried to. None of the other members of our therapy group had shown up. I chatted pointlessly with two attractive, inappropriately young women. They described themselves as actresses. I didn't want to unduly flaunt my position in the industry, so I allowed at least eighteen seconds to go by before I mentioned that I was a writer-producer of a major network comedy. This had its intended effect, which was to get me through several more minutes of conversation with them. Men more facile than I are able to convert these situations into something sincerely exploitive. My only motive was to not look foolish at a party by not having anyone to talk to.

I circled through the rooms of the house and back out onto the patio again, trolling for someone else to connect with. It was apparent that the woman who would take my breath away and change my life forever—the mysterious, perfect woman I'd been looking for since I was fourteen—was once again unable to make it. So I said my good-byes to Milo, who was giving neck rubs to two girls at once, and made my way up Beverly Glen to my car. In front of the Four Oaks restaurant, the cowboy urged young Denny's cooperation in getting into a Dodge van. Denny resisted with a drunken fuss.

"Do you want me to just let go of this chair?" said the cowboy. "Is that what you want? Because I just let my hand go, and you roll all the way down to Sunset."

Denny's answer was incoherent but defiant in tone.

The narrow lane was now purple with dark. Geneva Holloway was having car trouble. The Jaguar rolled over and over, whining without connecting.

"It's the battery," I said.

"Do you know cars?"

"No. I just know it's always the battery. Can I give you a ride back down to Milo's? You want to call the auto club?"

"I don't have the auto club. And actually, I don't have a lot of time." She assessed me. "Could you at all give me a ride? I live up in Trancas. Is that completely inconvenient?"

It could not have possibly been more inconvenient and still been in Los Angeles County, but I didn't weigh my decision for an instant. Beauty transcended geography. She stopped to retrieve a gift-wrapped package from her trunk and got into my car.

From Beverly Glen to the Pacific Coast Highway, Geneva Holloway recounted for me the details of her nascent career, including all the roles she went up for and didn't get and all the agents she considered signing with but turned down. She talked about herself for twenty-five minutes and kept me interested. This spoke highly of her potential, if not as an actress then at least as a star.

Around Chatauqua Avenue, she completed her run with the news that she had a callback at *Family Ties* the following Tuesday, as an "older woman" for Michael J. Fox. Then she was silent. She looked across me at the ocean, which was plum-colored under the October moon. I inhaled her powdery beauty for a few miles, catching glimpses of her when I pretended to be checking the other lanes. As we passed the J. Paul Getty Museum, she said, "Now you." She acted as if we were on a date.

"What do you want to know?" I said.

"Well, what's it like to produce a television show?"

As it turns out, I had been formulating an answer to that very question on my long drives home from work at the Burbank Studios in the middle of the night. So without the slightest hesitation I answered, "It's exactly like Chapter Thirty-seven of *Moby Dick*." (My overly literary writing partner had given me tapes of James Mason reading *Moby Dick* for my birthday.)

Geneva laughed.

"Well," she said, "I don't even want to know what comes after that." And she laughed again. Then she said, "I haven't had much of an education. What the hell does that mean, anyhow? Am I supposed to get it?"

"Not really."

"But what does it mean?"

"Well, in *Moby Dick*—are you familiar with the general thrust of the story? This sea captain, Ahab—"

"Gregory Peck."

"Right. He's after Moby Dick, this great white whale. And in Chapter Thirty-seven, he finally spots him—he has a shot at him.

And he gets a boat down in the water, a skiff or whatever the hell it's called. And he's got these Asian guys rowing the boat. They're not his regular guys—these are some kind of hotshot whaling experts. Anyhow, all these guys are rowing the boat. They really know what they're doing . . . they're Joe Whaler. And Ahab is standing in the back with this harpoon that he's been sharpening for three years. And Moby Dick is flopping around, like, two hundred yards away. And all of a sudden, these sharks surround the skiff. They're everywhere. And the sharks start taking bites out of the paddles of the oars. And the paddles are getting smaller and smaller, and it's getting harder for the guys in the boat to row, and the whale's not going to stay there forever, right?

"But the thing is, the sharks don't want the fucking oars. They want the whale, just like Ahab and the Asian guys. But the sharks, who want the whale as much as anybody else, they're the ones who make getting the whale impossible. You see?"

"Uh huh."

"Right. And here's the analogy. The whale is the television show. The hit series. Like, if it goes into syndication, everybody connected with it makes fifty million dollars. And the people in the boat, they're the writers and producers. They're the ones trying to get the whale, who know how to do it. And the sharks, the guys biting the fucking oars, they're the network guys, and the production company executives and the agents and everybody else who, when they don't know how to get to the whale, decide, somewhere back in the swamp ova of the human brain, well, Jesus, I should do *some*thing, why don't I try to sink the fucking boat? And that's exactly what it's like trying to produce a television show."

She liked this. Her eyes were very alive as she considered it, as if it excited her.

"And what about the actors? What are we?"

"Well, they can be in the boat, helping to row, or they can be sharks. If they're stars, the temptation is for them to be sharks. Usually, after your second *TV Guide* cover, you become a shark."

She lived at the end of Broad Beach Road. It was a small house, tiny really, but, given the area, managed to be a very pricey piece of real estate. It was stucco, the color of canned salmon if the exterior lights gave a true indication. There was a For Sale sign at the end of the driveway.

"Is this your house?" I asked.

"For now. I'm desperate to sell it."

"But it's yours? You own it?"

"There's an arrangement. Here, bring this."

She handed me the gift-wrapped package. A few moments later, I found myself on my knees before a rhododendron bed, digging a hole in the loamy soil while Geneva crouched beside me, tearing open the package. She pulled from the box a little plastic statue of a saint.

"Saint Joseph," she announced, handing him over to me.

"I know," I said, recognizing the venerable gent from my eight years at St. Malachy's School.

"I had it gift-wrapped, because I didn't want them to think it was for me, like I was Catholic. We plant him. Upside down and facing the house."

I aimed Saint Joseph head-down into the hole and considered the prospect that this beautiful young woman was insane. You can only ignore the evidence at hand for so long.

"My mother told me about this," she said as I refilled the hole. "She called me from Stockton this morning. They were talking about it on the radio up there. To sell a house, you bury a statue of Saint Joseph. Everybody was calling in saying it works."

After this brief session of liturgical husbandry, I was invited into the house for a drink. My choices were Arrow Peppermint Schnaaps or Hansen's coffee soda.

"I don't keep much in the house," Geneva explained.

"I'll have one of these," I said, and pulled the remaining miniature of Johnnie Walker Black Label from my pocket. She gave a whooping little laugh and took the bottle from me. As she banged around in the refrigerator for ice, something caught my attention in the window of her oven, and I opened the door. The oven racks were filled with sweaters.

"I don't cook," said Geneva.

We sat on her tiny sofa and she poured out her dreams to me, at least as they related to breaking out of commercials and into network television. And then, suddenly, we were kissing. I know I initiated it, but I doubt I would have started anything without a clear and unavoidable invitation. She kissed with great intention, aggressive, pressing kisses that tilted me backward. She came to a quick boil, filling the space between kisses with passionate, sucking breaths. She put her mouth over my ear and burrowed with the tip of her tongue. As I considered how to deal with her party dress, cumbersome as a wedding gown, she pressed her open hand down the front of my pants and just helped herself to Jimmy and the twins. I remember thinking, I know why I'm doing this, but why is she doing this? It was not my general habit to arouse immediate animal lust in unapproachably beautiful women. If this were the casting couch, then, given her performance, she should get the job.

We were interrupted by the crunch of tires on the gravel and the flash of headlights off the glass of a knickknack cabinet. "It's Russ," said Geneva, looking at me very frankly. She gave my erection a farewell pat. "Russ is early."

We reassembled ourselves in an undignified hurry.

"We have to be nice to Russ. He's going to jail soon," said Geneva. "The house is in his name."

She led the way outdoors, where a large white Lincoln had pulled in next to my Mercedes. As we crossed the lawn, Russ got out of his car very slowly. He was portly, and a little gray. His head rose above the level of the car roof and he squinted in our direction, like a grizzly who's on to a suspicious scent.

"Russ!" said Geneva, investing the word with great warmth. "This is Jimmy—" She turned to me. "I'm sorry . . ."

"Jimmy Hoy," I said.

"Jimmy Hoy. Jimmy, this is Russ Borgreave."

Once I heard the name, I recognized the face. Russell Borgreave was about to do time for illegal insider trading in association with the Beverly Hills office of Drexel Burnham Lambert. He was particularly noteworthy because his activities had led to the collapse of a statewide savings and loan institution based in Santa Monica.

"Of course!" I said with inappropriate warmth. I remember thinking, as I pumped his hand, This guy is a major crook, and I'm acting like I'm being introduced to Elie Weisel. Russ shook my hand, but he didn't say anything.

"Jimmy was nice enough to give me a ride home. Something's wrong with the Jaguar," said Geneva.

"The battery, I would say," I said. "My partner calls the guy who designed the Jaguar's electrical system the Prince of Darkness."

Russ didn't laugh. "We should go," he said to Geneva.

Geneva sent me off to my car with a friendly handshake. As I backed up the driveway, I saw her give Russ an arms-around-the-neck kiss. They were getting into his car as I backed out onto Broad Beach. On the Pacific Coast Highway, I became nervous when I saw a pair of headlights bearing down on me. What if Russ was the jealous sort who, provoked by the merest slight, would drive up alongside a fellow on the highway and shoot him. I understand that there are people in Los Angeles who will do that. The headlights passed me. It was a Toyota four-wheeler. My anxiety was not immediately allayed. But after several minutes of looney scanning, I realized that there weren't going to be any white Lincolns following me.

Later in the week, while I was in a casting session, Geneva Holloway left a message with my secretary: She'd gotten a firm offer on her house from a Korean who was going to pay cash. I called back several times, but there was no answer and no machine. Eventually, the number was disconnected.

The next time I saw her, it was on the cover of *TV Guide*. Her first time.

# *Chapter*

# *2*

A young man who was raised in the entertainment industry told some friends at college, "My father made forty-five million dollars in the record business in the sixties. And then he lost forty-five million dollars in the record business in the sixties. And in those days, forty-five million dollars was a lot of money."

◆ ◆ ◆

Slow dissolve to Christmas, four years after the memorial service for Milo Lally's dog. My partner Neil Stein and I sat at our desks in the Clara Bow Building at Paramount eating lunch, reading (the trade newspapers in my case, Virginia Woolf's *Orlando* in Neil's), and waiting with a certain amount of dread for a visit from Malcolm Dant. Malcolm was best known to the world at that time as Uncle Mose on *Saga,* the Depression-era black family miniseries that had been covered with glory at Emmy time. Neil and I had an overall development deal with Polonia Productions in Culver City, but we were housed at Paramount because we were about to start production there on six episodes of a half-hour comedy starring Malcolm, *Lou Duffy,* to air on CBN. There is a saying in television: "The good news is, they bought my show. The bad news is, they bought my show." We were in the bad news part of the experience.

"What does he want?" said Neil who, in the most relaxed of circumstances, is anxious around actors.

"He wants to discuss the story ideas."

"We should have never sent him the story ideas."

"It's in his deal."

"He better not have his gun."

"I don't think he will. I don't think he carries it all the time."

"Will Andre Broz be with him?"

"I'd rather have him bring the gun."

Because his reputation as a nice human being was in desperate need of shoring up, Malcolm Dant had behaved rather decently during the shooting of the pilot episode. The only problem had been the gun, a Smith and Wesson Model 66 stainless combat magnum. He produced it on camera blocking day, when everyone's nerves were frayed, and began waving it around. Brandishing it, I believe is the word. Ostensibly, Malcolm was kidding, but it was a menacing joke from an angry man.

I was not in the studio at the time. Neil was up in the control booth with Howie Kurtz, the director. Neil has an absolute dread of guns. ("There are certain things Jews just aren't good at," he told me later. "Guns is one. Ice fishing is another.") And yet as the executive in charge, it was up to Neil to deal with this six-foot two-inch, 220-pound former nose tackle for the Baltimore Colts who was waving a loaded combat weapon around the set of a half-hour comedy. Neil chose to delegate.

"Howie," he said to the director. "Go down there and take the gun away from him."

"No, Neil," said Howie. "You're the producer. It's your job to take the gun away. I'm the director. I just tell him where to point it."

Eventually the social worker on the set, a serious young woman there by law to protect the child actors, gave Malcolm a severe scolding and took the gun away from him.

Allow me to give you a little take on Malcolm Dant. He may or may not have set his girlfriend on fire. The charges were eventually dismissed. I have no comment. But he did, in fact, bring over a twelve-year-old boy from Zaire with all sorts of attendant publicity in *TV Guide* and *Ebony* and *People* about giving the lad a home in America and educating him. Then, for the next two years, he used the kid as a houseboy. The city of Beverly Hills was actually ready to cite him under an antislavery statute when the honchos over at Landover Productions stepped in and hushed everything up.

So there are bad things about Malcolm: Girlfriend burning, child enslavement. But on the positive side, as a performer he gets every laugh he comes near. There are some who would say that that makes it all even.

"If he has the gun, I'm not staying," said Neil.

"He won't have the gun. Distract yourself. Put down that literature. Here, read the trades."

Our secretary Sharone—that's how she spelled it—came into the office with her lips pursed and her eyebrows raised. There was the barest suggestion of Egg McMuffin streaked across her pretty pink cheek.

"Can we have a tree?" she asked.

"Does that mean, 'Will you give me money for a tree?'"

"Yes. I need seventy dollars for anything decent. But I saved the decorations from last year. I have them at home."

"Neil?"

"What?" He was buried in the *Hollywood Reporter*.

"We're getting a Christmas tree."

"I'm in."

"Deal," said Sharone. "Oh . . ." She was distracted by the copy of *Orlando* on Neil's desk. "Virginia Woolf . . . I'm thinking about going to Florida in March. Did she just write about the Orlando area?"

"Just the Orlando area," said Neil. We have an agreement between us not to laugh at Sharone, because she's had a hard life.

Sharone did a little hoofer's twirl—she had been a Los Angeles Raiders Raiderette for a while—and left the room.

"Jesus," said Neil.

"I know. I once bought a car for seventy dollars."

"No. Here in the *Hollywood Reporter*. Fucking Greg Paul, man."

My partner was a tribute to the entertainment industry adage, A sad Jew is a happy Jew. He routinely invited pain into his life by taking seriously the public pronouncements of Greg Paul, the creator of a sappy half-hour comedy called *Relative Differences,* who had just sold his series into syndication for figures in excess of the gross national product of a small Balkan nation. Greg, Neil, and I had worked together for a season on the first *Arnie Lewellyn Show,* and Greg's subsequent good fortune was bitter gall to us both. His routine, formulaic family comedy was slotted behind the phenomenally successful *Teen Dreems,* giving Greg a free ride. Neil once gave an objective evaluation of Greg's abilities: "He steps in shit and slides uphill."

Neil delved further into the interview, neglecting his "spa cuisine" lunch in the Styrofoam container from the Columbia Bar and Grill. (Neil sent out for this spa crap regularly. On the afternoon in question, I believe it was a *tian* of steamed vegetables and grains with a red pepper sauce. Every day, Neil ate his dainty lunch, then spent the rest of the afternoon making trips to the kitchen for Pringles and Cheez Balls and handfuls of trail mix with M&Ms in it.)

Neil groaned after every sentence he read, a deep, primal groan that had its origins three centuries ago in some little village on the Polish-Russian border.

"*What?*" I finally said. I was eating a Chinese chicken salad from the commissary.

"He credits his wife for keeping his sense of values intact."

"It's galling, isn't it?" Greg Paul was a major pussy jockey. He'd go through the Victoria's Secret catalog and circle the models he liked. Then it was his secretary's job to find them and bring them in for "interviews," so Greg could try to nail them.

"This is such fucking bullshit," said Neil. "Every interview is the same fucking thing: He presents himself as this let's-all-make-it-a-better-world flower child who stumbled into television by accident."

"I know," I said. "He doesn't care about money, right? He could care less about money. Every single interview talks about how totally indifferent this man is to money. And in every single interview, the sum of fifty million dollars just happens to come up. That is the specific sum that he has, to which he is totally indifferent, and about which he manages to talk ceaselessly."

"Why couldn't we get that lucky?" said Neil.

Neil Stein supported a wife, three children, his mother, one of his brothers, his wife's sister and her son. He lived in a house in lower Bel Air the size of Buffalo, New York, where he employed a housekeeper, a nanny, a three-times-a-week gardener, a twice-a-week pool man, and a Vietnam veteran who came in every Saturday and washed the cars. He consulted with a very expensive psychiatrist in Westwood twice a week. His wife Renata did not believe in therapy—unusual in a cause-oriented liberal—but made time in her schedule for visits to the house by a masseuse, a personal trainer, a tennis instructor, and a nutritionist.

In short, my increasingly pear-shaped partner had financial needs. It pained him to see Greg Paul, a man less talented than he, a man surely less honorable—a man, let's face it, with two first names—achieve such heady financial security at so early and undeserving an age as thirty-six.

Neil looked across the desk at me with sad, watery eyes. His face was round, as if someone had pumped a little air under the skin.

"All I want is fifty million dollars," he said. "Is that so wrong?"

I couldn't say it was. Most of us writers look forward to that day when we've accumulated our "fuck you" money. Writers in Hollywood, after all, are little more than upscale assembly line workers. The studio captains and network heads hold them in the thinly veiled contempt that the powerful reserve for those upon whom they depend. This generates a certain amount of disquiet. It is said that on silent, moonlit nights, when you stand on Mulholland Drive and look out over the glister of the San Fernando Valley, if you listen closely, you can hear the sound of writers whining.

Sharone swept into the room—really, she did—holding a regal stance as she closed the door slightly behind her. She might have passed as an executive secretary at IBM, except for the corduroy slacks and suede boots with fringed tops.

"Malcolm's here," she said, with a certain amount of elation in her voice for Malcolm's benefit.

"Oh, good," I said more loudly than I needed. Then I whispered, "Is Andre Broz with him?" Sharone shook her head. "See," I said to Neil, "it'll be fine. We'll just kiss his ass a little, to make him happy." As Neil passed his Styrofoam container over to me to toss into the trash, Sharone pretended to spray us with machine-gun fire. Neil mouthed the words, That's not funny, and Sharone put on a straight face and twirled out the door.

"They've been waiting for you, Malcolm," I heard her say.

Malcolm entered. He loomed much larger in a room than he did on a set. He wore a dusty maroon polo shirt that displayed his muscles to good advantage; a chocolate brown vein as thick as an extension cord bulged down his upper arm. There were curls of gray, like iron filings, at his temples. He glowed with personality.

"Working hard or hardly working?" he said. But don't judge him by that; when we wrote for him he was much funnier. Neil and I came at him from both sides, as if we were going to frisk him, which was probably not far from our minds. We greeted him heartily, offered beverages, paid him the obeisance owed a star. We sat him on the sofa and pulled up chairs to face him. He held our pages of story ideas rolled up in his hand like a diploma.

"So, Malcolm, what did you think of the stories?" asked Neil. He asked this with a certain amount of confidence, because, the gods having smiled on us, we'd come up with some pretty good stuff.

"I won't shit you guys" said Malcolm confidentially, as if he were letting us into a club. "These are unacceptable."

"Uh huh," said Neil, and from his perfectly flat affect you would never guess he had just taken a chest-crushing blow. "Which ones?"

"All of them. Everything written here is unacceptable."

"Uh huh," I said. "What is it that bothers you, Malcolm?"

"It's shit, that's what bothers me."

"Uh huh," said Neil. "Could you give us some examples, so we can get an idea of your thinking?"

Malcolm got a little testy at this, giving us an I-knew-you-guys-would-cause-trouble look.

"You want an idea of my thinking? It's shit. There's an idea of my thinking."

"I guess what we're saying, Malcolm, is, what should we do? Where do we go from here?" I said.

"Come up with different stories, that aren't shit."

After a silence filled with rich textures of violence Neil said "Uh huh" again, but this time with a brittle asperity. "I guess we can't be sure how to go about that, Malcolm. We thought these stories were pretty good. The network liked them very much. They're talking about putting us on at eight-thirty Wednesday night, right after *Close to Home,* because they liked the stories so much."

"Don't attempt that shit on me," said Malcolm, upset by Neil's recourse to logic and reason. He stood up and paced in a heavy, agitated way. The floorboards creaked under the putty green carpeting. He slipped into street argot, meant to lure us into forgetting that his father was a dentist in Georgetown. "Look, cuz, ain't no way I'm be doin' these. Rea' dis shit." He shuffled the story outlines with his hammy fists. "'Max's Problem,'" he read. "'A Man from Bonita's Past'... 'Sophie's Big Day Off'... 'Max Demands a Raise'... 'Bonita and Sandra, Attorneys-at-law'... It goes on like that. Where's Lou? Where the fuck is Lou Duffy? The show is called *Lou Duffy.*"

Neil and I made discreet eye contact. In our rush to get stories approved quickly, we had violated an elementary tenet: Never let the star know that there are other people in the world. The solution to this big story crisis was really quite simple: Change the titles. Had we written, instead of "Sophie's Big Day Off," "Lou Gives Sophie a Day Off"; instead of "A Man from Bonita's Past," "Lou

Meets a Man from Bonita's Past"; instead of "Max's Problem," "Lou's Friend Max's Problem"; had we thought to use these unimportant story titles as additional bricks for the shrine we build to our star, then Malcolm Dant would not have been standing in our office in a quasi-martial arts pose glaring at us like an upset Tonton Macoute.

"You got a copy of the pilot?" asked Malcolm. "Put it on. I want to show you something."

"Malcolm," said Neil, "I think you're at the center of every story. Everything revolves around you."

"Put on the pilot."

Malcolm addressed me as if Neil were not in the room. He had decided early in the relationship, for reasons emotionally comforting to him, to look upon Neil as the heavy in our writing-producing team. In fact, to the degree that there was a heavy, it was me.

"You want to watch the whole pilot?" I asked.

"Just put it on. Put it in the machine."

The three-quarter-inch VCR sucked in the cassette. After a few moments of color bars, there was a fade-in to the cold opening, that little tease before the credits start. After the exterior establishing shot of a small town police station, we cut to the interior where a few policemen and civilian employees are at work in the bull pen area. A young policewoman, Sophie, enters and spots a very plump fellow officer, Max, consuming powdery jelly doughnuts. Sophie says, "Max, look at you. Chief Duffy is coming back to work today. He told you to lose twenty pounds before he got out of the hospital." Max says, "I still have forty-five minutes." Laugh. The camera pans right. Malcolm enters on crutches, his leg in a cast. As he surveys his employees, who do not see him, there is an audience reaction on the sound track—a hushed "Ahhh," then hearty applause.

"Okay. Right there. Stop!" said Malcolm. I hit the button and Malcolm's face was freeze-framed in an unflattering, open-mouthed position.

"That's what I'm talking about," said Malcolm. "Did you see what just happened? I walked out onto that stage, and immediately, there was a murmur of recognition from the audience, and then applause. Big applause. I'm the star. People know me. They want me. I'm the reason this fucking show is on the air."

I sat back and looked thoughtful. Part of me was deliberating on how to tell Malcolm what I had to say in a way least likely to lead him to kill me. Another part was racing in eagerness to start spreading this story around town.

"Malcolm," I said, and I could have been Wilfred Brimley selling oatmeal, "I know you're the star. There's never been any question about that in my mind. Because, remember, when we did the pilot, we shot that cold opening on a Sunday, to get it out of the way? Without an audience? Obviously I know you're the star, because I'm the one who was down in the sweetening session. I'm the one who put in that murmur of recognition from the audience, with a machine. And then I put in the prerecorded applause. Big applause."

Malcolm glared for the barest of seconds; then, incredibly, his face softened.

"All right, then," he said, as if he had just won a major point. "We agree. So now just come up with better stories that aren't shit." He looked at Neil, who was ashen, and nodded. He laid the story outlines on our coffee table carefully, as if not to show disrespect. "And you might as well know, I want Andre on the show as an executive producer. He's talking to Polonia about it today."

Malcolm referred to his "personal manager," an old Army buddy who had a perplexing influence over Malcolm. Andre Broz was a white man who had decided to become black; he had had his hair processed and said things like, "We African-Americans . . ." but retained the name Broz, a Yugoslavian surname he shared with the late Marshal Tito. As a human being, he was a slug, a worm, a true bottom feeder. The commonly accepted explanation for why Malcolm Dant sacrificed a percentage of his income and reputation to a lowlife like Andre Broz was that the two had made a pact in the Army, under the influence of LSD, that whoever made it first in the world would bring the other along.

Malcolm exited. Neil leaned over in his chair far enough to reach the door and swing it closed. Then he called through it: "You own a car? Get killed!" He looked over to me. His lips were tightly pursed, as if he were enduring a gas pain.

"I have an incredibly simple solution to all this," I said. "We walk."

Neil smirked in contempt. "We walk? From six on-the-air, possibly behind *Close to Home*?"

"We walk."

"We just walk away?"

"This is how he is on the honeymoon. What happens in the second year? He starts *out* with a gun. And Andre. You want Andre Broz around with his drug connections and mob connections?"

"I've never walked off a show."

"Neil," I said, "I can deal with mean, I can deal with stupid. I can't deal with crazy. This guy is crazy."

"You think he's actually crazy?" asked Neil.

"If you haven't noticed he's crazy, then you give the term 'non-observant Jew' a whole new meaning. Of course he's crazy. He'll never make it through the first year. We'll work our asses off, then he'll explode in our face. I want to put my efforts into something that will pay off."

Neil looked at me as if I were crazy. And then something went on behind his eyes. Suddenly, he seemed to be considering that maybe *he* was the one who was crazy. He burst into a giddy laugh.

"Sharone!" he called. "Get Polonia Productions on the phone! We're busting out of this crypto-fascist puke hole!"

# *Chapter*

# *3*

■ Julius and Philip Epstein, identical twin brothers, were
screenwriters long associated with Warner Brothers. They
wrote *Casablanca* with Howard Koch. After Philip died, and Julius
appeared on the lot alone for the first time, Jack Warner passed
him and said, "Hello, boys."

◆ ◆ ◆

Perhaps it was an understandable flash of hubris in the wake of
fresh success. Perhaps it was a weighted business decision calculated to keep stars' salaries in line. Or perhaps he just felt like
it. But when Joe Danko, the president of the Continental Broadcasting Network's entertainment division heard that Neil and I
were walking off *Lou Duffy* and why, he said, "Malcolm Dant has
just fucked himself in the butt."

This may come as a surprise to the uninitiated, but it is not all
that common for the head of a network to back the writers over
the star. In fact, it is more common for it to rain in the lobby of
the Chrysler Building. Yet here was Joe Danko, the unlikely ar-
chitect of CBN's recent catapult to first place, with no earthly
reason to be nice to writers, being nice to writers. I hesitate to
make this accusation against a network executive, but it may have
been his sense of decency at work.

Joe Danko was a thirty-eight-year-old bohunk from Pittsburgh
who looked like an ingot with a shirt on. He was an educated man

in the packaging of a street tough. He had never shaken the blunt, working-class lilt in his accent, and it probably had never occurred to him to try. When he squinted at you through his glasses, you expected to see adhesive tape wrapped around the nose bridge. He dressed expensively, but never managed to look well assembled. He was not judicious in choosing his words of rejection, but there was never anything personal in it, and at least you knew exactly where you stood with him. If you happened to meet with him late on a Friday, you would be invited to join the round of liar's poker he organized as an end-of-the-week ritual. In an era when two of the network programming chiefs were named Brandon and one was named Kim, Joe Danko was an unusual piece of goods.

"We had this same shit with Dewain Lester," said Joe, referring to the costar of a black father-and-son show whose personal demons—cocaine, alcohol, gambling debts, ex-wives—caused him to miss several tapings. Joe spoke from the tall director's chair he favored, which placed him a few feet above everybody else in the room. "I promised myself when I fired his ass, 'Never again.' Do you know what Dewain Lester is doing these days? *Norman, Is That You?* in Las Vegas."

"I hear he's very good," I said.

Joe laughed. Everybody in the room laughed: The CBN vice president of development, the CBN vice president of current comedy, the CBN vice president-casting, the Polonia Productions vice president of comedy development, the Polonia Productions vice president of current comedy, the Polonia Productions senior vice president-comedy and drama. Nine people. Five white males, one black male, three white females. One gay. Two ponytails, both on males. A total of seven earrings.

As everyone laughed, I enjoyed watching the eyes of David Putzman, the ranking Polonia executive in the room, slide around like eggs on a plate. David had a plan, indeed a mission. The last words of Leo Becker, the president and cofounder of Polonia, had been, "Come back with your shield or on it." Putzman had no idea what that meant, but he picked up on the implications. The purpose of this meeting, from Polonia's point of view, was to enlist the persuasive—or, failing that, the brutal—powers of CBN to convince Neil and me to work with Malcolm Dant on whatever terms he wanted. Our well-being, health, and physical safety should be put in second place to Polonia's wish to make two hundred million dollars. It seemed like a reasonable request to everyone who made it. That Neil and I were intransigent proved, in Leo Becker's words, what assholes writers are.

But now Joe Danko had altered the situation beyond David Putzman's immediate ability to comprehend. Putzman's wide, round face was a plain of agony over which he tried to impose a winning smile.

"Excuse me for being a realist here," he said, "but Polonia and CBN both have a lot of money on the line. Malcom Dant may have his difficult aspects, but he's a great performer. He lights up the screen."

"He also lights up his girlfriends," I said.

Putzman held his concentration as everyone else laughed. Because he didn't have a sense of humor, this was his least favorite sort of moment. He had a great fear of appearing foolish. His father had been a purveyor of mixed nuts, and the advertising slogan, "Putzman's Fancy Nuts," had haunted David throughout his youth. At Beverly Hills High School, Putzman ran with a clique of Jewish princes whose fathers were well connected in the entertainment industry. Through this exposure, he developed a certain élan, the appearance and attitude of a winner, and it sometimes took as long as five minutes of face-to-face conversation to see through him. (The director of two of the highest-grossing film comedies of the late eighties is now additionally famous for telling Putzman, after a half-hour meeting, "David, either you are extremely cunning, or you're the most stupid person I've ever met.")

Putzman brought us all back to order. "Look," he said, "we've got a great show here, with a great star. Do we just walk away from that? Do we abandon a great performer because he's a little problematic? It's not fair to ourselves, and it's not fair to Malcolm Dant."

"Get somebody else to star in the show," said Danko.

"What?"

"I like the show. Just get somebody else."

Danko's logic fell across the room like a tree across a road. Putzman's eyes widened. He smiled, for the first time in that meeting sincerely.

"Then fuck Malcom Dant," he said.


"I can't believe somebody actually sided with the writers," said Neil as we made our way through the sets that cluttered the corridors outside the CBN sound studios. "I like this Danko. He doesn't just kill a guy, he burns his village."

"Neil, would it be all right with you if we didn't go out for a triumphant lunch?"

"What?" The pain in his face was so cute.

"I told this girl I'd stop by."

"That Kiki Burmeister?"

I nodded. Neil sighed. Kiki was an actress recently out from New York, but originally from Texas, whom I'd dated for a couple of weeks. She gave every indication of being major trouble, so I dropped her. But apparently without complete success.

We came out of CBN through the artists' entrance, causing us to cross through the snaking line of timmies waiting to get into a game show. "Timmies" was Neil's word for the awkwardly attired lay citizens, usually from other states, who make up the bulk of any studio audience. Professional audience procurers troll for them at the Farmer's Market, Mann's Chinese Theater, the Hollywood Wax Museum, and Universal City. As a matter of California law, every fifth member of a studio audience must wear contrasting plaids or, failing that, a T-shirt showing a cartoon cat holding a martini glass, with the slogan "Happiness Is a Tight Pussy." When Fred Allen did his first radio broadcast from the West Coast, he took a peek at the audience from behind the curtains and said, "It looks like Iowa sprung a leak." He was looking out on an auditorium of timmies.

For people who have been standing in line in a parking lot for two hours, two men coming out of a building is a major entertainment. They surveyed us with intense interest as we passed through them. Neil pretended we were in an urgent conversation, and spoke so everyone would overhear: "If it gets out that Bill Cosby's living with a seventeen-year-old male lover, we're screwed. The whole project will fall through." He enjoys little stunts like that.

But when we were clear of the timmies, he said, "What are you going to see that Kiki for? You were doing so well."

"She called me this morning when I was still asleep. She said she hungers for me."

"Don't get a disease. At least, not one that affects your writing."

I rang the bell at Kiki Burmeister's house, a little stucco bungalow on a Hollywood side street that ran between Melrose and Third. It wasn't actually Kiki's house. It belonged to a sound editor named Leroy Butley, with whom she lived.

Kiki did not tell me about Leroy until the first night we made love. She explained the situation to me while I stood barefoot on the wet grass in front of my house and tried to coax her back inside to my bed.

"There's someone I have to be home for," she said. "It's a platonic situation. There's this guy I live with, Leroy, and we have an agreement that we sleep in the same bed, but it's not sexual."

"Is he—what, gay, asexual?"

"No, he'd like to have sex all right, but that's not part of the agreement."

The agreement, she explained with a straight face, was for her to live with Leroy, rent free, in his house, and sleep with him in his bed, and for him to keep his hands off her.

"How's it working out?" I asked.

"So far, so good," she said. "How do you like the car?"

"It's beautiful. What color is it?"

"They call it steel blue. I spent a little more than I planned."

"Who doesn't?"

"See, it's just that Leroy has trouble sleeping when I'm not there."

"I think I'm going to have a little trouble sleeping myself tonight," I said.

Kiki made a U-turn, blowing me kisses all the while, and puttered off into the night. I knew that I wouldn't be getting Mom's engagement ring polished and reset for this one.

I gave up on the idea of Kiki, but she didn't give up on the idea of me. I avoided her calls or remained aloof when she caught me on the phone. But that morning, she got to me. When you come out of a warm sleep to answer the phone and this husky, little-girl voice says, first thing, "What are you wearing?" it has a certain effect.

Kiki came to the door all hair and eyes and lips. The hair was long and curly and chestnut; the eyes were agate blue; the lips, I believe, were what Thomas Hardy had in mind when he spoke of "peony lips."

"Oh, hi," she said, surprised, although I'd arrived exactly when scheduled. We kissed politely. "Come in, come in." She wore a Laura Ashley smock and was barefoot. She looked like the little girl in a picture that hung in my second grade classroom at St. Malachy's, a little girl on a footbridge who was being protected by a guardian angel during a storm.

"I have a lunch ready," she said, and produced sandwiches from Greenblatt's Delicatessen. "I fussed. Hope you like brisket," she said, and we toasted each other with the corners of our sandwiches. I appreciated her for having all the earmarks of a vegetarian without being one.

"So, what is this?" she said. "You don't return my calls, you act like you're avoiding me." She rested her feet on the coffee table. The little pink daubs of polish at the end of her toes looked like frosting.

"I am avoiding you. I think you're trouble."

"Well, I hope I am trouble to some extent. I want to be interesting."

"Some people can be too interesting. I've had women I've gone out with in this town tell me all sorts of strange things: That they used to ride with Hell's Angels, that they got herpes from two different est trainers, that they can levitate. And your story about your relationship with Leroy puts you right up there in that pantheon."

Kiki got teary, as if she were calling upon a great storehouse of disappointment within herself.

"See, the problem is, I lied."

"Ohhhh, really?"

"No, I lied about the car. It's Leroy's car. I didn't want you to know I don't have a car. And I think you picked up on that, and now you don't trust me."

"But what about Leroy?"

"He didn't need the car. He never goes anywhere at night."

"But what about him as a man?"

"I explained all that. It's nonsexual. We grew up together in Tyler, Texas. He used to go out with my twin sister."

"This is a very strange situation."

"You'd have to meet him. I don't want to talk about this. I want to have sex. Oh, and I didn't offer you anything to drink."

Kiki looked at what happened to her body during sex with frank interest, more like a lab partner than a lover. When we were on her bed—hers and Leroy's—and I played my lips over her nipples, she looked on as if I were a lifeguard giving someone artificial respiration. (She pointed out to me, like a tour guide, that she had the beginnings of a third nipple just below her left breast; the Burmeister twins had originally been slated to be the Burmeister triplets.) When I ran my tongue up her leg in the direction of her bronze panties, she shifted her body to get a better view, like a bystander at a parade.

At her inner thigh, where a generous application of Lubriderm caused my tongue to slide, I was jolted by the sound of someone on roller skates barging into the bedroom and thundering across the floor. I yelped and pushed myself upright onto my knees and swirled my body in both directions, preparing for an attacker. The sound surrounded the bed, but I saw no one. It was a phantom skater, a peculiarly southern California ghost. The steel rollers surged down the alley between the bed and the wall, and then there was the sound of wood crunching against wood. The lamp on the nightstand, a female toreador done in lime and black, wobbled on its base. Then there was silence, except for the hum of ball bearings.

Kiki leaned over the side of the bed.

"She's stuck."

I looked over the side of the bed also. It was a very large turtle—a turtle the size of a Volkswagen tire—strapped to a skateboard.

Kiki got out of bed to unwedge the turtle and turned it around.

"This is Natalie," she said. "She's a desert tortoise. I felt sorry for her . . . it's such an effort for her to get around. So Leroy put these straps on the skateboard. She really flies. We've sent some tapes to *America's Funniest Home Videos* but we haven't heard anything yet."

Kiki straddled the tortoise and gave it a healthy launch, her breasts flopping in opposite directions as she shoved the beast off toward the door. I lost sight of the tortoise, but I could hear the paddle of its naily fins against the linoleum.

Kiki knelt on the bed and crossed over to me, smiling apologetically. "I forgot she was in the house. Now you're going to think I'm way too interesting for you."

She took me in her mouth, making loud, wet sounds. As I

became erect within her, she interrupted herself to explain, "I'm a sucker for animals." Then she held away her hair with her left hand as she slipped her mouth over me again. She applied herself to me with open-eyed curiosity, like a technician wondering when a beaker will come to the correct temperature.

The phone rang, and rang again, and Kiki brought herself up from me.

"I better..."

She took the telephone into the closet, as if it were impolite to be seen talking on the phone.

"Hello?" she said. "Yes." A gasp of recognition. *"Yesss."* She spoke mostly in restrained "uh huhs" and "yesses." "I'd love to. Of course."

She came out of the closet eyes vivid, lips pursed, as if afraid to speak and make what just happened not true. She shivered with excitement, her nipples now hard as flooring pegs. Perhaps some good acting news had just come her way.

"That was Nathan Fisher," she said, referring to an actor who had been a national heartthrob for twenty minutes during the early eighties. He starred as a private eye in *Cold Steel* on CBS, and then went on to make a few movies. "He wants to see me! Nathan Fisher!"

Her enthusiasm was so genuine and unaffected that I got caught up in it. "Really?" I said, like a father whose daughter has been invited to the prom by the captain of the football team.

"I met him last night at this screening at the Directors Guild."

"You just bumped into him or what?"

"I went up to him. I was with Leroy. I told him how much I admire him and that I was an actress. I gave him my phone number. Wow. Wow, wow, wow. I should call my sister." She picked up the phone.

"Kiki, just a second..."

"Oh," she said. "I'm sorry," not quite sure of my objection.

"I don't have that much time."

"Oh." She came back to bed and crawled across to me. "I'll call her later." She played with me with her hands, slapping me from palm to palm as if she were molding clay.

"What does he want to see you about?"

"A job, I hope."

"He's probably going to hit on you."

"He better not try."

She went back down on me. Through the spray of chestnut hair that covered me I heard her say, "Jesus, Nathan Fisher."

# Chapter

# *4*

Wilfred Lawson, an English character actor with an enthusiasm for strong drink, sat in a West End pub one evening and overheard two young American actors speaking passionately about their craft. Lawson, his speech a little imprecise, approached them and asked them if they'd like to see, at that very moment, some acting that would surprise, and perhaps even jolt, them . . . acting of a sort that they had never seen before.

The younger actors agreed, and Lawson led them across the street to the alley entrance of a theater, and up the stairs to the balcony. There they watched a few minutes of a play in progress. The acting was fine. But suddenly, the mood on the stage changed. The actors varied their rhythms in unusual ways, and held their bodies in arresting poses. There was an air of tension and expectation on the stage and in the audience.

One of the American actors leaned over to Lawson and said, "This is amazing." After a few more moments of observing, he leaned over again and asked, "What are they doing?"

Lawson said, "They're waiting for my entrance."

◆ ◆ ◆

I like to think that even after eight years in the entertainment industry I am still, as I was once described to my liking, refreshingly non-Hollywood. But then how to explain that I was flying back to Los Angeles from New York on MGM Grand. MGM Grand screams out, "Kill the rich." My excuse for flying it is, when you land, you don't have to wait for your luggage.

I was screwing around, trying to get my seat right. It slides fore and aft, and some German guy behind me keeps slamming into me, like we're playing dodgems. There is no communicating with this guy. I don't know who he is, but he probably owns Bavaria or something. He looks like he might be a direct descendant of H. L. Mencken. They share many of the same physical features: the neck, the cheeks, the cigar. Across from me, Barbara Walters has curled herself up for a demure nap. I can smell a perfume ad from her open copy of *Vanity Fair*. What is the point of these ads? "This is how our perfume smells on cardboard"? Up ahead of me, Paul Newman sits across the table from some agent I recognize from the trades, a young woman. He's been talking at her for three hours straight. Behind me, past the bar, I see Richard Widmark. Distinguished, tan, coat and tie. What is he, seventy-five, eighty? He's got a little shopping bag from Alfred Dunhill resting at his feet. Rod Steiger comes up out of nowhere and starts helping himself to the cheese wheel on the bar.

Jesus, I think, if this fucker went down, what a great headline. I could see the faces of news anchors in every market provoked into sincerity: "Tonight, Hollywood mourns . . ." And where would I figure among these various accounts? I wouldn't rate a mention on television, of course. Maybe in the newspapers, after the jump, under the subhead "Also Among the Deceased: Writer James E. Hoy and Some German Guy."

I'd just spent three days in New York trying to lure a prominent African-American movie star out to Los Angeles for unimagined glory and money as the lead in the *Lou Duffy* show, to replace Malcolm Dant. You'd be surprised at how many people are willing to turn that down. You have to catch movie stars at exactly the right time to get them to do television. I thought I had a shot with Carl Lee Greene. He'd already starred as Malcolm X in the controversial miniseries about Muhammad Ali a few years earlier. He took his Emmy and went back to feature films. But the leading man roles had given way to character parts. The young black directors, the new rap pack, weren't much interested in tailoring roles for a heavyweight like Carl Lee Greene. I thought he might be ripe.

We met for lunch at Le Bernardin, Carl's choice. Apparently he's some sort of gourmet. Maguy Le Coze, the hostess, made a refined fuss over him when we came in. He urged the scallops aux truffe on me—"one of the ten best dishes in New York"— and selected a perfect Meursault to go with it. I think I still have the cork somewhere. He told me Burgess Meredith had sparked his interest in wine years earlier when they had done a production of *Lost in the Stars* together.

I was anxious in his presence, until I came to realize I was seeing him as Malcolm X. The face of Carl Lee Greene had superseded in my mind the face of the historical figure. His Malcolm was much scarier than Denzel Washington's later version in the Spike Lee picture. Maybe that's why his feature film career had softened. His performance in the miniseries was so powerful that producers had come to see him as the actual Malcolm X; they were afraid of him. It was only after he ordered the wine that I relaxed. I realized that a guy who can say, "The 'eighty-two Chambolles des Musigny" is probably not going to hurt me.

I think I had Carl sold at that lunch. I described the three-camera system to him: Reading the script at the table, three days of rehearsal, the run-throughs, camera blocking day. And then filming in front of a live audience. "It's like doing a one-act play every week," I said. This appealed to him very much; he came out of the theater. I reminded him how it was television that exploded his name into the very big time a few years ago. His mouth was watering. He admitted his agents were pushing him toward a decision. Agents like to see actors working. When we said good-bye, in the blinding midafternoon light outside the Equitable Center, he asked, "Do you have any idea what the show would be called?"

"Well," I said, "I think a good name for this particular effort would be *The Carl Lee Greene Show.*"

"Really?" he said. It was almost as if he were touched.

I went back to the Ritz-Carlton and called David Putzman at Polonia. "He's ripe," I reported. "There's nothing left now except for you to move in and fuck up the deal."

"Uh huh," said Putzman, which was his way of expressing enthusiasm and gratitude. "Listen, while I have you, Leo was talking to Larry Foreman, and Larry has this six-on-the-air commitment at NBC, and he thinks you and Neil would be perfect for it."

Larry Foreman, the former chain-smoking, heavy-drinking president of two major networks, was now a chain-smoking, heavy-drinking independent producer specializing in "high-concept" sitcoms. "High-concept" is a technical term most easily translated as "stupid."

"Our plate's a little full, isn't it, Dave? Come on, I'm delivering a very big name here."

"Yeah, but this is six on-the-air. You could schedule yourself. It's a real cute idea."

"We don't do cute."

"No, I mean classy cute."

"What did Neil say?"

"I haven't talked to him."

Neil frightened Putzman. Gentle, soul-eyed Neil Stein for some reason went on the attack around David Putzman the way a normally sweet-tempered terrier might suddenly go crazy in the presence of a vacuum cleaner.

"I want you to at least consider the idea."

"You want to pitch it on the phone?"

"Just briefly. The space shuttle—it's a half-hour comedy—the crew goes up, everything's under way, and this guy, the captain or whatever, finds out his mother has stowed away on board. His fucking mother is up in space with him. A Jewish mother. And they're going to be up there, God knows how long."

"Five seasons. How does his mother manage to stow away on a United States space shuttle?"

"Hey, you guys are the writers. What do you think? What should I tell Leo?"

"Tell him I think his wife is fucking the pool man."

"I mean about the idea. And don't even kid about his wife."

"Putzman, it's a horrible idea. It's stupid and base. It's one hundred and eighty degrees away from anything Neil and I would even be slightly interested in."

"Well, think about it."

Early that evening I was in the Ritz-Carlton bar having a Campari and soda and listening to Norman the bartender expound on Japanese-American relations to a few Japanese businessmen who didn't understand a word he said, when I was paged to the phone. I expected it to be my dinner date, the ex-wife of an old friend, who was already about fifteen minutes late. But it was Carl Lee Greene. That's why the hotel made an effort to find me. Carl Lee Greene was on the phone. So many star fuckers, so few stars.

"Great lunch," he said, but people don't usually call you at dinnertime to rave about lunch. "The thing is, I wanted to catch you before you went back tomorrow."

I'll give this to Carl Lee Greene: He was straight with me. A lot of stars like to string you along, pretending they're still considering your project. They love to be courted. Carl told the truth early. And he made the call himself, instead of laying it off on his agent. The galling aspect of it was that the truth was so stupid. He and his wife had signed up for a cooking class with Marcella Hazan in Bologna, Italy. They would be gone for six weeks, right in the middle of production. They had been on the waiting list for two years. They didn't want to give it up.

I played all the angles, but Carl was as firm as wood. So I said I was sorry not to have the opportunity of working with him. Which was true: Here was a major and authentic star with all the earmarks of a decent guy. My regret was acute. "Well," I told him as we signed off, "I guess you have your priorities straight." And as soon as I hung up, I thought, Yeah, that's one way of looking at it. But another way of looking at it is that this asshole was walking away from fifty million dollars so he can learn how to cook spaghetti.

So there I was in the faux deco surroundings of MGM Grand. It was like flying over the continent in a steak house. *The Barkleys of Broadway,* chosen by passenger vote, was playing on the video screens. Wine so early in the day ("We're pouring a Sterling Napa Valley Chardonnay, 1986") left me untypically reflective. One thing I was reflecting on was the failure of my mission: I was coming back to Los Angeles without Carl Lee Greene, the one major black star left whom we knew could carry the show. I felt as if I'd let down my team, especially Neil. The project seemed to be going away. Which would mean that Neil and I, instead of being able to concentrate our energies on an entirely new project, would require them to fend off the relentless pressures from Leo Becker and David Putzman and Larry Foreman to do a show about a Jewish mother in space.

Certain production companies make a deal with you—buy you—with flowers and dinners and soft words of respect for your creative talents. They support your goals of quality; they even allow language to that effect to find its way into your contract. But once you're signed up and delivered to the minimum security prison called "a development deal," the tune abruptly changes to, Produce anything, just get on the air. And thereafter, the writer has continual and direct exposure to people whose first instincts are to be thugs.

So this is what I reflected upon as I watched Fred, in tails, and Ginger, in a bizarrely fringed outfit that suggested she was the daughter of a tribal chieftain, gracefully flit about on the screen above Paul Newman's head. But being a balanced person, who knows that life is more than work, this was not my sole thought. I also reflected upon the likelihood of my success were I to suddenly bolt from my chair, grab the German guy behind me by the throat, pull him to the floor, and bang his head against the cabin partition until he went insensate.

Instead, I decided to get up and walk back to the bar and see if Rod Steiger had left any cheese. I spread something yellow and blue-veined on a water cracker. The aroma of chocolate chip cookies wafted over to me from the microwave; we were pretty close to Los Angeles if they were baking the cookies already. The flight attendants, all in black tie, were busy knocking down tables and stowing carry-ons for landing. I wandered farther back, toward the curtained off private cabins just beyond the bar, giving Mr. Widmark's Alfred Dunhill bag a little bump. A loud giggle caught my attention. I saw through a not-quite-closed curtain two people in a cabin meant for four, kissing. It was a bold display for such a relatively public place. The man worked the woman's left breast with his hand, twisting it as they kissed as if he were trying to bring in Radio Moscow. Both wore expensive tailored sweatsuits of matching white. Their faces were obscured by the woman's cascade of yellow hair, but clearly she was Geneva Holloway. A tiny white dog sat opposite them eating toothpaste from a tube, squeezing it out as best it could with its little black nose and clumsy paws. It looked up at me sheepishly as it pawed its treasure.

I withdrew, out of respect for the dog's privacy. Geneva and her friend didn't seem to care who watched. It had been over four years since Geneva sent me off into the misty Trancas night, aroused and confused. Her boyfriend Russ Borgreave had been convicted of securities fraud under the RICO laws and was in his third year at Allentown. Geneva for her part had struck gold. After a year playing Lee Major's secretary on *Horseplay,* Aaron Spelling put her in *Bel Air Terrace,* the nighttime soap, as Chelsea Huntington, the poor little rich girl. By the end of her second season she'd been through a brain tumor, vaginitis, prescription drug addiction, and a sexual identity crisis. There was an Emmy nomination, the *TV Guide* cover, a couple shots on *Arsenio Hall.* Geneva was about six years away from having her own brand of perfume. But Joanna Calhoun, the star of *Bel Air Terrace,* got her nose out of joint, so in the last episode of the third season Chelsea disappeared over the Atlantic in a Piper Comanche on her way to Virgin Gorda to rescue her father from an island insurgency. It was supposed to be a cliff-hanger. Will Chelsea survive? Will Geneva Holloway be back on *Bel Air Terrace?* Fodder for all those entertainment news shows hosted by women and men named Robin. But in the meantime it was well known in the industry that Joanna Calhoun would walk off *Bel Air Terrace* if little Chelsea rose up from the Atlantic Ocean, and that Geneva's agency, Triumphant Artists, was trolling her through the networks, looking for a series commitment.

You know how when you get off an airplane, there's always a crowd of people at the gate waiting for their loved ones, their faces hesitant, ready to break out into a smile when the right person emerges? A similar group greets you at the MGM Grand terminal—the same searching looks, the same air of expectation. Except at MGM Grand, they're all chauffeurs, fifteen or twenty guys in dark suits, about half of them holding cardboard signs that say "Epstein," or "Daley" or "International Model Search." All right, let he who is without sin cast the first stone: I had a guy waiting for me, too. This guy, Louis, whom I usually get when I order a limo. He's fifty-five, squat, rolls through airports like a Sherman tank. I like Louis because he doesn't feel compelled to chat.

"Hi, Louis," I said.

"Any luggage?"

"Yeah," I admitted, apologizing a little. Louis doesn't like to stop for things. He started off toward the outdoor baggage area, assuming I would follow. Having Louis meet you at the airport is like having your dad pick you up at school when he would rather be doing something else.

Within minutes the luggage arrived, a few carts bulging almost exclusively with Louis Vuitton, but with a few saltings of Bottega Veneta or Hermes, which showed that there were some fashion rebels on board. Louis scanned impatiently; he knows my luggage by sight, battered canvas pieces with scuffed belting leather trim. I waited with my fellow passengers for the carts to be unloaded; most of us were overdressed for the bright winter sun, with topcoats over our arms. Geneva and her companion, in their luminous white sweatsuits, looked like circus performers. They were greeted by a chauffeur and a lanky young woman in sandals, whom I took to be Geneva's assistant, because she was given charge of the little white dog. Geneva zeroed in on the young woman, full of animated chatter. She was close to me, just behind me, and I decided to turn and interject "Geneva?" into her conversation. She stopped in mid-simile and looked at me. Her eyes were little green pools of inquisition. The young woman looked at me unpleasantly, because I was taking the celebrity's attention away.

"Jimmy Hoy," I said.

"Help me out," said Geneva.

"I gave you a ride home from a memorial service for a dog once. You lived in Trancas."

"Oh, sure," she said. "I see your name all the time."

"And I guess I can say the same to you. Everybody's in suspense about what you're going to do next."

"Including me. We were just in New York for meetings."

"That was my husband's dog that died," said the young woman. "I met you before."

"Oh, God, wait . . ." said Geneva, suddenly inspired. She reached to her fellow circus performer, who was bending over a confusion of Vuitton pieces, matching up baggage tags. She pulled back the waistband of his sweatpants and thwacked the elastic, a little too hard. Somehow, after that indignity, he managed to concoct an expression of amused indulgence by the time he turned to face us. He was Milo Lally.

"Jesus Christ," he said.

"Remember this guy?" said Geneva.

"Milo," I said, "you dropped off the face of the earth."

"Not really," said Milo. He was uncomfortable.

"Well, you dropped out of group. We never heard about you again."

"Did you ever know I got married?"

"This is Milo's wife, Ashley," said Geneva, pushing Ashley forward.

"Of course. I did meet you. You were at the memorial service for the dog," I said. "You had long boots on."

"That's when Milo and me just started going out."

"Milo's my manager," said Geneva.

"Really? How long have you been handling her?" I asked, without allowing the slightest trace of irony into my voice.

"What is it, two years now?" said Milo. At some level, he was begging me not to call him out for the fraud I knew him to be.

"This one?" asked Louis, holding out my suit carrier with the embarrassing stains on the canvas.

"And one more. So, are you zeroing in on anything?" I asked Geneva. "You're so good."

"Oh, thank you. Not really. There's a certain amount of fear involved, because this next step is so important."

"You should do a comedy." I said this with authority, as if I'd been giving a lot of thought to her career. But as soon as I heard myself say the words, I realized that I believed them. She would be very good in a comedy.

Geneva and Milo looked at each other as if I'd guessed a secret.

"We were just talking about that on the airplane."

"You should absolutely pursue it. I see you in something where you're up against somebody strong. Because you're powerful, you have to have somebody strong to play off. It should be a situation where you're one down, where you have to fight your way up."

Geneva gave me that generous, focused attention people offer when you talk exclusively about them.

"This is very interesting," said Geneva.

"That's it?" said Louis, with no hint of patience.

"I have to go or my driver will beat me up. Milo, what a treat. Seriously, Geneva, think about comedy."

As my car went around the oval, Geneva walked toward a limo with her chauffeur and her dog, while Milo went off in another direction, his young wife hanging on his arm. Milo had complicated his life a great deal since we last met. Of course, he had seriously advanced his hyphenate status as well, from actor-masseur to manager–boy toy.

As my car passed Geneva, she flagged us down. I opened the window, and she held out a business card. "Here," she said. "In case you get any great ideas for a comedy."

It was a simple black-and-white card with her phone number, and then her name and title:

> GENEVA HOLLOWAY
> TELEVISION STAR

"Jesus, Louis, I'm sorry," I said when I realized he was already on the San Diego Freeway. "I forgot. I'm not going home. Santa Monica. Rustic Canyon." I'd promised my ex-wife I'd stay overnight with her son. Louis acknowledged me with a slight smirk of peeve. I love this guy.

Rustic Canyon hews to the cleavage between Santa Monica and Pacific Palisades. Avenues saunter down through it like friendly streams, and would empty into the mighty Pacific were it not for the six lanes of highway that blare past at its foot. A handful of years ago, when my wife and I bought there, the canyon was mostly an artists colony. But lately it's turned into a Beverly Hills for people who don't want to admit they have money.

Miranda Erikson, my ex-wife, continued to live in the boxy redwood-and-glass architectural statement that had been our love nest for the four years of our marriage. She met me at the door— the doors, really, two wide swaths of planking that always seemed out of scale to me—with a who-can-that-be air. Even when she knows what to expect, Miranda is prepared to be surprised. She took one of the bags from me.

"Should we take it into the bedroom?"

"No, this is fine," I said.

My haggard canvas bags rested on the flagstones of the entrance hall next to Miranda's luggage of trendy black vinyl.

"I'm not leaving until six. Emery has a meeting."

"Fine. A little overlap. We can visit."

Miranda offered me some tea and, sitting across from each other at the long yellow table in the cozy kitchen-dining room, we went over the drill for the care and feeding of her son Bennett, which was not very complicated. The tea had a soapy, herbal taste. Miranda drank hers out her favorite cup, which said 51% NORWEGIAN over the colors of the Norwegian flag.

"I appreciate this," she said.

"Glad to do it."

She slid a piece of paper across the table to me.

"This person called."

"Oh." It was Kiki.

"You're not going to have her over, are you?"

"I was thinking about it."

"I'd rather you didn't. At least, don't have her stay over. Bennett is a little confused as it is."

"Maybe I'll just have her over to go out to dinner with us."

"Thank you. So, what are you working on?"

"Have you ever heard of an actress named Geneva Holloway?"

Miranda considered this, to be a good sport. She had a minimal interest in popular entertainments.

"I don't think so."

"She's good. Not *funny* funny, but she has a nice quality. I'm thinking of doing a show with her." I announced this to myself as well as to Miranda.

Bennett came in the kitchen door, pushing himself in backward, using his nylon backpack as leverage. He was looking more like his mother these days, with her lively eyes and perfect skin and shy smile. He was almost pretty. No one would mistake him for my son. His father was an actor working on various American productions in Canada; his contact with Bennett was infrequent.

Bennett looked at his mother, then at me, gave off a barely audible "Hi" and left for another part of the house.

"Bennett!" Miranda called, looking off into the middle distance as she waited for a reply. "Bennett!"

"Yes?" came Bennett's voice.

"Jim's here."

"I know."

"Come here and say hello to him."

"I did."

"Come here."

Bennett reappeared without the backpack, embarrassed at being coaxed into observing the protocols of civility.

When we lived together, Bennett and I never quite broke the ice with each other. We depended on Miranda to be the buffer between us. Whenever she was away, we each kept to our own corner of the house, like strange cats.

Now that Bennett and I no longer lived together, I found it easier to relax around him. We still tended to keep our emotional distance, but when the two of us warmed up, we could have a little fun together.

"Bennett!" I offered my hand and he took it and shook hands shyly. He had the dank, slightly unwholesome smell of little boys.

"I'm in Research Group Alpha," he told his mother.

"Is that the one with the frogs or the bugs?"

"Bugs."

"Well, that's not so bad."

Bennett attended a public grammar school in the canyon where class divisions were called things like Research Group Alpha, instead of Robins and Bluebirds. His show-and-tell sessions, I recalled, were known as "communications."

"Hey, Bennett, I brought you something from New York." I took out my wallet and gave Bennett a five-dollar bill. He scrutinized it for some indication of what all this meant.

"This isn't from New York," he said.

· "Yes, it is. I got it in change from the bar at the Ritz-Carlton Hotel. Just yesterday."

"But it's not a gift or anything."

"No, Bennett, remember the last time I was here? You won five dollars from me at Super Mario Brothers."

Bennett searched his memory.

"Was that for real money?"

"Sure. I thought so."

"Okay," he said with a foolish smile and put the money in his pocket.

"Don't forget it's there or it will end up in the washing machine," said Miranda, and after Bennett left the room she added, "he has no sense of money."

"He doesn't have to yet."

"Who is this person?" she said, fiddling with the message she had given me.

"An actress. From New York. She has an identical twin sister in Tyler, Texas."

"She doesn't sound very substantial on the phone. I mean, she doesn't sound like a serious person."

"She's not worthy of me?"

"Doesn't sound like it. I mean, 'Kiki.' Give me a break."

"She's interesting."

"Everybody in the entertainment business is interesting. Nobody can be just a person. Why don't you cultivate friends who have normal lives?"

"It's hard. Why don't you introduce me to one of those normal women you hang out with?"

"I can't. When we were going through the divorce, I badmouthed you ruthlessly."

"That would probably just make me more attractive to them."

"I'm afraid you're right. Women can be very untrustworthy. Christ, what is he doing?"

She left the room to investigate an annoying grinding coming from the floorboards overhead, leaving me to bask in the comforts of her kitchen-dining room. Formerly our kitchen-dining room. Still half mine. We held the house in joint tenancy, as the lawyers put it, and I was in no hurry to sell. I enjoyed coming over every once in a while, sitting in the kitchen, conjuring up sentiments of intimacy without paying an emotional toll for them. The chrome yellow cupboards with the glass panes, the cacti on the windowsill, the blue-and-white platters of export ware in the glossy yellow hutch. (We had tried to evoke, with some success, Monet's dining room at Giverny, which we had visited on our honeymoon.) The Sub-Zero refrigerator. A controversial purchase, like the solar-heated hot water tanks on the roof. I'd never heard of Sub-Zero refrigerators, and suddenly, as we designed the kitchen, learned that I had to have one. Miranda, the antimaterialist, the social worker, lobbied for it, a six-thousand-dollar expanse of matte stainless steel more appropriate to an institution. Miranda insisted on it. She was contemptuous of show business; it bothered her that I made my money that way. But when it came to spending six thousand dollars of that money on a refrigerator, she had no compunctions. She never saw the irony in that. I often reminded her that Monet did not have a Sub-Zero refrigerator.

Miranda came back into the room and nodded, her lips pursed in mock frustration, indicating she had a story to tell.

"He's up there in his stocking feet, right? He takes all those little ball bearings out of that damn pachinko machine you gave him. Like, forty ball bearings. Then he *rolls* across the floor on them."

She shook her head. I smiled.

"So what time's Emery coming by?"

"He's not. I'm meeting him. I don't like him seeing you. He fawns all over you."

"He doesn't fawn."

"He acts differently. I've talked to him about it."

Emery was the minister at a very hip Episcopalian church down in Venice. A woman Christ on the cross, a gay and lesbian choir, that sort of thing. A very different way for Miranda to go after her actor-husband and me, Mr. Hollywood Pants. The first time Miranda displayed Emery to me, she was appalled at the sudden and keen interest he demonstrated in the mechanics of submitting a script to television.

"Well, it's not fawning," I said. "He's got an idea for a television series."

"No, he doesn't. He's above that."

"There's no sin in it."

"He's interested in television's power as a force for change."

"He's got an idea for a TV series. Everybody's got an idea for a TV series."

"No, he doesn't."

(Yes, he did. *Street Beat.* A dedicated young minister walks the streets of the city, ministering mostly to attractive young people in trouble. Emery confided this to me at a Christmas party over a cup of Miranda's glug, a wine punch long associated with the high suicide rate in Nordic countries. Emery let the information seep out reluctantly, as if he were telling me where Jimmy Hoffa was buried. He saw the show as a way to put forward humanistic ideals. I'm ashamed to say I toyed with him a little.

"This minister . . . could he solve some crimes?"

Emery looked puzzled. "I hadn't thought about that."

"Because if he could solve some crimes, you have more of a shot."

"Well, sure," said Emery. His lips were chapped, and the purple of the glug made them disgusting to behold. "He could be sort of a detective, I guess. I can see how that would work. But nothing violent."

"Unless it's organic to the story. I mean, there is violence out on the streets," I said.

"Yeah. That's true enough. But basically it's about his work with people."

"Right," I said. "Unfortunately, it sounds too much like a series Robert Blake did called *Hell Town*." Emery's cracked, electric purple lips twisted in disappointment. "But you're on the right track. I think there's something there.")

"You think television has this absolute hold over everyone." Miranda was berating me. "You're secretly proud of it."

"Not secretly."

"You probably won't believe this, but there are people in this city who have never heard of Roseanne Arnold."

"Not enough."

"You assume that television is ultimately irresistible."

"Apparently it is, Miranda. Everyone . . . *everyone* . . . has an idea for a series. That's the first immutable law of the universe. My accountant, my doctor's wife, people on airplanes, the lady where I take my dry cleaning. Last fall I go back to Cleveland for that testimonial to Father Erlingher . . . ? I'm sitting on the dais next to the bishop of Cleveland, we're talking blah, blah, blah— *he's* got an idea for a TV series."

"If Emery has ideas for television, it's for higher purposes."

"No, see, that's the worst type. I get that from TV critics and college professors and do-gooders. They come to me and condescend to do television. They won't admit to the lure of riches or glory, or just the pure excitement of it. They hide behind higher purposes. I much prefer guys who come up to me half tanked at parties and say, 'Boy, you ought to do a show about the carpet business. You wouldn't believe what walks into my store. We could go fifty-fifty on it.'"

Miranda stared at me.

"You're a fuckhead and I'm leaving." She said it with as much affection as you can say a thing like that. I heard her out in the front hall, fussing with her luggage.

"Where are you guys going to be?" I called.

"I left the number."

"But where is it? What are you doing?"

"Tahoe. Emery's doing a POC seminar."

Emery gave weekend workshops called the Power of Communication. They were for people who enjoy sitting across from a stranger and saying ten things they like about him. Emery charged participants a few hundred dollars and then basically humiliated them for two days. On the last afternoon, he turned it all around and sent them off elated and inspired.

Miranda came back into the room.

"What kind of series did the bishop of Cleveland want to do?"

"Not a bad idea, really, if this were a different world. The childhood of the saints—a different saint every week. I told him the Jews who controlled Hollywood would never let it on the air."

"You didn't say that."

"No, but that's what I told Neil I said."

"Why would you do that to poor Neil?"

"To torture him. Every once in a while, Neil requires a little torture."

# Chapter

# 5

■ George Jessel, renowned and much in demand for his flowery eulogies, was speaking at one of the many funerals he presided over. "A man whose devotion to his family was a glorious example for us all," he said, "a man whose tremendous success in his career was never as important to him as his very special love for little children. A man who—"

At this, Jessel happened to glimpse into the coffin. "Jesus," he said. "I know this guy."

◆ ◆ ◆

Neil and I sat in our office at Paramount brainstorming—which is to say, staring at each other. The plan was to come up with a solid idea for a Geneva Holloway series before the people at Polonia found out that Carl Lee Greene had passed. Because once they did, they would be on us like mold on cheese, arguing from every side the brilliance of a show about a Jewish mother lost in space. I dreaded particularly the moment that Neil, who carries personal guilt to the level of connoisseurship, would say, "You know, it's not a *horrible* idea."

As we sat sat looking for signs of hope in each other's eyes, Sharone entered in twill jodhpurs, several strands of her ash blond hair done in corn rows. She approached us reverently, bearing the Sunday overnight ratings like an offering. This was her dramatic homage to the creative process.

"James . . ." said Neil, finally breaking the awful silence. I looked over to him as at a long-awaited sail on the horizon. "Who wrote *Tom Jones*?"

His mind had been wandering, and he was man enough to admit it.

"Henry Fielding," I said.

"And Tony Richardson directed," offered Sharone, very respectfully, on her way to the door. Neil and I, equally respectful, waited until she was gone before we laughed.

Sharone Torberg's entire frame of reference was show business. She honored the industry that had so brutally betrayed her the way some women defend the men that beat them. She had come down from Bakersfield at seventeen without a high school degree; I get the impression there was a stepfather with roving hands in the background. She intended to "act or model." She evaded the immediate traps of the streets and drugs and supported herself selling herbs and crystals at a shop on Melrose. She pursued dancing, her true passion, then had the misfortune to be chosen as a Los Angeles Raiders Raiderette. This made her an object of desire, which edged her away from the values to which she had been hewing. She soon found herself in compromising positions at parties in expensive hotels, and often decided it was easier to sleep with a guy than not. This led to turning tricks. Then she took the est training with a girlfriend, just before that whole thing had played out in southern California. She and her friend were inspired by the training to become the best prostitutes they could be, to "come from service." This led to five years in Las Vegas, ending in a suicide attempt. Sharone was now closely involved with a support group for young women trying to stay out of "the life." Apparently, like any habit, it has a strong pull.

After a brief interval of bemused smiling at one another, Neil and I started our thinking again. Again, he was the first to break the silence.

"How do you know she'll do a half-hour?"

"She will. I sense it. I practically sold her at the airport."

"Is she crazy or anything?"

"I haven't heard any horror stories."

"Because here's what I was thinking..."

My pear-shaped partner positioned himself on the high board of an idea. He jumped.

"We still do the Malcolm Dant show, but with Geneva Holloway."

"You mean we make her the police chief?"

"No, the wife. We make her his wife, and she's a judge. She becomes a judge in the pilot. The Valerie Bertinelli thing."

We'd developed a pilot for Valerie Bertinelli about a woman who finds out you don't have to be a lawyer to become a judge, you just have to take a test.

"So she's a judge and he's the police chief?"

"Right. But now *she* hires the ex-con, because she's working, she needs help around the house."

In *Lou Duffy*, Lou, who needs help around the house, hires an ex-con whom he had put away, because he feels sorry for the guy. But the ex-con is incompetent, a continual source of annoyance to Duffy.

"This is better," I said. "Because now it drives the police chief nuts to have an ex-convict in the house."

"We make the convict very competent now—a real domestic wizard."

"Maybe even a threat to the husband... a little sexual tension in the air."

"This feels good," said Neil. "What do you think?"

"Is it too soon to whisper the word 'Emmy'?" I said.

Oh, golden the hour in which we first presented our idea to Geneva Holloway. Oh, glorious the writer who shares in even an echo of such success. Oh, happy the memory of the production company head who was host to this wondrous meeting.

Geneva positioned herself in the center of the long, teal blue sofa in Leo Becker's office. She wore a blowsy white jumpsuit. Her feet, in sandals, were up on the coffee table. Her toenails, her fingernails, and her lips were all of the same glossy hot pink. The low winter sun coming in the window behind her formed a nimbus around her famous tawny hair, which was all teased and curled. She had a cup of hot tea and a glass of mineral water in front of her, and two saucers of lemon sections.

Milo Lally, in a jacket and tie, blue jeans, and cowboy boots, sat far to Geneva's left at the end of the sofa, trying his best to look, if not like an equal, then at least like an adult. I imagined him fighting off the urge to stand up and offer to go out and wash everybody's car.

Leo Becker, in an Italian cardigan with an assertive design, running tigers I think, sat behind the antique refectory table that served as his desk and beamed across it like an indulgent father. His face was blotchy and his nose bulbous, giving him the air of Rembrandt in the later self-portraits. To disguise his baldness, he grew his gray-and-black hair very long on one side, then combed it all the way over his barren pate, giving the impression that he had strips of bacon resting on top of his head. David Putzman, secure in full Armani, sat close enough to Leo to align himself with the Polonia president without actually annoying him.

As usual, I made the pitch. Neil Stein, my faithful Jewish companion, annoyed me during my presentation by going two or three times too often to the glass-covered jar that contained Hershey kisses. He redeemed himself, however, by reacting to everything I said as if it was the first time he'd heard it, and subtly racheting up the level of appreciation in the room.

I concluded. Geneva sat silent, unreadable. Then:

"You do these things in front of an audience?"

"It's like doing a one-act play every week," I said. "The audience gives you an energy. You'll love it. It makes you feel like you're back on the stage."

"Yeah, the thing is, I was never on the stage."

"If you don't want an audience, we'll do it without an audience," said Leo Becker. "Whatever you want."

"I might like an audience," said Geneva. "I've noticed that people like me in person."

"I see a spontaneity in you that would be good to tap into," said Neil, diving into the pitch.

"It's true!" said Geneva, as if Neil had offered a thundering insight. "I am spontaneous. I spoke at this political thing last week for some senator— Milo, who was that senator?"

"Alan Cranston."

"And it was the first time I've done that, but everyone loved what I said. It wasn't the actress, it was the caring. That's what people heard."

"Exactly," said Neil.

Geneva was silent again, thoughtful, covering her upper lip with her lower lip.

"What would it be called?" she asked.

"We'd thought of calling it *Sea Hunt*," I said.

Geneva raised her eyebrows, puzzled. There was no room in her head for irony; too many hair roots.

"Excuse me at this point," said Leo Becker. "This is a creative meeting, and that's not my department. But I think the show should be called *The Geneva Holloway Show.*"

Geneva nodded in the face of this logic. Here was a good idea. "When would the network want this?"

"By May first," said Leo. "That's the deadline for pilots. We should be in production by early April."

"I'm in London until March thirtieth on a movie of the week."

"No problem there," said Leo. "We'll just have everybody wait for you."

Geneva looked at each man in the room, as if for the first time. It was sort of a general flirt.

"I've never played hard-to-get," she said. "This is all very exciting. I think we should make a deal."

David Putzman shifted his ample buttocks at the mention of the word "deal."

"I'm delighted," said Leo, standing and coming around his desk as if he were about to swallow us all up, which in a way he was. There followed an interval of gay chatter, all of us standing in a circle and filling the space in the middle with layers of expectation. Geneva spoke across the circle, selling with her eyes.

"I almost see myself talking to the camera sometimes," she said. "Addressing the audience directly. That might be fresh."

"Great!" said Leo, before I could respond.

"It's certainly something to consider," I said.

"Yeah," Neil whispered to me. "And let's have film in the camera, too. That's another fresh idea."

Actors love the idea of talking directly to the camera. It comes up a lot. Neil and I were once invited to hear a pitch by a hot young actor who had a series commitment from NBC. We went through the small talk, and then the actor said, "Well, you ready to hear my idea?" And I said, just as a little joke, "Certainly—as long as it doesn't involve having you talk to the camera."

The young actor looked confused at first, and then his eyes narrowed. Then he left the room. And then his agent and his development person left the room. And then, three other people left the room. And it was *their* room. (By the way, that series went one hundred and twenty episodes. He talked to the camera for the first three shows, and then the idea was dropped. Eric Rothman ended up producing it. He made about fifty million dollars.)

"Have your business affairs people call Bobby Meyerhoff," said Geneva, referring to her agent at Triumphant Artists. "I don't know why he wasn't at this meeting. He's probably fucking some young boy in the mailroom."

Leo laughed heartily at this as he walked Geneva to the door. "Don't worry," he said. "If there's anything I do well, it's make deals."

"By the way," she said, "how much rewriting do you do?"

"As much as you want," said Leo.

"I can just keep changing things, up to the last minute?"

"Of course. Whatever you want."

There was a flurry of good-byes, and then Leo turned back to the room.

"Well, boys," he said, "it looks like you already have your work cut out for you."

"Yeah, Leo," I said. "And it looks like you already have your cut worked out for you."

The pitch to Continental Broadcasting was a cup of coffee. Joe Danko got on my side early in the presentation, laughing out loud a few times in an immature sort of honk. That brought his fellow executives along. Geneva, again resplendent in white, her eyes greener than usual owing to an allergy, reigned over the room. She sucked up to Joe Danko with eye contact, a flattery that embarrassed him in the right sort of way. And while she interrupted my pitch several times, not showing a particularly judicious sense of comic timing, her interjections did more good in demonstrating her sincerity and enthusiasm than they did harm by throwing off my rhythm.

I finished, and then Geneva rambled on for a few minutes about how she'd probably be talking to the camera, and then came that awful space of silence when it was time for the other side to respond.

"Wellll . . ." said Continental's vice president of comedy development, daring to speak first. He was a very young man—ten years old? eight years old?—and the bleached out moustache he wore made him appear even younger. He looked around at his teammates. "This sounds very good. Let us get together and talk about it."

"What's to talk about?" said Joe Danko, and there was an edge of dismissive contempt in his voice. "It's a great idea. We'll buy it."

Neil elbowed David Putzman. "David, wake up. Take your order book out." He got his laugh.

Geneva poured it on for Joe Danko before he left, gushing all over him. The network people wandered off. David Putzman told Geneva what a great job she did, ignoring me. This was his standard approach toward writers: Say "please" a lot, but never say "thank you." He thought that an expression of appreciation was in some way a display of weakness. He'd make a great father some day.

Geneva put her arm around my waist and drew me to her. "This is the star today," she said. Putzman snorted a little.

We went as a group down the CBN halls, talking loudly and disturbing the hardworking young men and women who were in their offices concocting amusements for the American people. We crowded into the elevator—Geneva, Milo, David, Neil, me, and Bobby Meyerhoff, Geneva's bushy-haired agent—and speculated wildly on the value of our offering to the network. We handed our plastic passes back to the henna-haired receptionist and chatted in the lobby, showing off a little for the people passing by. And then it was time to part.

"Well, David," I said, "why don't you start fucking up the business deal, and Neil and I will get started fucking up the script."

"I want good writing, guys," said Geneva. "Good writing. Please."

"How good?" said Neil, and Geneva laughed.

Milo went to get Geneva's car, and the others said their goodbyes, and I was left standing alone with my star under the canopy. It was the first time I'd been alone with her since that night of near ravishment on the sofa of her house in Trancas. Geneva smiled pleasantly at me. Nothing in her manner, no little corner of her eye, acknowledged that we had passed a rather dramatic eighteen minutes together six years ago.

Milo came around the parking lot in a monstrous black Jeep with KC headers on the roof.

"Is that you?" I asked.

"Yes, but it's Milo's car. It's his he-man woman-hater machine."

"So what are you driving these days? Do you still have that Jaguar?"

She looked puzzled for a moment. Jaguar? Then she remembered. "Oh, that XKE. No, Christ no. I had to give that back to Russ."

Milo stopped and opened the passenger door.

"Well, get writing," said Geneva.

"There's something I've been wanting to ask you, about that night I drove you home," I said.

"What's that?" she asked, with a chill in her voice.

"Do you suppose that little statue of Saint Joseph is still buried in the ground up there?"

She smiled.

"The fuck if I know," she said.

# Chapter

# 6

■ The vice principal at Paul Revere Junior High School in the elegant Brentwood section of Los Angeles once got a note that read: "Please excuse Tiffany for being late today. The electric gates wouldn't open."

◆ ◆ ◆

The parking lot at Morton's restaurant provides a satisfying indication of how, at any given moment, the monied classes on the west side of Los Angeles are solving the problem of transportation. On the Monday night in question, the lot was a sea of Range Rovers, almost all of them olive drab. I assume these immense, four-wheel-drive, all-terrain vehicles are absolutely essential in managing that tricky incline in the garage of the Rodeo Collection. Amid them, Neil's yellow-and-white 1954 Buick Roadmaster convertible really looked like something. It had accommodated Neil and Renata Stein, the lovely Kiki Burmeister, and me from the Stein spread in lower Bel Air to the trendy Melrose eatery. Neil unveiled the Buick only at night, because he didn't want the sun fading the paint and the smog decomposing the rubber.

Kiki and I met at the Steins' for drinks and the mandatory inspection of the children, Paige, Brittany, and the sensibly named Jonathan. The girls were little sylphs in white cotton nightdresses. Jonathan presented himself in Mutant Ninja Turtles pajamas, swinging an illuminated plastic sword that hummed and buzzed.

His father coaxed the weapon away from him by giving him a dollar bill.

Renata Stein matched herself against Kiki and finding herself at an advantage in beauty, intelligence, and dress, decided to relax and be friendly. Renata presented herself as a perfect person, which served to keep her at a distance. She could be warm and charming and welcoming at times, but only because that's how she thought a perfect person would act under the given circumstances. She struck me as someone looking for the right role to play in life. She had no job. She once started work toward a law degree, but gave up on it. Currently, her enthusiasm was focused on the environment and the banning of handguns, for each of which she sponsored expensive fund-raising affairs at her Bel Air home.

My ex-wife's take on Renata had been "She does all the right things, but for all the wrong reasons."

Neil served us Kir Royales, while he himself threw back a vodka martini (Wyborowa, on the rocks with two olives). It made me anxious to see my partner drinking hard liquor, because of his past problems with chemical dependencies. We'd gone through a bad patch a few years earlier, when Neil's appetite for Tylenol with codeine disoriented him to the point where he drove into the guard booth at Universal. That merited him a night in jail and a few months in a drug rehabilitation program.

Renata told us an amusing story of how Steven Spielberg followed her all the way home from the Beverly Hills Hotel, actually pulled up behind her in the driveway. He said he had to know who she was.

"I said, 'I'm the mother of three. Where were you ten years ago?'"

Renata laughed. Neil, still over at the bar, manufactured his second martini.

Pam Morton gave us a warm welcome because we were with Leo Becker's party. Or perhaps she gives everybody a warm welcome. I tend not to go to Morton's unless I'm the guest of someone powerful. Geneva, surprisingly, was already at the table.

She was chatting with Avery Schine, the gray ghost of Polonia Productions. Leo and Avery were partners in the founding of Polonia, but most of the money was Avery's. And that money, according to *The Wall Street Journal,* came from unsavory sources in the environs of Cicero, Illinois. Polonia money was clearly Avery's, to do with as he saw fit. In recent years, that included wasting a lot of it in the movie business. The saying around town went, "What Leo makes in television, Avery loses in movies." Avery was, like so many oil barons and shopping mall billionaires (or, in his case, pinball machine distribution czars), enamored of movie stars. Making movies was a good way to meet them.

Avery had gray hair, but in curly abundance, and a youthful build. His face was artfully misshapen from a youth in the boxing ring, which gave it an interest it would not have merited on its own. There was a bottle of Tattinger Blanc de Blanc on the table, but Avery was drinking from a tall glass of ice water, probably to refill his veins.

Avery was unaccompanied. Geneva was with a manufactured "date," an aspiring actor with the good looks of a male model. I don't think he said eighteen words over the course of the evening. Avery greeted us warmly, pretending for Geneva's benefit that he had some sort of ongoing close relationship with us. Neil and I, being as good at star fucking as the next comedy writing team, went along with it. Geneva made a particular effort to extend herself toward Renata and Kiki.

Leo Becker arrived on our heels with his bride of several months, the former Cassandra Bowfinkle, smiling rapturously on his arm. Cassandra, at thirty-two, was twenty-eight years younger than her new husband. As she crossed the room, she made clear that it was possible to overdress for Morton's. Her dress was flowing, yellow and cream colored, and off the shoulder. She looked like a flan.

Avery explained that the press of business did not allow him to join us for dinner, but he offered a toast. "My partner and I place the highest value on our relationship with Geneva Holloway," he said, raising his champagne flute.

"So do my partner and I," said Neil, now on his third vodka martini.

Avery went off into the night, perhaps to a devil worship, and Geneva spent the course of the meal establishing herself in our eyes as a star. She did this by not allowing attention to pass from her for more than thirty seconds at a time. She made exceptions to this rule only when Leo Becker chose to speak. She deferred to Leo. Stars often like to designate a "father" in the production company, a Santa Claus of the mind whom they hold in reserve as a comfort.

Cassandra Becker rode into the conversation on Leo's coattails. She seemed to expect everyone to be inordinately taken by the fact that she came from Pittsburgh, as if this was a fascinating achievement. She talked about how much nicer the better neighborhoods in Pittsburgh were than the better neighborhoods in Los Angeles. Geneva got her revenge by confusing Pittsburgh with Philadelphia.

"I loved the *Rocky* movies," she interrupted. Cassandra corrected her, and Geneva pretended not to understand.

Renata Stein tried twice to bring up the story of her pursuit by Steven Spielberg, but couldn't muster enough authority to hold the floor. Kiki laughed at almost everything that was said, but addressed all her conversation directly to me. Such as:

"What's this?"

Her fork was piercing a stalk of asparagus.

"The asparagus?"

"*That's* asparagus?" As in "*That's* Greta Garbo?"

"You've never had asparagus?"

"I think my sister has."

Neil scraped the floor with his chair, and I couldn't be sure if he was patting me on the shoulder or just using me to brace himself. " 'Scuze me," he said.

"Is he going to the bar?" Renata whispered across to me. "I'm not going to turn around. Is he going to the bar?"

"Yes. He seems to be."

At this, Renata turned around and then turned back. "Another martini."

"Yeah. What's going on?"

"Didn't he tell you? About the operation?"

"What operation? What's wrong? Is he sick?" Geneva, who was in the midst of directing a story at Leo Becker, darted her eyes nervously at me because I wasn't paying attention.

Renata shook her head.

"Jonathan. Jonathan has an undescended testicle. He's going in Friday, and Neil hasn't told him. He's afraid to tell him. He hasn't prepared him."

"Why don't you prepare him?"

"Neil's supposed to. He's the father, for Christ's sake. It's one of the few things I've asked of him. I showed Jonathan that Mister Rogers tape about going to the hospital, but Jonathan didn't understand that it had to do with him."

Neil came back to the table with his new martini as Cassandra Bowfinkle Becker, disparaging the watercress on her plate, told about the absolutely first-class watercress that grew wild in a stream on the Mellon estate in Rolling Rock, Pennsylvania. Geneva pretended to be riveted to Cassandra's words.

"Cassandra, I have to ask you something," she said as Cassandra concluded. "The Liberty Bell. Is it anything? Is it worth seeing?"

Cassandra flushed. "No, again, that's Philadelphia."

"I'm sorry . . . you're not from Philadelphia?"

"No, again, Pittsburgh."

"Pittsburgh. Of course. Tell me, I can't seem to think . . . what does Pittsburgh have?"

"Well . . . we have the famous three rivers."

"Right. With all that watercress."

Leo Becker proposed a toast when the dessert was served,

and then Geneva said she'd like to speak seriously for just a moment. She held her champagne flute out like a beacon, and addressed us.

"I'm trusting you guys with my life," she said. "No, it's more serious than that. I'm trusting you with my career. I'll tell you something Vincent Minelli told me." Geneva turned to Cassandra at this and said pointedly, "He was a very famous director," and then returned to the group at large. "I met him at a party once. He was very frail, but he struggled across the room because he wanted to tell me how great he thought I was in *Horseplay*. And then he gave me a very good piece of advice. He said—"

We never found out what he said, because Geneva was suddenly startled by a little gray orb that darted onto her chest, adhered for a second, and then rolled down between her breasts. She looked up for its source. We all turned and saw my partner Neil Stein with his head resting on the far end of the table. He had the olive pits from his martinis lined up like little soldiers, and he was flicking them with his finger without paying any special attention to where they might land.

Before we could react, Neil got off another shot. This time the olive pit plotched against Geneva's cheek, right around where Elizabeth Taylor has a beauty mark.

"Neil!" gasped Renata.

Neil looked up as if he was surprised to find other people at the table. He saw Geneva swat an olive pit off her face in disgust. "Oh..." he said. "Very sorry."

The party wound down quickly. Renata took Neil to the car, while I tried to cover for him with Geneva.

"He's not a drinker," I explained. "He's under a great deal of pressure. His little boy is going in for surgery."

"Ohhh," said Geneva. "What's the matter with him?"

"An undescended testicle." I tried to make this sound as much like a brain tumor as possible.

Geneva and Cassandra Becker both said "Ohhh" together. "Well, we won't hold it against him," said Leo.

On the way to the car, Kiki said to me, "Now that's something I have had. Testicles."

"Testicles?"

"Sheep's testicles. At least that's what this guy told me after I ate them. They call them prairie oysters."

"You've had testicles, but you've never had asparagus?"

"Well, now I've had both."


I took the wheel of the Buick on the homeward leg of the journey. Renata sat in front with me while Kiki pretended to neck with Neil in the backseat. Mrs. Stein had no sense of humor about this. We drove into Hollywood to drop Kiki off at her stucco bungalow. Her housemate Leroy Butley had called her at Morton's to announce a *crise de coeur*. He wanted her home.

Kiki insisted we come in. Leroy, for a man in crisis, was awfully hospitable, as if we were visiting him at an Alaskan outpost and he was glad for the company. Upon meeting him, particularly upon shaking his hand, I came to believe that what Kiki had been telling me was true. They did not make love. It wasn't that he appeared asexual; it was that he had an aura of defeat about him, a man who would agree to unfavorable terms in exchange for small comforts. He was wispy, blond, and slight. You might be able to see through him if he stood in front of a strong light. He had a nautical look: He wore a T-shirt with horizontal blue stripes and white bell bottoms, and sandals, but with stockings. I felt an immediate affection for him, which probably sprang from my sense of relief.

Leroy, delighted as he was by our surprise visit, was also overwhelmed. He went around the house looking for interesting things to show us—his collection of chess sets, a machine that told fortunes, his computer, the desert tortoise on the skateboard—like a little boy trying to win over visitors with his toys. His Texas accent was far more pronounced than Kiki's.

Kiki made apricot tea and looked for some kind of alcohol to pour into it, for Neil. She finally produced a sticky green crème

de menthe. To my partner's credit, he declined. I expressed interest in and respect toward everything Leroy produced, while
Renata gushed over him seductively. The flirting confused Leroy
and he responded to it by pretending that Renata wasn't there and
addressing all his remarks to me.

We gathered in the kitchen for the tea and Kiki excused herself
to go to the bathroom.

"Don't ever leave me alone with Kiki," Neil whispered. "If I
got the chance, I'd fuck her." He often said this to me when he
was drunk, about whomever I was with. Renata bristled at the
whispering, sensing that it was not flattering to her. Kiki returned
from the bathroom with amazement on her face.

"Wow," she said. "That asparagus makes your urine smell
weird."

Kiki saw us to the car while Leroy stood in the doorway with
a benign smile. Neil pulled Kiki into the backseat, and she pretended to kiss him passionately. Renata said, "Let's go, let's go."

On the drive home, I tried to distract from the ill humor in the
car by speaking of the strange arrangement between Kiki and
Leroy, how they slept together without sex.

"I've done that," said Renata. "I would take my clothes off for
boys, but I wouldn't let them touch me. That's what my father
told me: 'Let them look, but don't let them touch.'"

"Your father told you that?"

"Yes."

"And that's still her philosophy today," said a slurred voice from
the backseat.

Neil had me stop the car at the foot of his driveway. He got
out to make an adjustment to the electric gates so they would
close after I left. Renata crushed herself against me.

"Kiss me," she said.

"Jesus."

"Kiss me. Please. Just one kiss. Give me a kiss."

"Renata, come on. Don't do this."

I saw Neil through the rearview mirror, watching to see how

this little scene played out. Renata continued to press her case. Neil made his way up to the house through the cactus garden. I got out and followed him, to encourage the lusty Mrs. Stein out of the car.

The next day, Neil came into the office after lunch.

"It led up to a trip to the UCLA emergency room at three o'clock this morning," he said. "And that's absolutely all I'm going to say about it."

# Chapter

# 7

◼ A nonwriting producer of single-camera film comedies called his creative team on the carpet and waved before them a scene that had just been submitted.

"Fellas," he said, "this isn't funny! I told you, we needed funny here. This isn't funny!"

The writer, Artie Julian, and the director, Hy Averback, were confused. They had thought it was pretty funny stuff. "Maybe if we read it out loud," suggested Julian. He and Averback began reading the scene, and when they were a few lines into it, the producer started laughing. By the end, he was pounding his desk in delight.

"Well, sure," he said, "if you're going to read it like that."

◆ ◆ ◆

Geneva Holloway owned a beach house in the Malibu Colony, and two weeks after our dinner of celebration at Morton's, I found myself there, presenting the story Neil and I had crafted for the pilot episode of the series. In fact, I performed it. I changed the pitch of my voice to portray different characters, and I moved across Geneva's dining room–lanai to indicate staging. I used a few of her things as props; I remember picking up a crudely sculpted wooden dog from Mexico and pretending it was a phone. Occasionally I took a dramatic pause, and the surf outside sounded like far-off thunder.

Neil sat lost among the overstuffed pillows on the rattan sofa. At just the right moments he improvised funny character lines and lobbed them in like grenades. Geneva watched me with her mouth open, fascinated by this story that was all about her, which she had never heard before. Milo Lally spent most of the time looking at Geneva, monitoring her face for reactions. He was in shockingly nonprofessional attire, given his weighty position as personal manager to a star: beach slaps, cream-colored corduroy shorts, and a T-shirt that showed off his work with weights.

Geneva wore a short white tunic dress with a gold chain around the waist. Her eyes were locked on me. She followed me closely as I moved around the room. In fact, I might say I commanded her complete attention if it wasn't for the brief, distracted glances she threw toward her feet, where a young woman in a halter top and jeans was fussing over Geneva's toes.

I would have to set this moment aside as some sort of nadir in my career, this being made to perform like a monkey for an actress who is sitting back and having her fucking toenails done.

David Putzman was the one who broke the news about the pedicure. He enjoyed telling me. Neil and I were already pissed off because we'd been finessed into having the meeting at Geneva's house in the first place; it meant a major schlepp up to Malibu in late Friday afternoon traffic. But this business about the pedicure was beyond the pale.

"She feels very awkward about it," said Putzman. "She's apologetic." He could hardly contain a smile. "This is the only time she has before she leaves to do that movie in England. It's our only chance to pass a story by her."

Neil was over at the Paramount store buying a sweatshirt for a nephew's birthday. But I didn't need his input.

"We're not going," I said.

"Aw, come on," said Putzman.

"We're not going. There's no discussion."

Neil entered, a bag puffy with sweatshirts under his arm.

"So, what's this?" he asked.

"We're not going to the Geneva Holloway meeting tomorrow. If you want to go, go. I'm going home." I turned to Putzman before my exit. "You tell him."

Neil called me at home about forty minutes later. Leo Becker wanted to meet with us.

"We're not taking that meeting with her," I said.

"Fine," said Neil. "Good. But don't make me meet with Leo alone."

I drove over to the Polonia studio in Culver City.

"Would you go?" I asked Leo. "Would you go out to her house in fucking Malibu on a Friday afternoon while she's having her fucking nails done?"

Leo wouldn't answer the question. He insisted on presuming it was rhetorical.

"Look, I'll say in her defense, she's *aware* of how offensive this appears. That's why she asked, 'Would it be all right . . . ?' What did she say exactly, David?"

"She said, 'Would the guys mind . . . ?'"

"You see, 'Would you mind . . . ?' She's not acting like a queen or anything. She's in a bind."

"Would you go?" I asked again. Neil nodded his head, seconding me.

"Look," said Leo, his face bulging and red, "what are we going to do? She gets to approve the story. It's in her contract. She's leaving for London. This is the only time she has."

"She says."

"Right. She says. So, still, what are we going to do? Not have a story? Miss out on a whole development season because she's having a pedicure?"

I like to think that Leo Becker was smart enough to know that he was putting a chill into our hearts with that threat of missing out on a development season. For a writer in development, there's nothing worse than the months of downtime. Neil and I exchanged looks.

"I want Putzman to come with us."

"Of course," said Leo. "David will be there."

When we left Leo's office, we pretended we had not sold out the last vestiges of our manhood. "At least Putzman has to be there, too," I said. On the drive out to Malibu the next day, we both remarked on how light the traffic was for a Friday afternoon.

Milo answered the door. Geneva already had one foot on the pedicurist's knee, with little white clouds of cotton separating her toes. She apologized.

"You guys are really great to put up with this," she said.

"We decided we can pitch a story during a pedicure," I said, "but we draw the line at a gynecological examination."

"Speak for yourself," said Neil.

Geneva favored us with a piercing laugh, and the ice was broken.

"David Putzman called," said Milo. "He can't make it."


Once I dove into the story, it wasn't so bad. I found myself checking the pedicurist's face for reactions. Little smiles, eyes wide with interest. I played to her as much as to Geneva. At length, but not at too great a length, I came to the blackout of the last act.

"And then the housekeeper says, 'We'll be wearing shoes for dinner,'" I said. "'You do have a pair, don't you?' And then you look down at your bare feet, then you look back at him, and you say, 'I'll check.' And then the housekeeper gives your husband a little squeeze on the shoulder and he says, 'This is quite a girl we have here,' and he exits to the kitchen on your reaction. That's it."

I took a deep breath. Geneva had a very somber look, as if she'd been watching a documentary on world hunger.

"I love it," I was very glad to hear her finally say.

"I think it's all there," I said, still selling.

"No, I love it," said Geneva. "Milo, what do you think?"

In the hierarchy of humiliations, waiting for Milo's opinion of my idea was just a little below the pedicure. Milo, to his credit, did not milk the moment.

"It's all there," said Milo. "I love it."

"She's bright and she's strong," said Geneva.

"Isn't she?" I said.

"But she has to be vulnerable, too."

"Oh, she'll be vulnerable," said Neil from somewhere among the sofa pillows. "That will all be in the writing."

"You know, guys, what I hope will come across..." Geneva looked away, scanning the coarsely hewn beams of her ceiling for just the right words. "The thing I would very much like you to convey in the words... The thing is, I live a very simple life here at the beach. I truly do. And I'd like to be seen that way in the series. Because when I go out into the world, I'm perceived as a star, a glamour symbol, blah, blah, blah. That's not me. This is me, out here at the beach, living in the rhythms of nature. Actually, I live a very spiritual life here."

She robbed us of further insight into her spiritual dimensions by suddenly screaming at the young pedicurist.

"Fuck, Kristen, *no*! Make that one just like the other one. I want them the same!"

The toe stylist lifted her head. She had a sweet, vacant face under honey-colored bangs. "It's hard to do," she said. "There's been damage to the nail bed."

"Just make them the *same*," said Geneva. She sat back and formed her face into a pout, to indicate that she was thinking. She looked over to me.

"Let's make the housekeeper black," she said.

I pretended to consider this. "Uh huh. Yeah, well, Geneva, I don't think we want to do that. There's a lot of sensitivity about that."

"It would be a lot funnier if he was black," she said. "Black people watch a lot of television. Wouldn't that help our ratings? I'm asking."

"Maybe. But the thing is, he's an ex-convict—"

"Oh, like there's not black ex-convicts. He could be one of those rapper types. A lot of jive talk. That's funny."

"Uh huh. But see, we don't want to depict a black on television as a housekeeper and an ex-convict, do we?"

"I don't see why not."

Neil pulled himself up from the cushions to help me out. "Also, Geneva, we're banking on a certain amount of sexual tension between you and the housekeeper. Just under the surface. A black guy would make that confusing."

"Oh," said Geneva. "Well, no, he can't be black."

"But we do want to have a regular character who's black. We thought the district attorney."

Geneva was not paying attention. She looked at Milo seductively.

"Sexual tension," she said.

"Tell me about it," said Milo.

She put the palm of her hand against Milo's inner thigh. "You have sexy legs," she said. "Did anyone ever tell you that?"

"Yeah, this guy at the bathhouse one night," said Milo.

"*Right.*" She slid her fingers up his thighs until her knuckles were covered by the leg of his shorts. She kept her eyes on his, looking for a reaction, as the pedicurist continued to pumice away.

The phone rang and Milo jumped up to answer it. I was still standing from my presentation, so I took the opportunity to sit down next to my partner. Milo covered the mouthpiece.

"It's Daniel France from London," he said.

"Oh, Christ," said Geneva. "Is he in London? Guys, I have to take this. Milo, take them outside."

We stood on the beach in the late afternoon sun like fools. I wore these stiff cordovan saddle shoes from Carroll and Company that sank right into the sand, and whenever I tried to reposition myself, they threw me off balance. Milo prattled on about the newly constructed barricade of raw lumber that hid the first floor of Geneva's house from view.

"Technically, it's illegal, because of the zoning laws," he said. "But they're doing it all up and down the Colony. During the big storms, she had water all over the first floor. Remember those storms last year?"

The young pedicurist came out of the house and down the railroad tie steps to the beach. We watched her as if she were descending from a stage and she smiled self-consciously. She balanced herself against the stair rail and took off her sneakers. There was a tan Band-Aid around one toe.

"Those plywood slats there slide right out," said Milo. He craned his neck over the slats in a nervous way, looking for a signal from the house. "You can just slide them right in there when there's a storm coming. But right now they're in there because—" He was interrupted by the loud skirl of sea gulls close overhead. They moved on. "Because she just had it built. It all has to be stained."

Neil turned to the ocean and folded his arms. The pedicurist held her face up to the sun, her eyes closed.

"The two fairies who live next door want her to change that corner on the far right," said Milo. "They say the post blocks the view of the sunset from their tea room. One of them's a lawyer, and he—"

"Milo," I interrupted, "are you going to stand here with a straight face and talk about tea rooms? We were in the middle of a business meeting, and now we're standing out here on the fucking beach."

"I know," said Milo sheepishly. This was my first shot at him away from his protectress, and I pressed my advantage. Neil turned back toward us. "What are you talking about plywood for? Are you her general contractor, or her manager?"

"I'm her manager," he said.

"Does she like the story or not?" said Neil. "Can you help, Milo? Can you do us any good?"

"She likes the story."

"And what the hell are you doing poking her? What about your wife? Are you totally unprofessional?"

"Hey, come on," said Milo, and then he was filled with a sudden nervous energy. "Hey, she's off the phone." I saw Geneva waving from a window, just her head and shoulders visible above the barricade.

Milo scooted us toward the house. He called over to the pedicurist, "She's off the phone."

Geneva sat on the puffy sofa now, her feet up on the glass table, the little mushrooms of cotton still between her toes. She was taking a break from her pedicure.

"I was just thinking while you were outside," said Geneva. "What about the little boy?"

"I'm sorry," I said, "what little boy?"

"Remember, I said I wanted her to have a little boy about five years old?"

I floundered. This was the exact opposite of what we had agreed upon.

"What we discussed . . . what I recall is that you didn't want to have any children. You thought it would be poignant if she wanted children but couldn't have any."

"No, no, no. *Remember?*"

It's difficult to account for the force of that single word, "*Remember?*" But when I heard it, I had a feeling that the course of my life had just changed. This "*Remember?*" was a Stalinist ukase, erasing a recent past we had all been witness to. I had no resource within me to match its power.

There was a silence.

"It's what we discussed," said Milo. Fucking Milo.

"We don't have a story if there's a little kid," said Neil, speaking very reasonably. He didn't get it yet. "The whole thing rests on the fact that you've just been married three months."

"But she has to be vulnerable," said Geneva. "I've always said that, right from the very beginning. I've stressed it. You agreed to that. That's why she has to have a little boy."

Neil pressed on. "But doesn't that look bad, that they would have an ex-convict in the house with a little child?"

"I don't even see why we need the housekeeper," said Geneva.

And now Neil's eyes widened, as if to let in the pain. This was turning into a prairie fire. I intervened.

"Well, this is going to take some reconfiguring," I said. "I guess we can hold off the network for a while while we rework things. You'll be available by phone in Europe, won't you, Geneva?"

"I'll make myself available. This is very important to me." She was giddy with the drama of it all.

We crossed to Neil's Jaguar sedan in the little gravel cove set aside for visitor parking. We walked in dazed silence, our digestive tracts drained of blood. I worried about Neil. This ordeal would require at least two Xanaxes on his part. His blood pressure was high anyhow and not responding well to beta blockers.

I could have told Neil that, in a few days, Geneva would probably forget all about wanting a little kid. Failing that, we could stick a little neighbor boy into the pilot, and give her a scene with him. Dumping the housekeeper, of course, was out of the question; without him, there was no show. The network would back us on that. We'll just take it one day at I time, I could have told Neil.

I could have said all that to comfort my despairing partner as we crunched across the gravel to his green Jaguar, covered now with dozens of purple bells from the jacaranda tree. But instead, to show you what a prick I can be, when Neil looked at me soulfully over the roof of his car as he unlocked the door, I said, "Hey, Neil, why don't you take a pass at the first draft on your own?"

# Chapter

# 8

The screenwriter Robert Riskin once approached Frank Capra with 120 pages of blank paper and fanned them under his nose.

"Here," he said, "put the famous Capra touch on this."

◆ ◆ ◆

There is a ritual among certain bored and disenchanted Inuit youths in Alaska known as a dynamite party. They drink several beers, and one volunteers to be buried in the earth. His fellows plant a few sticks of dynamite six or seven feet away from him and light the fuses. The ensuing blast blows the internee several yards into the air, giving him an intense and concentrated thrill. Sometimes, of course, he is killed.

Neil and I came to refer to our ordeal at the beachfront pedicure session as our Inuit dynamite party. We didn't actually get killed, but it felt like it.

When Leo Becker heard of Geneva's story changes, he turned the color of an overheated brick.

"If David Putzman had been there to help out, maybe we could have kept her under control," I said.

Leo called Bobby Meyerhoff, Geneva's agent, and reasoned with him, beginning the conversation with "While you're out smoking dick, your client's running a pilot commitment from CBN right over the fucking cliff." Leo went on to threaten Bobby in so colorful and personal a manner that the agent placed a matchstick under the hood of his car that night, and checked to see if it had been disturbed before he started the ignition in the morning. He did this for three days, until he flew off to London to talk to Geneva.

Bobby's chat with Geneva was a success. It then fell to Neil and me, as relayed by David Putzman, to simply make a few cosmetic changes in the story, which would allow Geneva to save face.

"Anything," said Putzman.

A transatlantic telephone appointment was arranged. Milo Lally and David Putzman came to our offices at Paramount to witness it. The voice that came over the speaker phone was that of an old, dear friend, an equal, our fellow laborer in the vineyard of entertainment.

"I *miss* you guys," said Geneva, after I said hello. "Where's Neil? Neil, are you there, too?" She cued him to respond several times during the brief conversation, to underscore his importance to her.

"We've thought about your reactions to our story," I said, "and I think we have something that will work for us all. We give you a five-year-old neighbor boy. He comes over to visit you a lot. He likes you, you like him. Whenever it fits in, we do a scene with him."

There was a silence that lent itself to various interpretations. We all looked at the speaker phone like men waiting to receive a kickoff. Finally, Geneva spoke.

"*Brill*-yant." The word blasted out of the little white box and surged through the room.

"It gives you a kid, but without throwing off the other elements of the script," I said.

"I see that," said Geneva. "Milo? Are you there?"

"Yeah, babe." Milo straightened his posture respectfully as he turned to address her.

"Isn't that great what the boys came up with?" Neil and I exchanged glances on "the boys." "And what about the housekeeper guy?"

"He's the same," I said.

"A white guy," added Neil.

"Brill-yant," said Geneva. She went on to endorse us in terms more appropriate for the discoverers of penicillin. As she did, Neil pantomimed masturbating himself.

"And how about you?" I said. "How's that movie of the week going? What is it, anyhow?"

"It's a Daniel France production, that's all I can say. He wants to keep it under wraps."

(We went to a screening of it a few months later; the time to keep it under wraps was *after* it was made.)

When Geneva signed off, Milo Lally said, unprofessionally, "We did it!" Relief gushed from his eyes. He sat down and stretched his arms along the back of our sofa, looking for all the world like he expected to be offered a cigar.

"All right," said David Putzman, which is as close as he ever danced to an accolade. He adjusted himself to leave.

"Excuse me, Milo," I said, "not to be indelicate, but you don't work here."

"You don't work anywhere," added Neil.

Milo broke off from his ecstasy. "I was kind of settling in here, wasn't I?"

"You ought to manage that client of yours a little closer," said Putzman as he walked to the door with Milo. "I was talking to this guy over in our London office? He says she's fucking her way across the English countryside. She's jumping on everything that moves."

I thought I could hear Milo's heart go thunk through the walls of the outer office.

\* \* \*

And so Neil and I began the actual writing of the script. As writers, Neil and I are well matched. While we might not be right up there with Beaumont and Fletcher, I think we hold a firm place in the midrange of high-end comedy writers. I do the words, Neil does the music. That is, my strengths are story structure, organization and well-written jokes. Neil specializes in inspired lunacy, the wild perspective, the achingly funny line. They say Mack Sennett brought asylum inmates to his set and had a stenographer record their ramblings. The hope was to come up with funny ideas. There's a famous scene where Laurel and Hardy carry a piano over a narrow rope bridge and, halfway across, encounter a gorilla. That scene was contributed by one of the madmen. Neil is my madman.

This might be an opportune moment to offer a little background on the comedy writing team of Hoy and Stein. I met Neil while we were working together on a Drew Corey Christmas special for NBC. It was one of my first jobs in the business. Neil, two years younger than me, was already an established professional. He'd begun selling jokes to comedians while he as at UCLA studying journalism. During his senior year, he made fifty-five thousand dollars free-lancing for variety shows, while I was still back in Cleveland writing a column called "Arcs, Sparks, and Flashes" for *Welding Design and Fabrication* magazine. At the time of the Drew Corey special, I was living at the Farmer's Daughter's Motel on Fairfax, and grateful for the free soap. Neil, at the age of twenty-seven, had a house in Laurel Canyon once owned by Don Henley of the Eagles; he was renowned for hosting weekend-long parties that featured imported drugs and young women more dazzling than a man of Neil's features and proportions could normally be expected to attract. ("Some girl will come up to me," Neil has told me in later years, "and I won't remember her name, but I'll remember that I bought her a fur coat.")

Neil came on the Drew Corey special during the final rewrites, to do punch-up work. He would "bicycle" over to us from the

Carson show late in the day. One afternoon, Drew threw out his opening monlogue. He said he wanted something "new, fresh, special." The producer teamed me with Neil to take a crack at it, because I was new and fresh, and Neil was an expert at monologues. Neil and I went to work without even kowing each other's last names. We soon found that we had a chemistry. In a few hours, we came up with a hilarious and touching piece of work about childhood and Christmas memories. We both still agree it's the best thing we've ever done. We read it to the producer and other writers. They howled. We gave it to Drew. He embraced us. *"This* is what I was talking about," he said. On the day of the taping, Drew got nervous and tossed out the monologue and instead told a long joke about a gorilla who could drive a golf ball five hundred yards.

But Neil and I knew we had something in each other. As he said at the time, "We're like algae and fungus. Individually, we're not much, but together, we can create lichen." We started writing half-hour comedies a few months later.

And speaking of half-hour comedies, I rise in defense of my craft: A well-honed half-hour, which creates its own reality and stays true to it, can, if well cast and directed, be very satisfying to watch. It's almost always better than the typically successful Broadway comedy. (Time and again I've paid fifty dollars to sit through something the New York critics gushed over only to stare at the stage with cobra eyes and wonder if my enthusiastic, over-incomed fellow theatergoers, for all their apparent advantages, had been deprived of exposure to, say, an average *Cheers* episode.)

Of course, many television comedies are not well-honed. They are, instead, predictable, manipulative, insulting, mawkish, stupid, and self-referential. The question for the time-pressed viewer, then, is "How do I tell a well-crafted half-hour comedy from the average piece of dogshit I'm exposed to."

My partner Neil Stein and I offer a few simple rules that have survived the test of time:

### HOW TO TELL A BAD SITCOM

1. Any show in which any character at any time during the life of the series says the words "Ta da!" is a bad sitcom.

2. Any show in which one character says to another, "What are friends for?" is a bad sitcom.

3. Any show in which a character says "Bingo!" in the sense of "Eureka!" is a bad sitcom.

4. Any show in which an actor or actress under the age of seven says cute things in close-up is a bad sitcom.

5. Any show in which an actor or actress over the age of seventy-five says vulgar things in close-up is a bad sitcom.

6. Any show that resorts to the use of Dr. Zarkov dialogue (named for the villain in the *Flash Gordon* series, where one character tells another character something they both already know, for the benefit of the audience) is a bad sitcom.

7. Any show in which a character, in the closing minutes, says, "I guess we've all learned a lesson," and then goes on to explain what that lesson is, is a bad sitcom.

And that's all. I'm sure that simply by avoiding these seven pitfalls, you, too, would be quite capable of constructing a fine half-hour comedy. I realize this is a little like Mark Twain's advice about putting together a library. ("To make an excellent library, begin by omitting all the works of Miss Jane Austen. Then, even if you have no other books, you will still have an excellent library.") But the rules work. I invite all readers who have often thought they might like to give television writing a try, to go ahead and write a script. And for a free, professional assessment, please send your work to Mr. Neil Stein, 14972 Lower Bellagio Circle, Bel Air, California 90049.

On the thirty-seventh day, we rested. It was time to send our script, known as "The Geneva Holloway Project—Pilot Episode," into the wider world. Writing a script, solving all the problems you've set up for yourself within forty or so pages, provides its own range of satisfactions. And these are the reasons you are a writer. These satisfactions are independent of and senior to the compensation, praise, condemnation, and misunderstanding that come after you've turned in the work.

Leo Becker was out of state when our script made the rounds at Polonia. This left David Putzman the point man. We couldn't get much reaction out of David. He circled the script suspiciously, sniffing it. It was as if we were trying to persuade him to try on a rather colorful native hat, and he was afraid it might turn out to be a tea cozy. But then Leo Becker weighed in with his opinion. "It's hilarious. It's perfect for her," he said, calling from a Gulf Stream jet somewhere over Mississippi. "Send it to the network. They'll plotz."

This focused Putzman's thinking. He sent our effort over to CBN, where it was favorably received. "We have a few minor notes," they told us over the phone. Sometimes minor notes from a network are "Does Othello have to be black, and does he have to kill her?" In this case, the notes were in fact minor, leading as they did to a mere two weeks of rewriting.

And so we had a script. As far as Neil and I were concerned, the actual work was over. Now all we had to do was produce the show.

# *Chapter*

# *9*

After World War II, a newly discharged GI from Chicago, Maglub Gorsibagian, decided to forgo the family carpet business and take a train west to Hollywood, where he would seek his fortune as a movie star. On the cross-country trip, he came to realize that Maglub Gorsibagian might not be the best possible name for a movie star. He worked long and hard trying to come up with a fitting alternative, listing his choices on cocktail napkins. And three days later, when he arrived in Union Station in downtown Los Angeles, Maglub Gorsibagian got off that train as Rex Beaumont.

◆ ◆ ◆

Geneva Holloway swept back into our lives, fresh from her European triumph in Daniel France's secret movie-of-the-week, and ready to devote herself to the casting of the pilot. She brought with her the sort of excitement a summer thunderstorm initially provides.

During an interminable round of casting sessions with Geneva, I came to realize that stars of the screen, like stars of the heavens, are best enjoyed from a great distance. Her mood was high, her energy boundless. It was like being trapped in a bomb shelter with a frisky young St. Bernard. Neil called these sessions "astronaut training."

The good news was, Geneva didn't have any strong opinions

on the people who came in to read. In general, she left the decisions up to Neil and me. The thrill for her, it seemed, was to have fellow actors and actresses fawn over her for a few minutes before she picked up her sides of copy and read with them. When they left, and Neil and I and the casting woman weighed their merits, Geneva's comments tended to be reflections on her own performance, sometimes to the point of expressing hurt that we were discussing the work of a stranger and neglecting the efforts of our own star.

The bad news was, there was one violent exception to Geneva's indifference to casting choices. She had strange ideas about the sort of person who should play Jack Mullin, her husband in the series. Geneva was emphatic in her assessments. In theory, we were all in agreement on the character of Jack Mullin: a rough-edged police professional in his late thirties, a little world-weary, capable of a slow burn. "Geneva" is his second wife and she has a rejuvenating effect on him. Living with a wise-ass ex-convict in his house drives him up the wall, but he indulges this woman whom he loves.

So on paper, we were ideally synchronized. But when an actual human being came into the room and presented himself as Jack Mullin, Geneva became bizarre and unpredictable.

For example, we brought in Nathan Fisher. Now, this was not my favorite thing to do. Nathan Fisher, the careful reader may recall, was the former star of *Cold Steel* who made a serious play for Kiki Burmeister during our early days together. But—such is my professionalism—we brought him in. Nathan was doing us a favor, really, by coming in to read with Geneva without making a deal up front. Nathan comes in. Geneva does a little gushing of her own for a change, out of respect. I am prepared to dislike him, but Nathan is charming; he and Geneva flirt a little. Then they pick up their sides and get down to business. The scene, a three-page husband-and-wife argument, comes to life. Nathan gets laughs *on the way* to the jokes; the jokes themselves he knocks out of the park. Geneva fights for her life; her performance comes way up. She sparkles. There is spontaneous and sincere applause

at the end of the scene. We thank Nathan profusely. He shakes
hands all around, he blows Geneva a kiss, he leaves.

Neil and I and the casting woman, tears still in our eyes, move
immediately beyond any discussion of the performance. We wonder, Can we make a deal? What kind of billing will he demand?
What kind of money? Will CBN give us overage if he comes in too
high? I'm thinking, should I ask Nathan if he'd like another shot
at Kiki?

This was the nature of the discussion, as God Himself would
so ordain after such a performance. But gradually our attention
was tugged over to the corner of the room, where Geneva was
rocking back and forth in a rocking chair. (The casting woman
depended on a rocking chair because of serious lower back problems, but Geneva had commandeered it early in our sessions.) It
was Geneva's silence, rare and troubling, that attracted us. She
pursed her lips. She shook her head with sad inevitability.

"What did you think, Geneva?" I felt directed to say.

"It's sad," she said. "He's so good in so many ways. But there's
nothing between us."

"It was hilarious," said Neil, almost dribbling over himself in
disbelief.

"I need somebody who relates to me on a sexual level. There
was no man-woman stuff between us."

The casting woman had a go at it. Her speech was a little
overdistinct; she had been taking prescription pain relievers because of a recent flare-up with her back problems:

"But Geneva, I really saw that between you. That's exactly
what was so great about it."

"No," said Geneva. From her tone, the casting woman was so
wrong that her error was beneath discussion.

Neil tried again. "I'll tell you, I like what I saw."

Geneva then introduced her black edge into the discussion.
"Look, guys, I know how people want to see me. Nathan Fisher
seems funny at first, but there's nothing *underneath*. By the end
of the first show the audience will hate him for talking to me like

that, because there won't be any sexual tension between the lines. And then they'll hate me for choosing a man like that for my husband. With Nathan Fisher, we don't have a show."

This was a typical Geneva Holloway tactic: An emphatic litany of convictions that sound strong and true, but don't stand up under the slightest scrutiny. But we were boxed in by the force of her personality. Suddenly, we were offering our star overlapping assurances: "We want you to be comfortable..." "You don't have to work with anybody you don't want to..." And from never-say-die Neil: "We'll just keep him in the back of our mind."

The next morning we were treated to an example of Geneva "I Know How People Want to See Me" Holloway's idea of sexual tension. Three of her old acting buddies from *Horseplay* and *Bel Air Terrace* showed up in a cluster. You begin to suspect that you and your star have conflicting notions of "rough-edged police professional" when you hear grown men giggling in the outer office.

Their names were Brent and Kyle and Bryce. They were all pretty boys, male model types. It was as if Geneva thought she were choosing a prom date. They had no substance. Two came and went in quick order. Their readings were so embarrassing I didn't know where to look. The third one could act a little—Bryce, whom Geneva had alerted us was "very special"—but he was addicted to that hallmark of bad acting, the dramatically portentous "uh..." As in: "Can I...uh...drive you over to the...uh... hospital? I...uh...have a meeting there. Perhaps we could have an...uh...early dinner and discuss Kimberley's...uh... amnesia."

My theory is that these abounding "uhs" came about in the early days of televised soap operas when actors didn't have much time to memorize scripts. The use of a skillfully placed "uh" gave the impression that the artist was giving special significance to the next word when in fact he was simply trying to remember it. But then the whole practice simply became a bad habit that younger actors mistook for a good habit. And now the pregnant "uh" is so ingrained as a trademark of "serious" acting that actors put it in even when they are reading directly from a script.

Which is exactly what this Bryce fellow came in and did. (I believe at one point he actually managed to hesitate in the middle of a pause.) And one thing all these little "uhs" do is destroy any chance of comedy occurring. This guy stood there and strangled our jokes like they were babies in a crib. One after the other, right down the line, with ruthless precision. I felt like MacDuff after he got the bad news about his newly revised family situation: "What, all my chicks? All my little ones?"

When Bryce left, the room was silent. The only question worth discussing, it seemed, was "Should we call the police?" I was slow to look in Geneva's direction. I wanted to compose myself so I wouldn't appear to be gloating. But when I did manage a turn of the head toward her, she was smiling and rocking with extreme self-satisfaction.

"Now that's what I was talking about," she said. "Tension." I have to admit, there was tension all right. "Annette, put Bryce down on the A list," she said to the casting woman, who was now wearing a metal brace around her back.

Neil and I stared across the room at Geneva. The casting woman's face registered a whole new level of pain. Geneva, interpreting the frozen horror she saw in our faces as residual awe left over from Bryce's stunning performance, invited us to lunch at the commissary.

"I'll make Milo pay. It kills Milo to spend money. Annette, you come, too."

"I can't walk that far," said the casting woman.

As we walked across the lot, Geneva chatted with a ferocity born of success. Her words were all about wardrobe, and the clear implication was that she was free now to concentrate her energies on wardrobe because the challenge of casting a husband for her had been met.

Neil's tendency, when an anxiety gnaws at him, is to speak up as soon as he identifies it; he says what he thinks, out of innocence, no matter what the political implications. My style is to ride it out for a while, until my anger becomes uncontrollable. And my anger does, frequently, become uncontrollable. I'll probably be found sniping from a freeway overpass someday. But in the meantime, it's usually Neil who gets us in trouble. We were passing Stage 12, where John Lithgow, on a break from filming, was standing outside at a payphone in a bathrobe and some kind of monster feet. Geneva, walking between Neil and me, had just said, referring to her character, "I see her wearing white; she'd wear a lot of white." She stated this as if it were the law of universal gravitation. And at that point, Neil blurted out, "Geneva, I have to tell you, I have a problem with this Bryce guy. I mean, he's not funny."

Geneva looked at Neil for a full two seconds, as if she were trying to remember whether or not she had the power to order him to be tortured and killed. Then she took him on.

"No, he's not fart-in-the-face funny. He's not obvious. He's an actor. His humor comes out of character."

"It's just that a lot of guys have come in and gotten laughs with those sides, and this guy—"

"We are sick to fucking death of that material," said Geneva. "Nobody could get laughs with that shit anymore. I know Bryce. I know what he can do. If you guys didn't see what was happening in that room, then I don't know if I can have any confidence in you."

Neil threw me a worried look behind Geneva's head.

"Uh, Geneva," I suggested, "casting is a very subjective thing. Maybe we're real wrong about this Bryce guy—"

"Bryce *Harbogovarian*," said Geneva. "He has a last name, for Christ's sake. Afford the man some basic dignity."

"Of course," I said. "I'm sorry. I'm just saying I don't think we want to lock in on him. I mean, we have to take at least two or three Jack Mullins into the network, anyhow."

"Unless we sign somebody automatically preapproved, like Nathan Fisher," said Neil, going too far.

Geneva saw the weight of logic mounting, ready to crush her. She skirted to the side of the issue.

"Look, guys," she said, in a voice that implied she was weary of making the same point over and over, "I'm not married to Bryce Harborgovan"—I'm sure she dropped a syllable from his name this time—"for Christ's sake. If somebody better comes in, wonderful. I'll fucking rejoice. But bring me somebody. Bring me some *actors*. And write a new test scene. Write something that a human being can *play*."

Milo met us at the entrance to the commissary and escorted us around the line of standees waiting for tables, as if he were the maître d'. He led us back to a booth he'd already secured. Geneva ordered a plate of carrot sticks and a bowl of chicken noodle soup, and asked the waitress how her daughter was.

"Still the same, doll," said the waitress, a bony woman whose face was creased from years of cigarette smoke. Geneva touched the waitress's hand and gave her a look that seemed to say, "I share your sorrow, but let's both be brave." The rest of us ordered.

Geneva focused on Milo and launched into a high-energy, totally beside-the-point extollation of a young actress who had come in that morning to read for the role of "Geneva's" assistant. The girl had been pretty good, but far too young. Geneva now described her as the second coming of Jean Arthur, and she reported it all to Milo with a new tone of respect, as if what he thought weighed heavily with her.

The waitress set a plate of carrot sticks in front of Geneva and proceeded around the table distributing salads. Geneva stared at the carrot sticks as if the head of her firstborn had just been set before her. She raised a finger above her head without taking her eyes off the plate.

"Doll?" said the waitress.

"These are wrong," said Geneva.

"I'm sorry," said the waitress, scanning the plate of carrot sticks for signs of incorrectness.

"These are chunky," said Geneva. "I want the thin kind. These are different."

Milo swept the plate from before Geneva's gaze and handed it to the waitress. "Bring the right kind," he said with quiet authority.

"Right away," said the waitress. Geneva started talking about wardrobe, as if that had been the topic at hand before the indignity of the carrot sticks. She spoke directly to Milo, but for our benefit. Her remarks, again, had mostly to do with the importance of the color white.

The waitress came up behind Geneva with a new plate of carrot sticks. She looked at us tentatively as if we might warn her away if she'd somehow gotten it wrong again. She set the carrot sticks before Geneva. They were on a bed of shaved ice this time, and garnished with parsley, and there were more of them.

"How's this, doll?" asked the waitress.

Geneva considered the carrot sticks and then turned to Milo. "These aren't right, are they?"

Milo, emboldened by the respect Geneva had been showing him for the last several minutes, made the mistake of saying what he thought. "Yeah, I think so, babe."

"They are?"

"They look like the ones you usually get."

Geneva reconsidered the little orange roots. The full impact of the conspiracy suddenly struck her. She turned back to Milo.

"No!" she said. "What are you doing to me?"

Geneva started out of the booth without giving Milo an opportunity to move. He scrambled out of her way and was left kneeling on one knee in front of the table as Geneva stalked down the commissary aisle. She came to a halt after ten yards and stomped her feet in frustration, as if she were marching in place. Milo rose and rushed to her. To say that all eyes were on them would be a misstatement only to the extent that the unsighted cast members of a series called *Blindman's Buff* were sitting together at a table oblivious to everything but their own conversation.

Milo hovered over Geneva speaking softly and urgently. His words were unavailable to us at that distance, but I assume he was trying to comfort her by in some way debasing himself. Eventually, he escorted her out of the commissary. It seemed as if somebody had to pay a price for our resistance to Bryce Harbogovarian, and Neil and I were both glad to have it be Milo Lally.

Neil picked up a carrot from the icy platter at Geneva's place and crunched into it.

"I thing things are going pretty well so far, don't you?" he said.


We trotted our handful of casting choices over to the network for final decisions. Both Nathan Fisher and Bryce Harbogovarian had been mutually sacrificed for the Jack Mullin role. Instead, we went in with two possibilities: a funny, solid, attractive character actor named Don Lasker, and another one of Geneva's male models, this one named Deems. In the reading, Don Lasker blew Deems back to *All My Children* where he belonged. Joe Danko, who sat in at the session, actually got angry that we'd brought this Deems fellow into the network. He yelled at us for wasting his time. "What were you thinking? Why would you bring him here?"

Geneva suddenly acted as if she wasn't with our party. I took the heat, with a certain private joy.

"I'm sorry," I said. "He had something in the room that he just didn't bring with him today."

"Jesus fucking Christ," said Danko.

So Don Lasker got the part, and CBN bought our first choices for all the other roles, and Geneva walked around taking bows as if this were a personal triumph for her. She had missed the real news of the day: For the role of the ex-convict, we cast Joseph Landry, a fresh face from the Broadway stage. We saw him as a very big talent who would grow in the role. Geneva had merely seen him as pleasant and properly deferential. In a few months, he would be stealing the show from her.

# Chapter

# *10*

In directing a hospital scene in a B movie for Warner Brothers, David Butler had detailed suggestions for all the day players who filled up the beds in the hospital ward. He told them how to hold their bodies, where to direct their gazes, when to react. He spent several minutes on these instructions, and then decided he was ready to shoot. Bette Davis, the star of the film, who played a nurse, and was the only one in the scene with any lines, had been looking on.

"But David," she said, "what about me? What should I do?"

Butler considered her, as if for the first time. He thought a moment and said, "Just fuck around with the sheets."

◆ ◆ ◆

The shooting of the pilot episode went rather well. Only one life was lost. That's not so bad, really, when you think of industries like logging or coal mining.

Someone died because of hair.

Actresses can drive you crazy when it comes to hair. Neil is much better than I at feigning empathy when an actress, looking perfectly presentable, stands before us in tears over the crime some hairdresser has committed against her person. Much better, I think at times like that, to have been the producer of *Combat*. An all-male cast. No hair problems: Helmets. (And if one of the actors became too troublesome, you could have a sniper take him out in next week's script.)

In the weeks before production, we pretty much emptied the bungalows of West Hollywood bringing in hairdressers to pass before Geneva. These interviews were like the casting sessions, except that Geneva took them more seriously.

She made her choice: Jerry Cardini. She gushed over Jerry. She adored him. To Geneva, Jerry was the logical culmination of Western civilization. Neil and I had worked with Jerry often before. He was not the smartest hairdresser in the world; he once admitted he wasn't quite sure if Paris was in France or France was in Paris. But he was a sweetheart, very good at what he did and, more important, a calming influence on fluttery stars.

Jerry asked to meet with Neil and me privately before he took the job. He came up to the office and sat on the sofa with one leg under him, anxious.

"You guys know I haven't been doing shows. I have this really good chair at Jose Eber."

"But Jerry," I said, "you're Mister Show Business."

"Yeah, right. The thing is, I've really been avoiding the instability of doing shows. I just came in and met her as a favor to you guys. I'm into stability these days."

"Stability?" said Neil with mock contempt. "Jerry, you're, what, thirty-five years old, no responsibilities."

"Actually, I have a daughter."

This news brought us up short.

"No, Jer."

"Do you, Jerry?"

"She lives with her mom in Sandusky, Ohio. They moved back there. Seven years old already."

"Well, Jer, that's great."

"A daughter," said Neil. "I have daughters."

"The thing is, this pilot is tempting, because I love Geneva. Do you think it will get picked up?"

"Who knows, Jer?" I said. "We have a star, we have a great cast, we have a good script. I wouldn't bet against it."

"I'm tempted to take a chance, because I miss working on shows. But to do the pilot, I'd have to give up my chair at Jose Eber's."

"Jer, you don't ever have to worry about working," I said.

"But the thing is, I can't afford any downtime. Do you mind if I smoke? I know it's terrible, but do you mind?" He took out a pack of Nat Sherman cigarettes, then put it back. "No, never mind," he said, "I should quit. Look, I don't mean to make this some heavy drama like *Death in the Afternoon* or anything, but the deal is—and I can tell you guys—I'm HIV-positive."

"Shit," said Neil.

"No symptoms, knock on wood. But I want to save up a lot of money for my daughter while I can. So my question is, is Geneva Holloway crazy or anything? Will she fire me in two days, and then I'll be out on my ass, or what?"

"Jer," I said, "are you happy at Jose Eber's? Do you love it?"

"It's money," said Jerry. "I love doing shows. But there's this stability factor. So, is she crazy or what?"

Neil and I looked at each other. Here was Jerry on our sofa, sitting on one leg and bouncing the other. To keep our consciences snow pure, we could send him back to his chair at Jose Eber's. But this was a guy who could make our star happy. So I sold him. I made sure I got all the negatives down on the record, but I sold him.

"Neil," I said, "would you say Geneva Holloway is crazy?"

"Yes, Jim, I would," said Neil.

"So would I." I turned to Jerry. "She's fucking crazy, Jer. She's a star. But she adores you. She'll kill for you. Also, she'll bust your balls. But if the pilot doesn't get picked up, Geneva said she will take you with her, wherever she works."

"She'll keep me working?"

"That's her promise. I mean, I have never seen her react so positively to anyone. Have you, Neil?"

"No, I truly haven't. You're her boy, Jerry. And I'll be frank. By coming on board, you'll make our lives very much easier."

So Jerry took the job.

There is a rule in television: Everything that can go wrong will go wrong, and then three more things will go wrong. During production, we came to find out that Don Lasker, the wonderful actor we had landed for the role of Jack Mullin, could not remember lines. That's not quite fair: He could remember them eventually, but it was usually long after the other actors had left the stage. His background was theater, where he had weeks to memorize lines, and single-camera film, where he only needed to know a handful of lines at a time. This was his first experience doing a four-camera show in front of a live audience.

We were on an eight-day shooting schedule for the pilot, reading the script on a Wednesday and shooting the following Friday. When Don was not "off book"—did not have his lines memorized—by Monday, Neil and I expressed concern. Don assured us he would have the lines cold by the run-through for the network on Wednesday. Jonathan Metzger, the director, backed him up. "He'll be fine," said Jonathan. "I'm working with him."

This carried some weight. Jonathan had been an actor and a stand-up comedian of some note. (He was known as "the yuppie comic." He still did occasional guest shots on Letterman. His trademark was a sweater worn over the shoulders, which probably eased his transition into directing.) Jonathan knew actors and their "process." We trusted that, under his coaching, Don Lasker would fall into his lines.

That didn't happen. He went through the Wednesday run-through without a script in his hand and struggled for every line. It was like sending an untrained dog after a bird you've shot down; by the time he gets it back, you'd rather not eat it. Don's hesitations and stumblings killed off any possibility of comedy. You could recite "The Song of Roland" between some of his pauses.

When the run-through ended, there was a disquieting silence in the bleachers where the network people and the Polonia executives were sitting. Jonathan Metzger came over to us and shrugged his shoulders so emphatically that his sweater should have fallen off. (I suspect he had the sweaters sewn onto the shirts.) "I'm at a total loss," he said. "I don't know what to do." This, by the way, from someone who was earning seventy-five thousand dollars to direct this pilot.

There were urgent consultations. It was decided to move shooting back a day, to Saturday. This gave Don Lasker an extra twenty-four hours to master his lines; and it gave us time to look for someone to replace him if he didn't.

Neil and I approached Don, who sat on the prop sofa over on the set. He was a big man with a handsome, Slavic face and a very short haircut. He looked at us as if we were unhappy coaches coming out to the mound. He was defensive.

"Geez," he said, "if I'd known it was going to be this hard, I wouldn't have taken the job."

"Don," I said, unhelpfully, "a large part of that money we pay you is for remembering your lines."

"Whoa, whoa," said Neil, calling me off. "Don, would you consider hypnotherapy? I know this hypnotherapist who works with actors. Would you be willing to try that? Hypnosis?"

"Sure," said Don, who at that moment was willing to try anything to end the conversation. We rushed him off to a shrink in Beverly Hills for some intensive work on the old wetware.

The hypnotherapist had a shamanistic effect. By Saturday, Don Lasker was on the money with every line. There was no need to replace him. As is so often the case, what we feared was our biggest problem dissolved into no problem at all.

Instead, our biggest problem took us completely by surprise. It came, appropriately enough, from our star, at the very last minute. And it was about hair.

To give credit where it is due, Geneva Holloway was remarkably reserved during production. She stuck the old needle in and twanged it a few times, but she fell appreciably shy of the monster behavior that her every breathing moment up until then had prepared us to expect. True, she commented critically on other people's performances, overriding the director. She persisted in referring to the six-year-old "neighbor boy" she had fought so hard for as "the little cocksucker," sometimes in his presence, which brought on threats from the social worker assigned to the set. She refused to acknowledge, either through word or glance, any of the other female cast members, which reduced each of them to tears at some point during the day.

While none of this was conduct that would reflect well on, say, a postulant in the Religious Sisters of Mercy, for Geneva Holloway it was acceptable and refreshing. Because, through it all, she took our words as we wrote them. I believe she accepted the script because she did not particularly notice the script. For Geneva, those forty-five mimeographed pages were nothing more than a springboard to the real work at hand: shopping for clothes. She held up rehearsals more than once because she was out shopping with Dawn Bulk, her wardrobe lady. She foisted upon us outfits hardly in keeping with her character (her rationalization of how a policeman's wife in Midland Heights, Ohio, came to own an eighteen-hundred-dollar asymmetrical Yohji Yamamoto double-breasted dress was a special pleasure to hear). But while she had long, uninterrupted stints at Maxfield's and Fred Segal and Harari, with occasional opportunities to abuse her fellow workers, we could write whatever we wanted.

And to her absolute credit, Geneva was very kind to Don Lasker through all his difficulties. Perhaps there was something in Don that sparked Geneva's genuine but untapped reserves of human decency. Or maybe it was just an acting thing.

After the camera run-through on Saturday, when Don Lasker finally knew all his lines and, for the first time, we saw how our little entertainment actually played, Neil called out, "All this needs is an audience. Bring on the timmies!" It was too late, of course, to call tourists away from such important business as seeing how snugly their fists fit into the concrete impression of Jayne Mansfield's breasts in front of the Mann's Chinese Theater. So we decided to shoot a version of the show just for ourselves, to have in the can before our prescheduled live audience showed up at eight o'clock. The cast was sent to wardrobe and makeup and the crew was put at the ready.

And then, as usually happens in life, we found that we had solved one problem only to replace it with another.

The crew assembled, the cast members took their places. We awaited our star. At length, she emerged from the refinements of coiffure and macquillage, and it was then that we saw God's plan for us: Geneva had chosen for herself a hairstyle that, depending on the angle of the camera, obscured anywhere from one half to three quarters of her face. She was too inattentive to Hollywood lore to be aware of Veronica Lake. I'm confidant that her inspiration must have been Connie Stevens's "Cricket Blake" character in *Hawaiian Eye.* I believe the offending feature of the hairdo is called a flip. It was, of course, impossible to film the show this way.

Neil and I approached Geneva with a false calm, trying to make a barely repressed trot come off like an amble. We intercepted her before she took her position on the set.

"Geneva, your hair," I said, in a tone that implied it was on fire.

"Yes?" she said.

"Well, we can't see your face."

She considered this for the barest of moments, then graced me with a condescending smile.

"It's fine," she said and started again toward the set. Neil, to my amazement, blocked her way.

"We can't film it like that."

Geneva looked at him as if a piece of furniture had spoken.

"Well, I'm afraid we'll have to."

"No," said Neil. "We can't." He was convincing. He was the timid man who suddenly draws a line: No, I'm afraid I can't allow you to rape my wife. "You'll have to pull it back," he said.

"This is how I'm wearing my hair," said Geneva.

As things heated up, Jonathan Metzger came close enough to us to give the other actors the impression he was in on things but not actually close enough where he might risk having us ask him to step away.

"People have to see your face," said Neil.

"Really," I said. "Geneva, it's not just that they can't see your face, it's distracting. People will wonder what's wrong."

I thought I might have an argument of some value in that. Geneva seemed to be giving it weight. But when she spoke, she said, "I could go back to my trailer and wait until you apologize. But I'm too professional for that." She walked around us and signaled to Jonathan. "Let's go."

Jonathan looked to me for guidance. I shrugged. Jonathan turned to the stage manager. "Let's go," he said.

"Places, everyone!" called the stage manager, stirring a universe of people into movement.

"Is this going to be usable?" said Neil.

"I doubt it," I said. "Where's the network? Where's Polonia? It's fucking amazing how *vital* it is for all those people to be here for every single fucking rehearsal and run-through all week long. I mean, we couldn't move forward without their brilliant fucking notes. During the week, you can't take a dump without heartfelt comment on texture and consistency from three or four vice presidents. So why, just because this happens to be a Saturday afternoon, can we be suddenly left to our own untrustworthy devices? Where, for the one moment in the history of recorded time when a network vice president might actually be useful, is the fuck one?"

"We should call somebody," said Neil.

"Exactly," I said.

"Quiet, please," shouted the stage manager. The alarm bell rang, signaling the start of shooting. I looked over to the set, and from my angle on Geneva there was no hint of face whatsoever. The general effect was that of a Lhasa apso that had managed to fit itself into a Donna Karan pants outfit. We talk about actors hiding, by which we mean they put a barrier between themselves and the audience, some layer of gimmickry or sentiment that signals, "This isn't really me. I'm really much smarter and very decent." If an actress is asked to "carry" a show for the first time, and she is untested in the half-hour format, and she shows up with her widely publicized and much sought after and quite beautiful face obscured by swards of hair, might that actress be "hiding"? I saw no need to place a long-distance call to Dr. Jung in Zurich for an answer.

Nor, as it turned out, was there a need to call Leo Becker at his beach house in the Malibu Colony and alert him that we had just begun filming a thirty-minute episode of *Guess Who the Star Is*. As the cameras began to roll, a voice boomed over us, coming down out of the darkness of the empty bleachers.

"Excuse me!"

The actors froze and squinted into the darkness. Jonathan Metzger yelled "Cut!" then wheeled around and glared. The floorboards of the bleachers wobbled and Leo Becker appeared in the far reaches of the stage lights. He wore white slacks with his multi-cabled white Italian sweater and, in that color and light, looked like something that might appear in a shrine.

"Geneva, dear . . . your hair," he called. And then, with a suggestion of irritation, "Where are the guys?"

"The guys" were standing right below him on the stage floor. His suede moccasin could have given my ear a little tap.

"Right here, Leo," said Neil, and Leo looked down at us, grasping the rail of the bleachers.

"Jesus," said Leo, gruffing out the word, "her fucking hair." And then he contorted his face into a suggestion of delight as Geneva approached. "Geneva, sweetheart, we can't see your face. Your hair is in the way."

Geneva did an interesting thing here. She assessed the situation and determined where the power lay, even as the words were still coming out of Leo's mouth. And then, like the most sophisticated chess player, she jumped two, or perhaps three, moves ahead. Not for an instant did I see on her face—what little I could see of it—any thought of fighting for her hairdo. In a heartbeat, she transcended those roiling emotions that just a few moments earlier had so completely overtaken her. She made a brilliant leap forward, into "blame."

"It's the goddamn hairdresser," said Geneva. "I asked him for a certain look, he swore he could do it, and he can't do it."

"Well, then, fuck him," said Leo. "We'll get rid of him. Guys, we have to get her a hairdresser who can work with her. We can't have this."

"I'm sorry," said Geneva. "I tried to go along with him, but . . ."

"Christ, it's not your fault. You have enough to worry about. Come on guys, we have to give her some support here."

Geneva, without shame, darted us a quick *"See?"* look.

"But what can we do right now to fix it?" said Leo. "We have to shoot this show. Can you get him to move it back, so we can just see your face?"

"That's all right. I'll just tell him exactly what to do," said Geneva, prepared to be brave now that someone had the basic decency to give her a little support. "I need ten minutes."

"Ten minutes, everybody" shouted Jonathan Metzger, who had worked his way over to us. "Don't wander."

Geneva started back to her trailer. I saw Jerry Cardini standing off to the side of the set, smoking one of his Nat Shermans and holding the empty Kleenex box in which he kept a few brushes and combs for touch-ups. He saw me looking at him and he acknowledged me with a smile and a raising of the eyebrows. He had no idea he had just been fired.

The first show went well but the second one, with the live audience, soared. Don Lasker took everything Geneva sent him and hit it out of the park, even getting laughs from the crew, who were hearing the material done the right way for the first time. Geneva started fighting for her life, which brought out the best in her. Joseph Landry, the young ex-convict, got laughs on his jokes *and* his straight lines. The rest of the cast, responding to the heat at center stage, caught fire as well. Neil and I shook hands after the final pickup. For the first time, it seemed like we could make this a decent series without Geneva turning us into jellied eel. It was really all very satisfying, if you managed to keep Jerry Cardini out of your mind.

I approached Geneva about Jerry later in the week, after we had screened the rough cut and she was in a good mood. But she was unwilling to show mercy. Her logic was this: I insisted on a hairstyle that covered my face. Jerry provided it. Leo didn't like it. Jerry must die.

It was time to break the news to Jerry. Neil and I took him to Chasen's; Jerry loved all that old Hollywood crap. He surprised us by bringing along a friend named Tommy, a picture framer with his own shop on Melrose. Jerry teased Tommy for flirting with the waiter. When the waiter walked away with the platter of shaved ice into which our communal seafood appetizers had been embedded, Jerry chanted:

> *Tommy and the waiter*
> *Up in a tree.*
> *K-I-S-S-I-N-G.*
> *First comes love,*
> *Then comes marriage,*
> *And then comes Tommy*
> *With a baby carriage.*

We ate hobo steak and chicken burgers—"real guy food," Jerry called it. Over coffee, Tommy excused himself to go to the men's room; he said he wanted to see the famous James Thurber drawings. Jerry then opened the way for what followed by asking, "Has the panther lady crawled back into her cage yet? We'll have to work something out when we get picked up because, frankly, I don't want my name on a crawl if she's going to look like that. She looked like a turd on toast, from what I saw of the rough cut."

"Jerry, the thing is, she doesn't want you on the show." I just came out and said it. There didn't seem to be a way to put it off.

Jerry looked down, as if a pudding had just fallen into his lap.

We scrambled to get Jerry on another Polonia show. When those efforts failed, Neil and I kicked in some money and told him that it was a severance bonus from the production company. And we swore to Jerry that we would get him a job as soon as the production season started in July. And on top of that, we bought him a CD player because he had mentioned he didn't have one.

He took a hairdressing gig in a small salon on the fifth floor of an office building on Cannon Drive. His clientele were mostly real estate ladies and attorneys and buyers from Saks and Magnins. I ran into Jerry at Musso and Frank one night and he said it was depressing because these businesswomen didn't dish with their hairdresser. They were doing business on their cellular phones all the time. I told him to hold tight; we were ever vigilant on his behalf.

In May, CBN picked up our show, which we had decided to call *All Rise,* for thirteen episodes, to begin airing in the fall. We were scheduled for Monday nights at eight-thirty, after *Bette and Bob,* kind of a soft time slot but not Devil's Island or anything. Neil and I got busy staffing the show with writers and working out stories. And the fact is, we were not terribly obsessive about finding work for Jerry Cardini. When you do somebody wrong, there is a tendency not to keep reminding yourself of that fact.

The week before we aired, the *Los Angeles Times* gave us the cover of their "T.V. Week," CBN promoted us heavily on their hot Sunday night lineup, and Geneva was all over the place doing interviews. So we were heard about.

One of the people who heard about us, apparently, was Jerry Cardini. On the Monday we premiered, he was on his own in the little salon on Cannon Drive with a three o'clock and a three-twenty. By a quarter to four he had them both under the dryers. He excused himself and went into the back room. The three o'clock was Elaine Driftmeyer of Jon Douglas Realty. She was busy on the phone about a three-bedroom Spanish colonial on the corner of Gregory and Peck (there is, in fact, such an intersection) that was starting to fall apart. At ten after four she realized her hair was more than fully dry. She put her office on hold and called out for Jerry. When he didn't answer, she said she'd call back, unhooded herself, and went looking for him.

The small back room, from which there was no exit, was empty. The window was open, and Elaine heard the squawk of a police radio bouncing off the white bricks of the building. She looked down and saw two squad cars, a paramedics van, and a small crowd. In the center of it all, evident by the melon green shirt he had been wearing, lay Jerry Cardini in a fetal position.

Jerry had had the bad luck to land in the valet parking area behind the Bistro Gardens within a few yards of Clint Eastwood. Clint was waiting for his Porsche when Jerry hit. Clint reacted, as most of us would, by saying, "Jesus!" Then, according to *Daily Variety,* he "took control of the situation." This involved running back into the restaurant and telling the maître d', "Some guy just jumped out a window."

Jerry, who was enamored of stars, was not well served by them in his life or in his passing. The slant on all the television news reports that night was "Clint Eastwood narrowly escapes death as a man falls five stories and just misses him."

# Chapter

# *11*

Why does that guy have it in for me? I never did him a favor in my life.

—MAYOR JIMMY WALKER

◆ ◆ ◆

We assembled a lean but effective writing staff. We hired Gino Buccanetti, a newcomer who'd written a very funny *Murphy Brown,* as story editor. Lisa Silverman, who was misspending her Harvard education in the field of comedy writing, was producer. When she first came to Hollywood, Lisa supported herself by going on game shows, and is distinguished among comedy writers for having posed nude in *Playboy* for a feature called "The Women of *Jeopardy!*" Don Monahan and Don Blatz, referred to jointly as the Dons, came on as supervising producers. The Dons had been writing together for about two years. Don Blatz's previous partner, Rick Agoda, had died of AIDS. Don Monahan came out of retirement because he needed the money. Toward the end of his career, Monahan had created a popular series called *House Boat Harrigan.* Monahan, a lifelong gambler, had counted on his profit participation in *House Boat Harrigan* as his retirement nest egg. But when the show sold into syndication, the studio cooked the books and managed to prove that the series was still "in deficit." Monahan's continual message to Neil and me was, "Take all the money you can get up front, boys."

We threw ourselves into breaking stories and getting writers started on scripts. We enjoyed going out to lunch every day; we knew that when production started in late July we would be chained to the lot for months. We enjoyed the wild hilarity writers can concoct when they're in a room together working toward a common end. And we enjoyed the long weeks of insulation from Geneva Holloway. Those were indeed enjoyable days, lulled as we were by the false idea that we had enough time.

But God being God, we soon had a serious problem to distract us. It came in the form of the July 13th issue of *Daily Variety*. Sharone brought it into the office while I was eating my morning oat bran muffin. She set it on my desk as if she were presenting me with a dead kitten. She was wearing a white buckskin jacket with particularly long fringe, but her demeanor caused me to forgo comment.

I picked up *Variety*.

Neil was reading interviews in *Writers at Work* to see if Philip Roth or Joseph Heller had any magic words for him. He had been encouraged to learn that Joseph Heller once wrote an episode of *McHale's Navy*. Neil, who aspired to write short stories one day, worried that his labors in television might corrupt his artistic sensibility beyond any hope of redemption.

He looked up and saw my chagrin as I read *Variety*. "What?" he said.

In an unduly prominent front-page article, above the fold, Neil and I were charged with various crimes against race, to which we had not been asked to respond. The chief theme was this: We had given to Geneva Holloway, a white actress, a role that properly belonged to Malcolm Dant, a black actor. Malcolm had graciously declined comment. The charges were being put forth by Orris B. LaVelle, president of the Beverlywood chapter of the NAACP, who had distinguished himself at the most recent national convention of his organization by stating, in session and in press release, that the Jews who control Hollywood were systematically blocking African-Americans access to positions of power in the entertainment industry.

While my name was mentioned in the article, the several direct quotes from Orris LaVelle cited only "Neil L. Stein." You could almost hear LaVelle's contempt for this Jew bound off the glossy white pages of the paper. Neil panicked. His eyes narrowed and he focused on the middle distance.

"It's bullshit," I said, but he did not respond.

Sharone came back into the office. "Renata on one," she said. Neil picked up the phone and greeted his wife.

I only heard Neil's end of the conversation, but it was clear that Renata was not offering wifely comfort and support. I presume Renata, who saw herself as one of the foremost proponents of racial harmony that Lower Bel Air had to offer, was asking Neil what the fuck this was all about. Neil seemed to be defending himself. "But *we* didn't fire him," he said at one point. "Joe Danko fired him."

Neil hung up the phone and looked at me with harbor seal eyes. We have an agreement: he can say derogatory things about Renata to me, but I am not allowed to concur or volunteer any unflattering observations of my own.

"Never marry a shiksa," he said. "All of a sudden, they're more Jewish than you."

The writing went better that morning than you might expect. Concentration seemed to allay anxiety. Shortly before lunch, we were interrupted by a call from Greg Paul, the multimillionaire creator of *Relative Differences*. The call was for me, but out of politeness to Neil I put it on the speaker box, to share my intimacy with this newly great man.

"James," said Greg.

"Greg . . . you sound like you're calling me from inside your bank vault," I said.

Greg gave a snort of appreciation. It was a remarkable little snort, Proustian in its levels of meaning. "Yeah, I do have fifty million dollars," said the snort, "but I wasn't going to be the one to bring it up." Or perhaps I was reading into it.

"Did you guys see yesterday's *Chicago Tribune?*" asked Greg.

Neil and I looked at each other. Yesterday's *Chicago*-fucking-*Tribune?*

"I think we threw it away already," I said.

"No, really, there's an interview with Malcolm Dant with the TV critic there. It was all about your show."

"And . . . ?"

"You should get a copy. He's claiming he was fired for racial reasons."

"No."

"He says when he spoke up about derogatory elements of the script, you guys had him canned. Get a copy."

"Greg? This is Neil. How did you happen to be reading the *Chicago Tribune?*"

"I was in Chicago. They gave me some man-of-the-year award there."

I mouthed the words, Don't-ask-who-gave-it. "Okay, Greg, we'll get a copy," said Neil.

"Thanks for letting us know, Greg," I said.

Greg was in the process of saying "The Chicago chapter of the B'nai Brith Anti-Def—" when I hung up.

"Putz," I said.

"Searching the world for bad news about us," said Neil.

We had to admit, however, that this was starting to look like an orchestrated campaign. We'd been expecting, all morning, a call of assurance and support from Leo Becker. Well, a call anyhow. This was the sort of thing that made Polonia look bad in the industry. We had a certain amount of dignity, which kept us from calling Leo first. But not all that much. We placed the call.

"Mr. Becker is not here," said a voice in Leo's office that I did not recognize.

"Is Iona there?" I asked. I make it a point to be on a first-name basis with the secretaries of the great.

"No."

"No?"

"There's going to be an announcement."

"What announcement?"

"Well . . . that's what the announcement is going to be about."

Sharone came in with a fax rattling in her hand. Important. All producers. Must attend. Screening Room 1, Polonia Productions, three-thirty.

And so we gathered, we cogs in the wheels of entertainment, in the cavernous screening room. Producers, executive producers, supervising producers, line producers, coproducers, writer-producers, filling row after row of faux-mohair seats. I don't suppose at that exact moment in time there was a larger concentration of Jaguar keys anywhere else in the world.

There was a certain amount of jocularity and waving across the room, but it all rode on a wave of apprehension. What if this was the day God appeared with a clap of thunder and said unto us: "You're all frauds. You make too much money. You've been found out. The people of the earth demand retribution."

Instead of God, we got Avery Schine, who stood at the podium and looked out over us with the warm, blue eyes of a cost accountant. He came to the point rather directly: He had fired Leo Becker. He didn't put it that way; instead he said Leo had ". . . chosen to seek other opportunities . . . enormous contributions . . . will be greatly missed . . ." But if you believe that, then I have some swampland in Florida I'd like to interest you in.

The back story was well known to everyone in the room. When Polonia Productions consisted of Leo Becker and a secretary in a two-room office on Sunset Boulevard, Avery Schine was the out-of-town money from Chicago. Forty percent of the stock was owned by Leo, the creative force with the show business background. Sixty percent was owned by Avery, who was staked by some gentlemen in the pinball machine distribution business. Avery started out one-up, and he stayed that way.

As Polonia grew, Avery took a more active role; which is to

say, he became intrusive. While Leo was out selling television shows, Avery decided he wanted to be in the movie business. He liked the idea of hanging out with movie stars.

As the company prospered, Leo grew resentful, Avery imperious. It came to the point where they leased a second corporate jet, because they refused to travel together. Leo's financial clout in the organization diminished when he divorced Greta Zale, whom you may remember from a sixties half-hour comedy called *Sis and Miss*. Greta, through the courtesy of California's community property laws, got a nice taste of Leo's Polonia stock: half. There was no immediate problem. She let Leo vote it for a few years. But when Leo married the young and unforgivably slender Cassandra Bowfinkle, Greta reconsidered her business arrangements. There were too many unhappy memories connected to those 500,000 shares of Polonia stock. She sought a buyer.

She sold her shares to Avery Schine, giving him absolute power over her happily remarried ex-husband. But in fairness to Greta, she did not do this out of spite. She offered the stock to Leo, but he was not in a position to cough up the seventy-four million dollars required. For Avery, on the other hand, it was merely a matter of going down to the trunk of his car.

So there was Leo Becker, confined, his dignity at risk. And there was Avery Schine, holding nuclear weapons. The inciting incident—referred to subsequently as "Sarajevo" as the story made the rounds of the production offices at Polonia—had occurred the previous afternoon in the executive offices on the third floor of the Franklin Pangborn Building. Leo noticed a handwritten note from Avery Schine that lay on the desk of Avery's secretary. Leo read the note aloud and scoffed. "My partner writes like a fucking third grader," he said. The secretary reported the remark to Avery. Avery went into Leo's office the back way, through the executive dining room they shared, and confronted him man to man:

"Did you say I write like a third grader?"

"You do. You write like a fucking child."

"You said that in front of my secretary?"

"Who needs to? She has to read your crap all day."

It escalated from there all the way to the point of glass breaking. I heard the details from Iona Shipper, Leo's secretary, who even showed me a note that Avery subsequently wrote to Irv Nitti, his financial lieutenant and hatchet man: "Leo Becker is leaving the company as of now. Initiate procedures as to this."

Awkward, but beyond the sophistication of a third grader.

Whenever I asked out loud what the hell Avery Schine was doing in the entertainment business, someone would always say, "Oh, he's a brilliant businessman." "Brilliant" seemed to precede the words "Avery Schine" the way "powerful" comes before "House Ways and Means Committee." You'd think someone with that reputation would, every once in a while, do something brilliant. I never saw it. For example, it certainly wasn't brilliant of him to make a movie about the invasion of Panama that cost more than the actual invasion of Panama. (The movie lost $45 million, but it did give Avery a chance to have his picture taken with his arm around Jacqueline Bisset.)

Getting rid of Leo Becker was not very brilliant, either. Neil and I sat in the screening room stunned. There we were, with a show on the air, suddenly deprived of the only Polonia executive with any influence, credibility, track record, or authority with the networks. And then Avery made it all much, much worse. He announced that David Putzman would be taking Leo's place. Surely Avery understood David to be the lightweight he was. He must have intended David's appointment as a calculated insult to Leo.

David stepped forward. His round, prematurely balding head made him look like the Gerber baby. He willed an aspect of forcefulness into his flat and unconvincing features. He addressed us with all the authority of the assistant manager of a car wash sent out to confront an unhappy customer. I still remember his first sentence, because it was the most amazing thing I ever heard him utter: "Last night after Avery and I talked about all this, I was reading Tennyson."

This lead up to "The old order changeth . . ." David rambled on with false sincerity and even more false humility until all the nerve ends in the room, which only a short while ago were alive with the anxiety of change, had been numbed. As he walked off the stage, I noticed once again what a high, round rump he had, a challenge to any tailor and one his own had failed to meet.

Avery stepped forward again and said he understood the concern these changes had generated. He encouraged any questions, which he would answer to the best of his ability. Any questions at all. There was a tension-filled moment, like those seconds before a kickoff. And then, before one of those windbags who do hour-long dramas could compose some abstruse declarations that would keep us there another half hour, I raised my hand in a preemptive strike.

"Yes, Jim," said Avery, as if we were colleagues used to working closely together.

"Yeah," I said, standing up, "that Toulouse-Lautrec poster in Leo's outer office—can I have that?"

Everyone in the room laughed except David Putzman. He saw a threat in my question before he saw any humor. He had already moved into Leo's suite and laid claim to everything Leo left behind.

When you produce a television series, the list of executives who can actually help you is very short—shorter than the list casting people draw up when they're told to look for "a young Cary Grant." Leo Becker was on the list. When he chose to be on your side, he could bark into a phone and work wonders. David Putzman, we were quick to find out, didn't even know there was a list.

Actually, "quick to find out" is not a good cluster of words to use in association with Putzman. It took us four days to get a meeting with him, while the attacks from Orris LaVelle continued in the trades. LaVelle said he was offended that "Mr. Neil Stein refuses to answer my calls." Of course, Neil was never called. It was Avery Schine who finally focused Putzman's attention in our direction. "This shit can affect the stock price," he said.

There was a black man waiting in Putzman's outer office when we arrived, a small man so infused with dignity that from the oversized wingback chair he sat in he looked like a king. Neil and I smiled politely at him and took seats. Putzman was already notorious in the company for running late. We assumed the old gent was an earlier appointment who hadn't been seen to yet. Then Orris LaVelle and Andre Broz, Malcolm Dant's evil manager, came tumbling in, locked in animated chatter. They sobered up abruptly, so as not to appear as chummy as they in fact were. Andre acknowledged us with a wave of his hand at waist level. Andre, the second-generation Yugoslavian who had declared himself black, wore his hair processed, and his skin actually seemed darker to me. I wondered if he was having pigmentation injections. Orris LaVelle gloamed onto the old black man, addressing him as Pastor Loomis, which made him—as we should have recognized— the Reverend Dewey Loomis of the Church of Christ Baptist Church in Compton. Reverend Loomis had been fighting the good fight back before the conflagration that caused Watts to become the best-known neighborhood in Los Angeles. He rolled up his yellow eyes to take in Orris LaVelle, looking beyond the calculating words and false charm. There was steel in the man, and the authority that comes from knowing what you want.

LaVelle called Andre over for introductions. What heart-stopping lies had these two scoundrels been telling to involve this local monument in what amounted to a shakedown?

At length, Putzman's secretary came out of his office with a tray holding a yogurt container and a half-eaten pear, and we were invited to go in. Putzman had redone Leo Becker's office in an American West design, a motif he favored so highly that he extended it to the naming of his daughters (Cody and Cheyenne). The technical term for what happened to us in that office is, I believe, "a sellout." Putzman began by expressing authentic disappointment that Malcolm Dant wasn't there. He probably wanted to get a picture of Malcolm shaking his hand, to add to the legends of show business already gracing his wall: Rich Little, Erma Bombeck, Jack Klugman. (Frankly, it was pathetic. The Santa Palms car wash in West Hollywood has a more impressive display than that. And the photos did not fit in with the lariats and bleached cattle skulls.) Andre Broz explained that Malcolm chose to remain aloof from the battle.

"His mind has moved on to other things," he said. (His mind may have moved on, but his career stayed behind in the toilet. Just three days earlier I had seen that Malcolm was a guest on *Win, Lose, or Draw,* a game show hosted by Vicki Lawrence.) "I'm here as a disinterested party, solely in support of Orris LaVelle and Pastor Loomis," said Andre, putting an interesting new spin on the concept of disinterest. "Yet a wrong has been done and must be righted."

Pastor Loomis immediately made it clear that it did not matter to him what Andre and Orris had on their dance card. He had an agenda of his own and took this opportunity to present it.

"There's a dispute among you and I am not privy to the facts," he said, his words coming out like beads on a string. You could hear the lilt of his Sunday speaking voice in them. "Perhaps this man Malcolm Dant was wronged. I don't know. If he was, he has the resources to take action on his own."

"But there's a broader issue, Pastor, is the point," said Orris, nervous, coaching.

"I agree," said Pastor Loomis.

"See, it's an issue of African-American representation in the industry," said Orris.

"Jobs," said Pastor Loomis.

"Jobs. The man said it," said Orris.

The two men, it turns out, had different meanings for the word "Jobs." Pastor Loomis meant people getting hired, coming to work, getting a paycheck. He had a healthy supply of people who needed jobs, through an organization he founded called the Compton Youth Covenant. Orris's idea of jobs was more along the lines of a substantial grant to Orris LaVelle, which he would use to think up ways of improving black employment at the studios.

At which point Andre Broz kicked in with his particular take on disinterest: a certain amount of money from Polonia to fund a project—perhaps a movie. It would be a joint venture among Polonia, Orris's organization, and Malcolm and Andre's Mandela Productions (a name chosen to invoke both Nelson Mandela and the Buddhist mandala, Andre once explained).

With Pastor Loomis's plan, given the way these things tend to work out, perhaps twenty-five or thirty African-Americans would get well-paying jobs. Under the Orris Lavelle-Andre Broz-Malcolm Dant plan, three black men would make a fortune.

Putzman sat and listened to everything with his hands folded at his chin, his index finger pressed together into a steeple that he bounced off his pursed lips. His round head loomed like a little moon. Now he spoke, the great white father.

"Mistakes have been made," he said, cocking the steeple toward the rest of us. "Certainly, there have been misunderstandings. I wasn't in on any of the meetings between Neil and Jim with Malcolm Dant. I'm like Pastor Loomis in that regard. I don't have all the facts."

"I'll give you the facts," I piped up.

"No, what I'm getting at is, let's set the facts aside."

"How far aside?" I said.

"No, I mean, let's start fresh. Let's forget about what happened and just deal with what we all agree are the ongoing problems. If there had never been a *Lou Duffy* project, I think we should be having this meeting anyhow. Polonia is willing to do what it can to increase African-American representation in the industry."

Putzman went on to concur that the best way to do that was pretty much along the lines that had already been proposed. He would give Andre and Orris a great deal of money, and pass Pastor Loomis along to the Polonia human resources vice president.

"We want to do the right thing," said Putzman. He actually used those words.

"Excuse me," I said, "but what are Neil and I here for?"

"You're part of all this," said Putzman.

"Just for the humiliation? Because we're writers, we have ample opportunity for humiliation all day, we don't have to come to special meetings for it."

We stood up. Putzman seethed, like a parent whose kids were acting up in front of company. Neil crossed to Pastor Loomis and shook his hand.

"It's an honor to meet you, Pastor Loomis," he said. "We met briefly once before. In 1978. I was in that 'lunch-in' you organized at the downtown Hyatt, for the food service employees."

Pastor Loomis beamed at the memory. "That one turned out pretty good," he said.

"It sure did," said Neil.

"Hey, guys, just a minute," said Putzman as we left. "Stay. You can't let ego enter into this."

Which was a strange thing to hear from a man who sat under a plaque that claimed to be the Putzman coat of arms.

# Chapter

## *12*

■ During the McCarthy era, two William Morris agents were talking about rumors that Delores del Rio was about to show up on the Hollywood black list.

"Is she really a communist?" asked one.

The other replied, "Well, she says she is, but you know actresses."

◆ ◆ ◆

We started shooting episodes of *All Rise* in August, 1988, with eight scripts in various stages of development. The gap between the start of production and the on-air premiere is a period of heightened loopiness on new shows. The network and production company executives scurry frantically, looking for things to find fault with. You get a lot of notes like "Does that wall have to be green?" As if a taupe wall would deliver an extra three quarters of a rating point. The cast, understandably, is on edge because they are making shows but not yet receiving any feedback from an adoring public.

Geneva reacted as if she were trapped in a wet trench during a very loud aerial bombardment. Neil and I consoled ourselves with the thought that she could not possibly sustain this level of testiness through the whole course of our thirteen shows. The mere human penchant for variety argued against it.

"She's just feeling a little insecure right now," we said to each other. "She'll calm down once we're on the air." But after a few weeks, we came to see that we were underestimating this lady's capacity to be unhelpful.

A particular episode stands out: In the first few weeks of the show, Geneva showed a preference for a blowsy look. We, and the network, would have preferred her in something more form-fitting. One afternoon, Neil and I decided to bring up the subject to Geneva. We wandered over to the stage after an editing session to suggest that the wardrobe we'd just seen in the rough cut wasn't very flattering to our star.

Geneva was knitting at the rehearsal table while Jonathan Metzger worked with Joseph Landry over in the kitchen set. Don Lasker sat several seats away from Geneva, scanning a copy of *USA Today*. Mary Beth Opdyke, who played Geneva's assistant, was over by the bleachers, teaching a tap dance step to the assistant prop man.

Geneva looked very appealing, the way a beautiful woman will look even more beautiful when she's focused on a task and unaware of her surroundings. She wore a sleeveless top that showed off her graceful, thin arms, like Debra Winger's in *Urban Cowboy*. She sat on a metal folding chair, her legs veed up on the chair next to it and looking all the more comely coming out of the wide, dark, legs of her baggy green shorts.

Neil and I greeted her with smiles and she greeted us back with a couple of nods of the head.

"We just saw the rough cut," I said, and Geneva cocked her head a little in polite acknowledgment.

"The scene with the gun collector comes off great," said Neil. "You really made it work."

Geneva looked up at this. "He's funny?"

"He comes off funny, because of your reactions," said Neil.

"We favor you in the editing," I said. "That really solves the problem."

"We probably should have replaced him," said Geneva of this guest actor whom she would not allow us to replace at the time.

I sat down on a metal folding chair. "You know, the network had a note, and when we were looking at the rough cut, I see their point. It's a wardrobe thing."

Neil sat down beside me. "Not the stuff you wear at the courthouse. That's a great look, the suit thing. But the outfits around the house."

"There should be some 'sexual tension'"—I made fun of the phrase as I said it because these were words we were all sick of hearing—"between you and Louis. Those long sweaters get in the way, and that skirt last week, it was so full."

"Noted," said Geneva, as she concentrated on her knitting.

"We should see a little more of you," said Neil. "Don't you think?"

"*No*-ted," said Geneva, ending the discussion.

An hour later, Jonathan Metzger called us from the stage. "Geneva went to her trailer and she won't come out," he said. "She won't talk to anybody."

"What's wrong?"

"I don't know. After you guys left, she started sobbing."

"Was it something we said?" asked Neil.

"I don't know. I don't know what you said. It's like she got bad news from a doctor or something."

"Is she in there alone?" I asked.

"No. Dawn Bulk is with her." Dawn Bulk, the wardrobe woman, was Geneva's confidante, and, as a result, probably the fourth or fifth most powerful person on the set. "What am I going to do? There's nothing I can rehearse without her."

"What if you broke for lunch?"

"It's only eleven-fifteen. We usually break at one."

"So break now," said Neil.

"Okay," said Jonathan. "We'll break for lunch."

Jonathan stopped by the office at twelve-thirty as Neil and I and the other writers ate a take-out lunch from a Japanese place in the Gower Gulch shopping mall. (A word of advice: Tempura does not travel well.) We generally avoided Japanese, but Lisa Silverman lobbied for it, and she was sensitive about being the only woman in this roomful of men, so we ordered Japanese this once. I don't know why it was such an issue with Lisa. She never actually ate lunch; she looked at lunch. She just liked to open the Styrofoam container, inhale the vapors, and then go get a handful of trail mix out of the glass jar on Sharone's desk.

Jonathan knocked on the open door to attract attention to himself, then entered the room shaking his head, answering the unasked question.

"Some food?" offered Neil.

"I ate with Don Lasker at the commissary," said Jonathan. "Tried to calm him down a little."

"What's he worried about?" I asked.

"The network run-through tomorrow. He's big in the show. He's got that long run about when he was a kid at camp. He needs rehearsal."

"Maybe we should hire somebody to run lines with him," suggested Neil.

Jonathan just shrugged. He ate some of Lisa's kappa maki and went back over to the stage. We went back to our writing.

"We could lose a whole day," Neil kept saying.

"So we lose a day," I said. "We're losing a day of writing because you keep worrying about losing a day."

"Should we call Putzman?" asked Neil.

"Don't we have enough troubles for one day?"

"Right."

At one-thirty the runner came over and told us we were wanted in Geneva's trailer.

You enter a trailer at a disadvantage, body off balance from the springy steps, head lowered to accommodate the inadequate height of the door. It's much like the hunching down required to enter the keep of a castle, where you're in a position to have your head lopped off if the defenders determine you are a foe. Geneva insisted on a trailer, instead of a dressing room, so she could have a private toilet. She loved talking about how often she had to pee. She went so far as to discuss it with Jay Leno on *The Tonight Show* once.

Geneva, Jonathan, and Dawn Bulk were at the far end of the trailer on the small, upholstered settees that formed a U around a Formica table. Dawn had her hand over Geneva's, showing off her very long, pink nails. (We called her Rosy-Fingered Dawn.) A little off to the side sat a man I'd never seen before. He wore gym pants and a tank top; his muscles were developed to the point of grotesqueness. His thick, curly black hair came down well over his forehead. The room was heavy with the odor of carpet glue and end-of-the-pot coffee. Jonathan invited us to sit down by extending his arm, and Dawn scooted over to Geneva's side to make room.

Geneva's eyes were red from her tears. Her look was stern and straight ahead.

"This is Emil Novak," said Jonathan, indicating the weightlifter. "He's a personal trainer and body worker. We called him because Geneva had a shoulder cramp." Emil acknowledged us by pointing a finger in our direction.

Jonathan took a breath. "Geneva has something to say," he said. "It's about her wardrobe choices."

Geneva turned to us and took us in with her eyes. "I am a survivor of rape," she said. "It was very brutal, a gang rape by soldiers. I was left for dead in a ditch." She clutched Dawn's hand.

"Jesus," said Neil. "When was this?"

"It was in a past life," said Geneva. We absorbed this with straight faces. "In subsequent lives, I've been given broader hips, as a source of protection. Some people think you're from peasant stock if you have broader hips, because it means you have a wider birth canal and can deliver babies more easily. But with me, it's strictly a matter of protection." She stared at us for a long beat, as if we were supposed to complete the thought.

"Uh huh," I said.

Dawn spoke. "Geneva doesn't want to draw attention to her hips. That's why she wears a fuller look on the show."

I nodded. Neil nodded. But then he took it further. "What were the circumstances of the rape?" he asked with complete reverence.

"It was during the time of the French Revolution. It happened in the woods of Malotte near Fontainebleau. I was the Comtesse de la Malotte. I say soldiers, but they were really riffraff in uniform. Three of them."

"There's nothing more to be said," I said, truthfully. "We'll handle the network. But right now, aren't we drawing attention to your hips by overdisguising them? Can't we do something about that?"

Both Geneva and Dawn nodded emphatically. "Daniel France knew how to dress me," said Geneva. This was one more of her frequent references to the chubby, apparently omnipotent producer of her forthcoming movie-of-the-week. "Dawn's going to talk to him."

On the way back to the office, Neil told me that there was another question about the rape that he had been burning to ask: "Have you reported this to the police?"


As our air date neared, Geneva seemed to lose interest in *All Rise*. Instead, she directed her enthusiasm toward this amazing and completely wonderful movie-of-the-week that she had done in England with Daniel France. She came late to rehearsals, or left early, or ducked out in the middle of the day, to give interviews promoting this dazzling, ground-breaking movie that was soon to replace *It's a Wonderful Life* as everyone's absolute favorite. She explained her neglect of the project at hand with a curt "Daniel France needed me," as if the mention of Daniel France was the equivalent of invoking the Holy Father.

Daniel France is young—late thirties, my age—and in a short period of time has earned a reputation as a mounter of atrocious productions. And no one stops him. His chief assets are high energy and a very good tailor. He sits in network meetings, rotund and animated and better dressed than the network vice presidents, and spins tales of gold. He relies on classics of the cinema with good starring roles for women, and remakes them with great attention to costumes and location and almost no attention to pacing or script. (Perhaps you saw his production of *Pride and Prejudice,* in which he reunited all the cast members of *Charlie's Angels,* including Shelley Hack.) He films these television movies in desirable places, usually in Europe, and insists that all the network executives visit the location. And he hands out very expensive gifts at Christmas—stuffed golden pheasants flown in from Dean and DeLuca, for example. I guess everyone has such a good time on a Daniel France production that in the screening room, no executive can bring himself to point out to his fellows that they are coconspirators in an assault on human sensibilities.

To his credit, Daniel France coaxes miracles out of actresses— not, unfortunately, in their performances, but in their willingness to cooperate. Witness the loyalty he commanded from Geneva Holloway. I think gay guys have an advantage in this department. They know the actual names of fabrics. They can intelligently use terms like "blush" and "foundation." They can empathize with an actress who goes on and on about her hair, and without pretending. A woman will do anything for a man who makes her look good.

So here was Daniel France, a man of impeccable personal taste, making perfectly dreadful popular entertainments. Neil said he should be buried next to Noël Coward, with the epitaph "He Had a Talent to Abuse." Often, it is especially sad to note, his movies get very high ratings.

At this point, I suppose it's appropriate to reveal the telecinema classic that Daniel France had given Geneva Holloway the honor of starring in. It was a remake of *Philadelphia Story.* There are those who claim that Daniel, in his pitch meeting at the network, had said, "I want to remake *High Society,* but without the music. I think there's a good basic story there."

And that's how *It Happened in Philadelphia* came to be. (It was Daniel's hallmark to rename the classic he was about to violate. *Pride and Prejudice* was called *Those Bennet Girls.*) Geneva Holloway reprised Katharine Hepburn's Tracy Lord, with Andrew

Stevens as Jimmy Stewart's Macaulay Connor. It fell to Harry Hamlin of *L.A. Law,* in the role of C. K. Dexter Haven, to make us all forget that there ever had been a Cary Grant. The press kit emphasized that "the entire production was filmed on location in England," an odd boast for a story that takes place in Philadelphia. As premiere week approached, and the network announced that it would launch it's *Sunday Movie of the Week* slot with *It Happened in Philadelphia,* Geneva's indifference toward *All Rise* became pronounced to the point of rudeness.

Daniel France, in association with the Hollywood chapter of Women in Cable (women in cable television, not a group of lanky slaterns in leather bustiers and spiky heels) sponsored a benefit screening of *It Happened in Philadelphia* at the Academy of Motion Picture Arts and Sciences in Beverly Hills. Tickets were $80 a person, with the proceeds designated for Bramble House, a center for mentally disabled children who had the additional disadvantage of physical handicaps.

Neil and I had each written our check for $160, to share with our star on this, her night of glory. If you watched *Entertainment Tonight*'s coverage of the event, and looked closely over the bare and fetching shoulders of Joan Van Ark as she was being interviewed, you may have seen our foursome hovering over the steam tables in the background. Well, not the entire foursome. The lovely Kiki Burmeister, actress and jewelry craftsperson, as was often the case at these large gatherings, knew just about all the unattached men there. While Neil and Renata and I were enjoying the crab claws, Kiki was catching up with all these men and exchanging new phone numbers. There was such innocence in this, at least on her part, that in my heart of hearts I truly didn't mind, although I sometimes pretended to be jealous to make her worry about me. Kiki was still living with Leroy. She had come to the conclusion that she hated Los Angeles. She called it an evil city. Her pursuit of acting had become dilatory. I once wangled her an interview with the casting vice president at CBN, and she never showed up. She seemed to prefer the pursuit of moneymaking schemes destined never to make money: selling homemade jam, designing hats, teaching ballet to preschoolers, or, currently, making earrings out of broken glass. I came to see that Kiki followed the grazing principle of life: She moved through the day like a cow, from one clump of enthusiasm to another, and at sundown she lifted her head to see where she was.

Neil and Renata and I were near the main entrance when Geneva Holloway emerged from a long white limo—is there anything more vulgar than a long white limo?—dressed like the bride in the window of a Latino department store. Her gown was natty lace and abundant white silk, and she wore baby's breath in her two and a half pounds of blond hair. The bridal theme continued with a halting, shy smile and a dreamy wetness in the eyes. She submitted herself to the U of photographers—the hardened mercenaries who sell to the tabloids, the video crews who free-lance for television entertainment shows, the few sad autograph collectors with their automatic Ricohs. She gave herself over to them with a look of wonder, amazed that she should be the focus of all this attention.

Milo Lally came out of the limo several seconds after Geneva, as if he had taken a wrong turn at the built-in bar. He wore his rich cowboy look: a burgundy velvet blazer; a creamy white western shirt buttoned at the neck with two pendulous collar points hanging down like spaniel's ears; jeans, of course; and boots with gold toe guards. A third person got out of the limo. It was, for some reason, Emil Novak, the body builder. He wore a sport coat that barely contained his bulging musculature. Milo stood by as Geneva basked for a few more moments in the photographers' lights, then he stepped forward and urged her away. Geneva allowed herself to be led, confused but flattered by last-minute calls from photographers who wanted her to look in their direction. Emil followed, craning his head side to side like a bodyguard.

As Geneva entered the high-ceilinged lobby of the Academy, by now dense with invitees, her face suddenly became more knowing. "Jesus," she said, "what a rat fuck."

Geneva circulated grandly, kissing and hugging. She greeted

Neil and me as if we were a couple of awkward cousins who had to be invited but really didn't fit in. Waiters circulated with napkin-wrapped bottles of Pinot Noir in one hand and fume blanc in the other, until the politely insistent gongs summoned everyone up the grand staircase and into the auditorium.

I suppose you could update the screen version of *Philadelphia Story* to the early nineties and cast it well and turn out a witty homage to your source. It's not an intrinsically bad idea. Most ideas for television aren't intrinsically good or bad. Everything rests on execution. And in its execution, *It Happened in Philadelphia* failed in every aspect. As the saying goes, when a movie is bad, even the hats stink.

Those with a direct relationship to the principals in the production forced occasional laughs, not quite correctly timed. Everyone else sat cobra-eyed as the horrors on the screen unspooled. An example of one of those horrors: Daniel France likes to put something from his own life into each of his films. That's why Elizabeth Barrett in his *Elizabeth Loves Robert* had, instead of a cuddly lap dog called Flush, a black Labrador retreiver called Bandit. Unaware that he was tampering with one of the most famous sailing crafts in cinema history, Daniel decided to change the name of the *True Love,* the yacht Dexter designed for Tracy, and a model of which he presents to her and George Kitteridge as a wedding present. Daniel thought it would be cute to honor the memory of a little sailboat he had owned in his grammar school days. That, and the fact that the cast understood the word "yar" to rhyme with "rare," did much to alter a cherished scene in which Tracy and Kitteridge (played by Richard Moll of *Night Court*) discuss the model Dexter has just given them at the swimming pool on the Lord estate.

KITTERIDGE: Look at Haven's idea of a wedding present.

TRACY: Why, it's a model of the *Bulgie.*

KITTERIDGE: The *Bulgie*? What's that?

TRACY: The *Bulgie* was a boat he designed, and built practically. We sailed her down the coast of Maine and back the summer we were married. My, she was yare.

KITTERIDGE: Yare? What does that mean?

TRACY: Yare means easy to handle, quick to the helm, fast, bright. I loved the *Bulgie*.

When the film ended, there was a round of awful, perfunctory applause and then an awkward stillness. There was a sense that any sudden movement might lead to a panicked sprint toward the emergency exits. People seemed unable to rise. You expected Red Cross volunteers to pass through the auditorium and administer oxygen.

People moved back down to the lobby for a buffet. Daniel France descended just before us, between Geneva and Andrew Stevens, arms locked at the elbow, like a poster for *Babes on Broadway*. A wonderful fragrance wafted up from Daniel, and I couldn't help noticing that he lessened the impact of his male pattern baldness by polishing his pate the same black as his hair.

As if we hadn't suffered enough, we were forced to gain access to Geneva and somehow comment positively on what we had just endured. You're familiar with such backstage double entendres as "You'll never be better than you were tonight," "It was incredible," and "I couldn't believe my eyes"? I took these texts as my inspiration for, "We saw a whole new side of you." Neil got away with clasping her hand in both of his and beaming a very brief "Delightful." Renata Stein, rather missing the point, said, "What a beautiful party," while Kiki, in spite of the press of people, tried to make a complicated connection between herself, Geneva, and some girl who used to be Jackson Browne's private pilot.

Milo Lally gravitated toward us. After the agents and network executives paid him the scant attention that was his due, he really had no one else to talk to. He held his champagne glass with both hands.

"What's with this Emil guy?" I asked.

"She was worried her neck would go out, because of all the stress of the premiere. So she brought him along in case it does."

"Milo, you're a masseur."

"No, I don't do that anymore. I'm a manager now. So . . . what did you think of the movie?"

We told him.

"It's a career buster," I said. "I just hope it doesn't pull down our show with it."

"I think she'll be looking for new management," said Neil.

"Don't shit me," said Milo.

"Milo," I said, "it's a disaster. Did you see it? Did you have your eyes open?"

"Shit," said Milo.

"You asked," I said.

The reviews were savage. It was as if a gazelle had strayed into a den of lions and asked, "Anyone peckish?" The film had stirred such passion in the nation's television critics that some of them were actually jolted into composing an interesting sentence. "Normally I'm opposed to capital punishment, but 'It Happened in Philadelphia' has turned me around," said *Newsday*. "Ian Carter directed in much the same way that Sherman marched to the sea," said *The New York Times*. "It airs near Yom Kippur, and has much to atone for," said the *Los Angeles Times*.

There was a distinguishing feature to many of the reviews: They attacked the actors. Generally television critics are forgiving of actors and blame everything on the writers. You can watch an actor absolutely sabotage a good script and then read reviews like "Unfortunately, even the impressive talents of Cheech Marin could not salvage Anton Chekhov's trite and meandering script." But in the case of *It Happened in Philadelphia,* the actors took their lumps, in some cases for the first time in their lives. Surely it had never before been said of Geneva Holloway that "she should be arrested for pandering," or "Ms. Holloway, like Lee Harvey Oswald, acted alone," or "Geneva Holloway combines the beauty of a young Katharine Hepburn with the acting talent of a young Hugh O'Brian."

The ratings, when the piece aired, were more forgiving than the reviews: a 24 share, by no means a disgraceful outing. Viewers increased each half hour, much the way spectators at the Indianapolis 500 return to their seats late in the race, when accidents are more likely to occur.

Our show, *All Rise,* debuted a week later, at eight-thirty on Monday night, with a 23 share. Although we came in a share point below the movie, we were seen as a success while it was considered an embarrassing failure. For one thing, we came up two share points from our lead-in, and almost took the time slot. For another, our reviews were mostly glowing. Of course, television reviews have about as much effect on the size of the audience as the phases of the moon have on a parked car. (Critics, like the homeless, are one of those problems a free society has not been able to rid itself of.) But people in the industry read the reviews, and it's always nice to have something to send your mother.

Nearly every reviewer contrasted Geneva's efforts in the television movie with her winning outing in the half-hour comedy. Most made remarks like "in more capable hands," "producers in tune with her talents," "the writing she deserves," blah, blah, blah. Thus Geneva Holloway, in the view of the rather limited world that pays attention to these things, was seen to have been redeemed by Jimmy Hoy and Neil Stein. It's as if Jesse Helms were drowning and had his life saved by a black man.

Geneva, given her gift for selective memory, could have chosen to rise above the bad reviews for the movie and forget the good ones for the half-hour comedy, and continue her reign of terror in our lives. But something happened in the lobby of the Academy that night that was even worse than what took place on the screen and it bound Geneva to us against her will.

At some point in the evening of the screening, Geneva was led away by her publicist to the corner of the lobby that *Entertainment Tonight* had staked out for its interviews. Geneva paid tribute to the film, and then said, "Let's not forget what this evening is really about. Those beautiful little kids at Bramble House." She spoke briefly and well about the courage and nobility of those severely disadvantaged children. As she did, one of them, Thomas Durkee of Woodland Hills, California, ten years old, who suffered from Down's syndrome and cerebral palsy, approached the periphery of the interview. Thomas was one of two children at the party representing Bramble House. They were invited to the reception but had not been asked to sit through the film, perhaps on the theory that they had already suffered enough in their young lives.

Geneva's publicist spotted Thomas and, seeing an opportunity, urged him forward, thinking to create a tender on-camera moment. As Geneva spoke eloquently, a tear in her eye, about "these brave little lambs, these little wonders," she suddenly felt Thomas against her leg. She looked down and was shocked to see a contorted body and overlarge face looking up at her through thick lenses.

Geneva screamed. She jumped back in panic. She yelled, "Get him away from me! Get him away from me!" The little boy started crying and was scooped up and carried away.

Perhaps fifteen people saw what happened, but soon everyone in the room, and eventually everyone in the industry, heard about it. Thus, *All Rise* became Geneva's only safe harbor.

# Chapter
# *13*

Ed Gardner, the creator of *Duffy's Tavern* and a man with an eye for women, spent his honeymoon with Shirley Booth on an ocean liner. One night she caught him coming out of another woman's cabin.

"Now you know the worst," he said. "I'm a jewel thief."

◆ ◆ ◆

In the days following the *It Happened in Philadelphia* debacle, Geneva Holloway managed a sea change that nearly exhausted her vast reserves of shamelessness. Suddenly, there was this merry imp scampering about our stage, abrim with goodwill and helpfulness. There were now welcoming smiles for the hair and makeup people who used to edge around her in dread for their jobs. She escalated her give-and-take with the crew members to new, crowd-pleasing levels of vulgarity. ("What's the difference between sushi and pussy?" she shouted out one morning. Nobody knew. "Rice!") She bought an expensive and scarce Nintendo game for Christian Nemec, our child actor. And her fellow cast members—the men she had held at a cold distance, the women she had taken turns torturing to the point of tears—her fellow cast members she now embraced with warm chat and pleasant inquiry, an equal among equals.

Neil referred to this as Geneva's "quips and pranks and wanton wiles/Nods and becks and wreathed smiles" period. People she had most victimized were soon speaking well of her, even in private. After a note session in which Geneva made a few suggestions that were not only useful but also, no matter from what angle you examined them, entirely selfless, even Neil and I began to wonder if the Good Geneva were here to stay.

"She just had to relax," said Neil. "We're on the air, we're doing well, the scripts are good. Maybe she just had to be sure she could trust us."

"You know what it is, it's like a horse," I said. "A horse has to walk in a circle and trample the grass a little, before it can lie down and rest."

"Horses sleep standing up," said Neil.

"Well, a wolf, then."

Of course, on the principle that there is nothing to be learned from the second kick of a mule, we did not lower our guard entirely. But in the face of such grand gestures as Pecan Sandy Day, we surely relaxed it: Geneva came to work one Monday morning with an enormous basket of homemade pecan sandy balls, for all to share. This was to celebrate our pickup order for nine more shows. She had recently moved into a new house in the Malibu Colony and she inaugurated her oven by making cookies for her coworkers. They were from her Grandmother Holloway's Christmas recipe, she said. They were light and sweet and perfect, with the occasional piece of pecan shell authenticating their homemadeness. We were all touched.

The Sunday following Pecan Sandy Day, I found myself out in the Malibu Colony, sitting on the deck of the oceanfront home of Edward MacKay, the beloved character actor. At the time of my visit, Mr. MacKay was upstairs in the master bedroom, dying. Emphysema. Age seventy-eight. He'd had a good run. Emery Dierdorff, my ex-wife's lover, had organized a brainstorming session to generate ideas for a deathbed public service commercial Edward MacKay had agreed to make.

Fierce Santa Ana winds flowed over Los Angeles that October, as if a large oven door somewhere up in the mountain passes had been left open. The skies were a deep arid blue; temperatures broke decades-old records. As the afternoon sun brought the back of my head up to the temperature of a refractory brick, I sipped iced passion fruit tea and listened to the drone of Emery Dierdorff's voice.

Given the cause of Edward MacKay's pending death, I assumed this public service spot would be a posthumous warning about the dangers of cigarette smoking. Emery was taking a damned long time getting to the point. He sat at the end of a chaise longue and formed his arms into spheres as he spoke. He wore a short-sleeved rabat of clerical gray and a creamy white Roman collar, in contrast to the Hawaiian shirts he favored when he conducted services at St. Luke's in Venice. He rounded off his look with baggy Girbaud jeans and thin leather beach slaps.

I was there at the invitation of Miranda Erikson, who reclined on the chaise behind Emery, and up the billowing pant leg of whose shorts I was now trying to look. The inner thighs of my ex-wife continued to hold inexpressible delights for me. I was as attracted as ever to those neatly formed legs that tapered down to exquisite ankles. Miranda turned her bare foot left, and then right, letting it play over the edge of the chaise, and I was reminded of Emma Bovary, my next favorite adulteress after Miranda, turning a foot in front of the fire. (Miranda and I separated after she told me she was having an affair with another writer. It was someone I knew, someone whose career I'd helped. Someone younger. It struck me as especially unfair that Miranda, whose major complaint against me was my preoccupation with my writing, should take up with another writer. Often, I've had people tell me, "I met your ex-wife," and then add, "She's very pretty." My response is "Yes, she is. I didn't break up with her because I didn't like the way she looked.")

Kiki Burmeister sat beside me. Other luminaries on the deck, listening to Emery Dierdorff's spiel as a large tray of sectioned fruits and cheeses browned in the sun, were: Flora MacKay, Edward's wife, birdlike, all in white with lipstick that was, well, lipstick red. Hobart Beane, who plays oil baron Carson Lloyd on the series *Denver;* he wore white jodhpurs and a linen helmet, and he pantomimed everything, because he had taken a vow never to speak on Sundays. Margot Wexler, the actress, who lived in the neighborhood, and who was in the news for storming off the set of a Kevin Costner movie. Josh Canter, the head of production at Sony-Columbia, with his trademark black bobbed hair. The two Wendy Karetskis, each an ex-wife of computer billionaire Del Karetski; their common names and impressive fortunes had brought them together as fast friends after their respective divorces from Del. Nadine Garamundi, the retired head of daytime programming for CBN, who was now almost blind from glaucoma. And assorted others, mostly television writers like me.

As I looked up Miranda's shorts, I caught the odd phrase from Emery: "Short time frame. . . . Maximum impact. . . . Powerful image. . . . Yul Brynner." Yes, Yul Brynner. That was a very impressive spot he recorded shortly before his death. "It's too late for me . . . but you still have time. Don't smoke." Edward MacKay's crusty, lovable Grandpa Morty character, from the *My In-laws* series, could certainly have an impact, delivering a message like that.

Then something Emery said commanded my full attention: ". . . one of the most important ballot measures in years." This did not track. What was he talking about? "Proposition Twenty-Seven is almost a perfect summary of Edward's lifelong political orientation. The Field poll says we're running twenty-eight percent for, forty-seven percent against, and those are numbers we can work with. Our big problem is the lack of recognition. Can you imagine the impact? Edward saying, 'I died. I can't vote for Proposition Twenty-Seven. You're alive. You can.'"

There was a silence. I would like to say there was a stunned silence, but I think that would only apply to me. Everyone else seemed to be mulling it over. I was relieved when Wendy Karetski Number Two, the younger one, in the Norma Kamali, asked the question I was burning to ask.

"Pardon me, but what is Proposition Twenty-Seven?"

There was polite laughter.

"I'm sorry," said Emery. "I get so close to these things, sometimes I presume everybody is right there with me."

"No, I know I should know," said Wendy Karetski. "But there are so many propositions."

"Exactly. That's our problem. You stated it eloquently. That's why we need the commercial."

"But what's the proposition?" piped up the first Wendy Karetski, coming to the support of her alimony buddy. "Enlighten us."

"Right. The purpose of Proposition Twenty-Seven, simply stated, is to declare October twelfth, in the Santa Monica-Malibu area, Indigenous Peoples Day. It would be an official holiday."

"October twelfth is Columbus Day," said the second Wendy Karetski.

"Right," said Emery. "We're going to change that, perhaps nationally."

I, personally, couldn't fucking believe it. But everyone else seemed to think this was a worthy enough goal for which to exploit a dying man. The brainstorming began in earnest. Emery displayed a heavy fabric globe of the world, like a medicine ball. People who wished to speak had to be holding the globe. It functioned like the conch shell in *Lord of the Flies*. When someone had completed his contribution, he tossed the globe to the next speaker. A young man stationed by an easel wrote down ideas and catch phrases as they were shouted out, racing across the pad of newsprint with a marking pen as thick as a cigar, dodging the globe as it was hurled back and forth.

Flora MacKay watched all this without screaming or throwing furniture or damning us all to hell. She had a bewildered air about her, as if she didn't quite understand what this was all about but had been assured that it was important for her to be there.

Nadine Garamundi called out a suggestion without waiting for the globe. "I was thinking he could say something like, 'Vote for Proposition Twenty-Seven—real Americans should honor the first

Americans, because . . ." And as she spoke, somebody tossed the globe over to her, to make her legitimate. Nadine's poor vision made it quite impossible for her to make out the squishy sphere as it sailed toward her head. It smashed into her warm, open face as she was in mid-sentence, sending her off the white plastic deck chair and onto the floor. People rushed to attend to her, and she was helped up, insisting she was fine, but her nose was bleeding and she had no idea what had happened. I took the opportunity to excuse myself.

"I'm going in the house and get some fresh air," I said to Kiki. I went inside and looked for a bathroom. Miranda came into the house carrying the large, near-empty pitcher of passion fruit tea. I followed her into the kitchen. As she refilled the pitcher from a large crock, she acknowledged me with a familiar lift of the eyebrows.

"Come on," I said.

"What?" said Miranda.

"Indigenous Peoples Day? Miranda, you can't take that seriously."

"You support the person you're with," said Miranda.

"That's something new you've learned," I said. "Come on, this guy is almost lunatic fringe. I think the Emery Dierdorff joke is over."

"Well, you're not exactly here with Diane Sawyer, are you?"

"Kiki is very sweet. She's a good person."

"I talked to her. She's an air fern."

"She's undemanding and nonjudgmental. I feel completely comfortable with her."

"Emery has a strong vision of what he wants. I find that very attractive. And I love his mind, and his commitment to larger causes."

"I really resent hearing you compliment him, because you never used to compliment me."

"I complimented you."

"Never."

"Oh, come on."

"Hardly ever. I attributed it to your Norwegian heritage. I used to say to Neil all the time, 'You know what the leading cause of death in Norway is? People choking to death on compliments.'"

Miranda, to her credit, laughed at this. She picked up her brimming glass pitcher. "I have to get back out there," she said.

I went out the front door of the house, to an enclosed courtyard. A nurse, a black woman in a slippery white uniform, smoked a cigarette and chatted with a young surfer type in tattered cutoffs, who was delivering fresh oxygen tanks and picking up empties. The nurse nodded in my direction and smiled, and tapped her ashes into a jade plant. It suddenly occurred to me that Geneva Holloway, my new best friend in the whole world, lived close by. If I dropped in on her by surprise, surely it would be taken as an inordinately winning gesture.

I didn't know Geneva's new address, but I remembered it was ninety-something. I walked up the black-topped lane that serves as the Colony's main drag, and eventually I came to Geneva's yellow Jaguar sedan. A new Range Rover was parked cozily next to it. It seemed that Milo had traded in his Jeep. I wondered how he managed to be away from his young wife on a Sunday afternoon.

Geneva came to the door in person, carrying the remote control to the television. She screamed in delight, as if she were on *This Is Your Life* and I was an old pal who flew in from my venison farm in New Zealand just to surprise her.

"What are you *doing* here?" she said. I explained that I had ducked out of the little gathering down the road. "Come in, come in," she said, as if there was a big party inside. She led me into the two-story living room, empty and still and filled with the afternoon sun. "Hey!" she called out to the empty room as if she were testing her voice in a cave. "Look who's here."

I heard someone shuffling in from the sun porch. In the archway, where I expected Milo Lally, the menacing bulk of Emil Novak appeared. From his demeanor—he looked like a deer caught in headlights—and from the Sunday sports section hanging down from his primate's grasp, it seemed clear that he hadn't stopped by to administer a neck rub. He wore a Won Sur Ton sweatshirt and was barefoot under his white gymnast's pants. He greeted me with "Hey," and then asked Geneva, "What time's that thing?"

"We don't have to go," said Geneva. "In fact, I don't want to go." And then, to me, "Let me show you around the house." Which she did. "It's basically the same layout I had on the other side of the road, so I didn't go crazy with new furniture."

The kitchen looked eerily crisp, as if it had never been used. "You don't do much cooking, huh?" I asked. "None," she said. She opened the doors to both binlike Gagenau ovens to amaze me with a display of expensive sweaters neatly stacked on the never-used racks. "Terrific storage," she said. "Mothproof."

"You kept your sweaters in the oven years ago, in your house in Trancas."

"Oh, God," she said, reflecting, "that's right. You know all my tricks."

Outside I asked her, "What about Milo?"

"What about Milo? He's my manager," she said, explaining nothing.

On the walk back down to Edward MacKay's place I reflected that Geneva Holloway was not, after all, the industrious little kitchen sprite who had baked all those wonderful cookies. I had to face a sad fact: Pecan Sandy Day had been a fraud.

When I got back to Edward MacKay's deck, the brainstorming session had subsided. The true purpose of the gathering was now revealed: Emery Dierdorff was making an appeal for money. I'm sure he had decided long before what he wanted Edward MacKay to say in the TV spots. He had called all these prosperous people together because he needed the dough to buy the air time.

I leaned against a railing with my arms folded as Emery finished his pitch. He was quite passionate as he described the benefits to Western civilization of a Santa Monica–Malibu Indigenous Peoples Day; you'd think starving children and cures for cancer were somehow involved. Kiki, I noticed, sat at the edge of her chair in rapt attention. Emery concluded. He took a deep breath, exhausted by his own goodness. "And now," he said, "who will be kind enough to make the first pledge?"

Emery eyed his prospects, waiting for the first offer of a thousand dollars, or five thousand, or perhaps from one of the Karetskis, ten thousand. As people shifted a bit in their chairs, waiting for someone among them to break the ice, I saw Kiki check inside her purse. Then, unaware of the sums expected, she waved in her lovely hand, for all the world to see, what for her was a generous donation.

"Five dollars!" she called out with the determined air of someone who was finally doing some good in the world.

# *Chapter*
# *14*

■ If I were to not perform, it would be like Salk withholding the vaccine.

—JERRY LEWIS

◆ ◆ ◆

Geneva's period of contentment and cooperation came to a quick end. As an old comedy writer once told me about his third marriage, "It was the happiest seven hours of my life." Geneva might have stayed happier longer if it weren't for the fact that there are other people in the world.

But there are other people in the world, and one of them was Joseph Landry, the twenty-seven-year-old actor who played Louis Belmont, the ex-convict who served as Geneva and Jack Mullin's housekeeper. It was an attention-getting role, and the right actor, with flair and good luck, could use it to turn himself into a household name. During our casting sessions, Geneva was strangely inattentive to this possibility; her emphasis was all on the role of the husband. But now she saw this lanky blond kid with high cheekbones emerging from what she considered her pack of supporting players, and she did not like it.

The situation crystalized on a Tuesday night after we had been on the air for six episodes. We were about to film the show before a live studio audience. Some of the people were there because they had been wandering through the Farmer's Market and an "audience procurement consultant" had given them free tickets. Some were there because they had been brought up by bus from the Camp Pendleton marine base, to enjoy an interlude away from their studies of the garroting and eviscerating of other human beings. But, for the first time, most people were there because they had already seen *All Rise* on the air and liked it. This was evident from their high spirits, and the knowledgeable questions they asked about the show during the warmup.

I came out and took the microphone from the warmup comic to introduce the cast. The etiquette here is that you bring them out in reverse order of their billing, building up to your star. I introduced little Christian Nemec, and the audience rewarded him for being small and cute. Mary Beth Opdyke, who played Geneva's assistant, received a warm round of applause and a few wolf whistles. Ed J. Wilson, the black district attorney on the show, was welcomed politely. But when I said, ". . . and now, a brilliant young actor from New York, here in his first network series, he plays Louis Belmont on our show, please welcome—" there was an outburst of excited applause at the words "Louis Belmont" and Joseph came out from behind the rolling screen that hid the actors from view. The attendant uproar drowned out the sound of his name. His fans stomped on the floor of the bleachers and young women screamed.

As Joseph milked the applause by doing a few of the comic hand movements he used on the show, I saw Geneva's face freeze, as if a private screening of *All About Eve* was passing before her eyes. I introduced Don Lasker, and he was embraced by the audience for his many appearances on *Matlock, The New Perry Mason, Murder, She Wrote,* and whatever else. As I began Geneva's introduction, her eyes remained locked into position, like an eagle who thinks it sees a herring about three quarters of a mile away. Her face was absolutely still. I wasn't at all sure she would come out. But the sound of her own name brought her around. A gracious smile warmed her face, and she danced out from behind the screen.

Geneva submitted herself to the audience with an expression of wonder. "All this, for me?" Her claque of gay fans, sensing her special need this night, cranked up their exclamations of delight to the point where I thought there might be trouble with the marines. Geneva willed the audience into outdoing their reception of Joseph Landry, at least in warmth and duration, if not in authentic excitement.

The following morning at eleven-thirty we gathered in Rehearsal Hall B in the Robert Mitchum Building to read the script for the next week's episode. A rehearsal hall is usually about the size of a "function" room at an Elk's club, windowless and low-ceilinged and lit by those cool white fluorescent bulbs unflattering to skin tones. It's a perfect place for a small Romanian wedding.

The script supervisor came by and said, "Myra has a dentist's appointment and is running about eighteen minutes late." Myra Foley was our guest star that week. "Where's Geneva?" I asked, and the script supervisor just shrugged her shoulders.

"We better get started," said Jonathan Metzger.

We were all seated at the tables waiting for two important empty chairs to be filled when Myra swept in, just about exactly eighteen minutes late, all smiles and gracious hellos. Neil and I rose to greet her. Myra carried a half-gallon jug of Canadian Tarn bottled water, which interfered with our handshaking. She shared this fear so many people in Los Angeles seem to have about being separated from liquids. As Myra stood there surrounded by well-wishers, Geneva made her entrance. She wore sunglasses and white mechanic's overalls, with her wild blond tresses hidden inside a white turban, the sort you associate with Lana Turner. Geneva, too, carried a half-gallon of water, Arrowhead Mountain Spring. The two stars called out to each other and crossed the floor with arms open. They embraced; we were lucky not to have lost them both, from the crushing blows of the water jugs.

Geneva was very "up," too up. She greeted Joseph Landry with a special hello, and when we read the script, wherever Joseph had a big joke, she led the laughter.

We read through once without stopping for comment, as was our habit, and it went well enough. After that first read-through Geneva offered symbolic applause in the direction of Myra, and then turned it toward Joseph, who was strong in the script that week. Then we read the script a second time, stopping for questions, suggestions, complaints and on-the-spot rewrites. It was during this process that Geneva began asking a series of deadly questions, each beginning with a disingenuous, "Wouldn't it be better if . . . ?" Each question was designed to take a joke away from Joseph Landry. "Wouldn't it be better if Don took that line? It's more in his character." "Wouldn't it be better without Joseph saying anything? You could just go out on my reaction." Wouldn't it be better if Joseph just stood there completely silent through the whole show, like a lox?

I didn't see Geneva's master plan at first, and took her questions at face value. But then, not needing a load of bricks to fall on me, I began making gentlemanly parries. "Let's just see how it works on its feet." "I'll have to think about that." "Why don't we wait until the run-through on Friday and decide then?"

Joseph Landry took all this with equanimity. In fact, he followed the whole process with detached interest, carefully crossing out lines in the script as if it had nothing to do with him. The first person who cracked the air of civility was Gino Buccanetti, the youngest member of the writing staff, the author of the episode under discussion.

Gino had been rewritten heavily, and few of his original lines remained on the pages. That's the process. You often see writers in tuxedos taking bows at the Emmy awards for scripts they don't have a page of writing in. It's the nature of the business. The first script Neil and I sold, a *Barney Miller* had a quote from an Edgar Guest poem in it. When the episode aired, I realized that Edgar Guest had more lines in that script than we did.

Gino was a little bull of a guy, short and round and black-bearded. When we had started down to the rehearsal hall for the reading, Gino, still new to this idea of extensive rewriting, was a very unhappy cowboy. But after the script was read, and Gino had heard all the laughs it got, and a few actors said "Nice work, Gino," suddenly, he was elated. During the second reading of the script, Gino got puffed up with the pride of authorship. He edged his chair closer to the producers, pointing at the script and making suggestions to us in a loud whisper. Every time Geneva put forward one of her damaging changes, Gino looked over to Neil and me with desperate, bulging eyes, a calf straining at its tether. Every time we granted Geneva her wish, Gino winced and clenched his fists. Finally, when Geneva suggested altering a feed line in such a way that it would kill Joseph Landry's joke in the next speech, Gino, in what you might call a modulated bellow, said, "No!"

Everyone turned to look at Gino. This did not stop him. He complained to me in an urgent whisper, "She's killing all the jokes."

There's something to be said for the truth. There were several glances in Geneva's direction, to see how she would react to this assault. I think Geneva misinterpreted the attention; she thought people were ready to gang up on her. She studied the script as if she had not heard Gino, as if she were not aware of the eyes focused on her. Then she looked up and announced the results of her concentration.

"You know, actually that line works the way it is." She smiled. "Why don't we just see how it plays on Friday?"

But damage had been sustained. And by the Friday run-through, Geneva had managed to erode Joseph's presence in the episode even further. Afterward, the network guy complained to me that Joseph was too light in the show. CBN loved Joseph Landry. Joseph Landry tested well. "Everybody likes to see him in conflict with Geneva," he said. "We think he's a break-out character."

I couldn't have agreed more. That night, during the rewrite, Neil and I put in a whole new scene, a fight between Geneva and Joseph. The scripts were delivered to the cast at home on Saturday morning, so they could learn their new lines over the weekend.

I got a call from Milo Lally on Saturday afternoon. It was very important that he talk to me. Official business. I agreed to meet him for a drink on Sunday afternoon in the Santa Monica Mall— or the Third Street Promenade, as they call it now. We met at a place called Fuzzy Coolers or Tropical Chillers or something like that. Behind the bar were ten or twelve tanks like the plastic juice dispensers at soda fountains, each filled with vividly colored syrups. They were trainer drinks for college kids, postadolescent Slurpies.

"A Pink Panties," said Milo to the bartender. "Make that two," I said, and we walked back up to the front and sat outdoors in the ironed-off patio. Milo seemed very nervous, like a low-level Mafioso who has just stolen money from his boss. His handsome face, weak at its best moments, was pitiable now. He tied his plastic straw in knots as he tried to explain his mission.

"Geneva got the new script this morning, and she's not happy," he said. "And frankly, I don't blame her. That new scene between her and Joseph Landry hurts the story."

"It hurts the story?" I said

"Yes, I think it does."

"What, out of the blue, you're an authority on dramatic construction? Suddenly it turns out that, on his deathbed, George S. Kaufman said, 'I leave it all to Milo Lally'? Milo, it helps the story. It strengthens everything by about thirty-five percent. How on earth do you think it hurts the story?"

"Geneva thinks it hurts the story," he said, backing off from his play doctor stance and playing his only card.

We parried back and forth for a few minutes, and finally I said, "Milo, CBN wanted a scene between Geneva and Joseph. We also wanted a scene between Geneva and Joseph. The American people want scenes between Geneva and Joseph. There is only one person in the known world who doesn't want scenes between Geneva and Joseph. She's outvoted."

"You don't know how she's been on me about this," said Milo.

"Take it up with Joe Danko at CBN. It's out of my hands."

Milo gave up. He tied a new plastic straw in knots. He bounced his leg until the plastic table shuddered.

"I have to hang around for a little while," said Milo. "Ashley is picking me up. I'm trusting her with my motorcycle."

"Milo, what's the deal with this Emil Novak?" I asked.

"I don't know," said Milo. "He's not managing her, I'll tell you that. I'm the one she calls at all hours, crying and screaming on the phone. You've seen what I have to do."

"Hardest job in the world," I said.

"You see!" he said, as if citing my testimony to a third party. "I paid my dues. I never lived off her. I never wanted anything I didn't earn. And then this guy comes along and just fucking *moves* in. Moves right into the house after, what, a month? I've been with her four and a half fucking years. I should be living in that house."

"Milo, you're married to Ashley."

"I meant theoretically."

"So," I said, "how is all this going to work out?" I guess my question was, Is this the end of Milo Lally? But that was a possibility Milo had not yet entertained.

"Between her and me, it'll be strictly professional management business from now on," said Milo. "Let Emil Novak run her errands. Let him fuck her for an hour and forty-five minutes every time she feels horny."

# *Chapter*
# *15*

During the rehearsal of a sketch on Jackie Gleason's variety show, a young and not very talented actress playing a nurse was mangling every line. Finally, Gleason exploded. "Who wrote this shit?! There's too many 'ohs.' Every line starts 'Oh' this or 'Oh' that! No wonder she has trouble! I want to see all the writers in my office right away!" And he stormed off the set.

The writers, humbled, assembled in Gleason's office. "Jackie, it's the girl," said one of them. "She isn't any good."

"Yeah, I know that," said Gleason, "but I didn't want to embarrass her."

◆ ◆ ◆

The Christmas season encroached upon Los Angeles. Wreaths of green sprouted on the grills of four-wheelers and paramedic ambulances. The L. Ron Hubbard Winter Wonderland, with flocked trees and artificial snow and a misty, dry ice atmosphere, opened on an empty lot next to the purple Church of Scientology on Hollywood Boulevard. A billboard-sized menorah and a giant Christmas tree went up side by side on Wilshire Boulevard in Beverly Hills. The head of Christ appeared on a lawn chair in East Los Angeles, attracting thousands of visitors. The Catholic diocese took no official position, but an auxiliary bishop fell back on a dependable quote during a television interview: "For those who believe, no explanation is necessary. For those who do not believe, no explanation is possible."

On a perfect Friday afternoon in that Christmas season, cold winds pushed away layers of smog, revealing a cobalt blue sky and clouds as white as riverbank snow. And under that perfect December sky, a handful of professional comedy writers made their way from Stage 6 on the Paramount lot back to their offices in the Clara Bow Building, discouraged and humiliated, each bleeding in his or her own way. Geneva Holloway had just cut them off at the knees.

Geneva had come to see that her campaign against Joseph Landry was a lost cause, but as soon as we relaxed about that, she outflanked us. Suddenly, she argued for increased participation for Joseph, bigger scenes, more lines. She could not have been more supportive of him if she had actually been sincere.

But her suppressed resentment toward Joseph had to come out somewhere; it came out in inventive attacks on the scripts.

"We can't give up the letter," said Neil, referring to a vital part of the current script that Geneva had just decided to undermine.

"The letter stays," I said. "We'll save it."

We were climbing the three or four hundred steps to our second-floor offices. The other writers plodded up behind us, as if they'd just spent a long day schlepping mortar boards of cement. Except for Lisa Silverman, the author of the script in question who, having been so jolted by the encounter with Geneva, hurried back to the office ahead of us, to telephone her psychiatrist.

"Where did she go?" asked Neil, stunned. "Where did the Good Geneva go?"

"I like to think God wanted someone to play with," I said, "and so He took her up to heaven with Him."

"Jimmy, I'm serious," said Neil, "I don't want to go over to that stage anymore. She makes me too uncomfortable. She directs all her remarks to me, like you don't exist."

"She thinks you're the good guy."

"I *am* the good guy."

"Right. And look where it's gotten you."

We gathered in our office with its chipped paint and sagging acoustical tiles and stared at one another, helpless. Geneva had just dealt a death blow to an excellent script.

Here's the episode: it's time for Judge Geneva Mullin to reach a verdict in the case of an elderly man who is being accused of stealing jewelry from a widow he's moved in with. The widow may well have been motivated to bring a false charge because the man has been paying attention to a neighbor lady, "a hussy with two wigs." For some reason, Geneva keeps putting off her decision. We come to find out that the old man reminds Geneva of her father; he was thirty-eight when he left Geneva and her mother for another woman. That was Geneva's last contact with her father, except for a letter he sent her shortly before he died. Geneva never read the letter. She keeps it locked up in a safety deposit box because she's afraid of what it might say. On one level, she had judged her father years ago and found him guilty. On another, she always harbored the secret hope that someday he would appear and explain everything and redeem himself. This letter was Geneva's last chance to find a father who was a decent man, a father who was worthy of her. To fulfill her expectations, it had to be almost a perfect letter. And Geneva knew that the chances of that were slim. She preferred to keep the letter sealed and live on in expectation.

Don Lasker, in his role as Jack Mullin, and Joseph Landry as Louis Belmont, get to the bottom of all this, and confront Geneva about it, and take her to the bank to read the letter. And she does. And, in an unexpected way, it is a perfect letter. Her father throws himself on the mercy of the court. He admits that there is no excuse for his behavior. He reminds her how she'd sent back all his early letters to her unopened—she'd forgotten about that. He speaks of the wall of animosity put up by her mother, which he could not penetrate, and he talks about pressures from his new wife. And he tells how he followed Geneva's progress in the world surreptitiously. He even attended her high school and college graduations. Copies of the graduation programs are included with the letter. He apologizes profusely for his failures as a father and as a man. And he tells her he loves her.

Then Geneva looks at the photograph of himself he's enclosed, and she says, "Not guilty."

As popular entertainments go, not a bad story. At the Wednesday reading, Geneva, upon first exposure to the script, read the letter in a moving and effective way. When she said, "Not guilty," I have to tell you, there wasn't, as an old vaudevillian used to say, a dry seat in the house. Even the macho prop guy, with tattoos on both forearms, started tamping down the tobacco in his pipe with great concentration so it could not be seen that he was on the verge of tears.

But now, at this Friday run-through, Geneva had fumbled through the crucial scene where she reads the letter. In the note session afterward she said, "Look, guys, I'm really sorry, but the letter isn't working." Given the way she'd just performed it, I had to agree. "I don't know who this man is. He's not a character. All of a sudden, I'm supposed to invest all this energy in a letter from someone I don't even know."

"But he's your father," I said, with a pathetic pleading in my voice.

"I mean I don't know him as an actress. Maybe she knows him, Geneva the character, but I don't know him. Who is he? I'll tell you the truth, I can't play it."

This was the lethal phrase Geneva had recently introduced to our transactions: "I can't play it." This was her variation on the old trick of pretending to defend your character's integrity when, in fact, you just didn't like the line. (A Hollywood actress of some celebrity, brought to New York to do *Macbeth* for the Shakespeare in the Park series, was heard to say, "Lady Macbeth wouldn't say that.")

We had a long discussion that went around in circles and was brought to an end only by our exhaustion in the face of Geneva's energy. Finally, we promised to rethink the letter scene, just so Geneva would go home.

"I'm not giving up the letter," Neil said again, once we were settled in the office.

"We can't give up the letter," I said.

"The letter is crucial," said Don Monahan. His partner, Don Blatz, was noncommittal.

I walked to the doorway and yelled, "Lisa!" down the hall, startling Sharone, our secretary, who was putting on her coat. She would do that on nights we worked late, put on her coat and stand in our doorway with her car keys in her hand, without actually daring to ask, "Can I go?" And then Neil and I would ignore her for a while, because of our secret belief that if we had to suffer, everybody should suffer. But usually we let her go, because we knew she went to this support group for former prostitutes, and we didn't want to get in the way of that.

"Lisa!" I yelled again, and I looked in Sharone's direction so somebody might see the full measure of my impatience. I noticed that Sharone had put up another cat poster, a very large one of a cat doing a pull-up on a crossbar. "This cat thing is getting out of hand," I said. Then I thought I heard a grunt of acknowledgment come from behind Lisa's door, so I went back into the office.

"I'm not giving it up," Neil was saying.

"It's perfect," I said.

"We shouldn't even *change* it," said Monahan. "Fuck 'em. You're never going to see any profits from this show anyhow. Do it the way you want."

"Right," said Gino, who had fallen back into his normal pattern of deference since his brave moment in the rehearsal hall a few episodes earlier.

"Sharone!" I yelled, and she popped into the doorway like Zorro appearing in a balcony window. "Go tell Lisa to get the fuck in here!" Sharone vaulted away in pure joy, knowing that after she performed this task I would tell her to go home.

"Look guys," said Don Blatz, "let's add a little reality to this mix. She said she's not doing the letter."

"Fuck she's not," said Neil.

"It's a beautiful letter," said Monahan. "Sharone," he said, looking up to Sharone who was already back in the doorway, "what do you think of that letter?"

"I cry every time I hear it," said Sharone, which set off a round of "There!" and "See?" among us.

"She'll be right here," Sharone articulated in my direction, and then added, waiflike, "You don't need me any more, do you?" I waved her away as if I were blessing her, and she mouthed the words "Good night."

Lisa came into the office, barged in, really, like this important executive late for a meeting with her underlings. "Where are we?" she said, as if she wanted an answer and wanted it now.

"What did your shrink say?" asked Neil.

"She said Geneva Holloway sounds like she has a narcissistic personality disorder. That gave me a great deal of comfort. Seriously, where are we?"

"The letter," explained Gino.

"The Dons are divided," I said.

"I'm just saying, she said she won't do the letter, and that's the actual reality," said Don Blatz.

"I'm not giving up the letter," said Neil.

And it went on like this, as it always does when a script endures a body blow. There is a necessary period of denial. It took about an hour of that sort of back and forth until we adjusted to the current reality. We had to do something about the letter, but we didn't know what.

"I'm not giving up the letter," Neil reiterated.

"Neil," I said, because I was the only one in the room with the authority to say it, "what if we just *experiment* with another version of the letter?"

"Like what?" Neil snapped.

"I don't know. We're experimenting."

"Maybe her father avoids the whole subject," said Don Blatz. "He gives her stock tips, advice about buying cars."

"Maybe the letter isn't even from her father," said Don Monahan, whose only words over the previous hour had been, "It's perfect."

We started pitching in that direction for a while. Neil was silent. Not sulking, but lost in thought. Rick Barnes, the runner, came in and distributed take-out menus from neighborhood restaurants. He wore his Oberlin sweatshirt. He had just graduated with a major in comparative literature, and was breaking into show business by getting us food and driving all over town delivering scripts to the cast members' homes. He was a very good-looking kid, with high West Indian cheekbones. We all decided to make his life easier and go Chinese.

After we ordered, we stared at each other, at an impasse. I started going through my mail. Lisa Silverman bounced her leg up and down in an agitated way, causing the candy dish on the coffee table to rock. Gino Buccanetti looked around the room, startled. He was new to Los Angeles and worried about earthquakes.

"On nights like this, I wish I was back on cocaine," said Lisa. "Remember cocaine? It seemed like such a friendly thing at first. You'd have a few toots, drink a glass of champagne, and then go out to the airport and greet people you didn't know."

"Look at this bullshit," I said, holding up a Christmas card I'd just opened. "It's from my agent. 'This year, in your name, we are donating a sum of money to the Los Padres Dog and Cat Ranch.' Who started this idea? 'This year, in your name, instead of buying you a nice gift, we're taking *your* money and giving it to our charity. That way, we get a tax deduction, we don't have to give any of our own money to charity, and you get stuck on the mailing list.' This incenses me."

"Yeah," said Don Monahan. "What happened to agents just giving you a nice golf umbrella, or a set of highball glasses?"

"My brother-in-law was the first one to pull this," I said. "We gathered for Christmas, and he announces, 'This year, instead of presents, we're giving money to the rain forest.' How touching. In the meantime, I'm stuck with a sixty-dollar Barbie water slide for his kid. I'm thinking, give your own fucking money to the rain forest."

"You think Geneva Holloway had a normal childhood?" said Lisa. "You think she played with a Barbie doll?"

"Yeah," I said, "a Klaus Barbie doll."

"Wait!" shouted Neil. He sat bolt upright, like a shaman awakening from a dream.

We all turned to him.

"Geneva *doesn't* read the letter. Her father reads the letter."

"He's not dead?" asked Don Blatz.

"A voiceover," explained Neil.

"Of course," I said. "We'll get somebody real good, like a Jimmy Stewart."

"You know who we could get?" said Neil. "Charlie Burton."

It was a wonderful idea. Charlie Burton had been playing crusty but vulnerable types since the thirties, when he debuted as the tax collector with the heart of gold in Frank Capra's *Give Us This Day*. Contemporary viewers of television had seen him as either the father or the grandfather of most female series stars, from Doris Day to Sharon Gless. And he loved to work.

We called our Polonia casting woman at home, who called Charlie's agent at ICM, who called Charlie at The Grill, where he was having dinner. Within an hour, we had a deal. All that was left, then, was to do the usual amount of rewriting we do on every script.

Then, instead of having Rick Barnes delivering revised scripts to the cast and giving our game away to Geneva, we got word around that the script would not be ready until Monday morning. We scheduled a rereading at 10:00 A.M., as we often did after a script was heavily revised. To solidify our case, we asked Charlie Burton to come in a little early, before he recorded his voiceover, so he could do the letter live at the table.

The changes we had made were well received. When we got

to the letter, and Charlie Burton started reading, and Geneva saw
that there were no changes in the text, she shot a look in our
direction, as if we were getting away with something. Which, in
fact, we were. We had, after all, left the letter unchanged and at
the same time taken a big scene away from our star. Small-minded
people might say that we had punished her. But Charlie Burton's
rendering of the letter was so well received, with teary-eyed
secretaries tucking their script binders under their arms so they
could applaud him, that Geneva was left with nowhere to turn.
And so she herself took an active part in the applause, and she
even blew a kiss of thanks over in the direction of the producers.
But, as we should have known, you don't get the better of Geneva
Holloway without paying a terrible price.

The next day, Tuesday, our shooting day, there was a bit of a
dust up on the set. Geneva complained that the snapshot of her
father, at which she was expected to look lovingly before she said
"Not guilty" at the end of the show, was not, in fact, a photograph
of Charlie Burton. A resourceful prop man, and all prop men are
resourceful, made a few phone calls and soothed Geneva with the
information that a photograph of Charlie Burton—indeed, an age-
appropriate photograph of Charlie Burton in his sixties—would
arrive in time for the dress rehearsal.

At the dress rehearsal, two hours before the audience would
arrive, Geneva was shown the new photograph and approved of
it with an emphatic "Perfect." The run-through proceeded apace
and went as well as these camera run-throughs go until, at the
very end of the show, after listening to the prerecorded voice of
Charlie Burton move us all once more with his rendering of the
by now, I admit, slightly tedious letter, Geneva looked lovingly at
the little snapshot of her father, and then abruptly broke character.

"This isn't going to work," she said, shaking her head in regret.
Neil and I rushed to her like trainers whose fighter has just walked
to the corner in the middle of a round.

"What is it?" asked Neil.

"This photograph won't work," said Geneva.

I looked at it.

"It's perfect, Geneva," I said.

She focused an amazing amount of contempt into one short glance at me.

"It won't *work*. This is a photograph of Charlie Burton as Charlie Burton. I need a photograph of Charlie Burton as my father."

"This is the most egregious fucking bullshit I've ever heard," I said. It just came out. Geneva bristled.

"Actually, we don't even need the photo at all," said Neil, but Geneva was completely focused on me.

"I am an actress," she said. "I am not a machine."

"Neil," I said, "I can't believe this. We didn't fucking think to have a photograph of Charlie Burton taken for this role fifteen fucking years ago. An unforgivable oversight." What I found interesting was that I wasn't yelling this. I spoke in cold blood.

"I can't play it without the proper photograph," said Geneva.

"What are you saying?" I said. "That you won't do the show? That you're walking out on the show? That you're abrogating your contract?"

"Hey . . ." said Neil to me. And then, to Geneva, "You don't need a photo to look at. You just put the letter down and you look off and say, 'Not guilty.' Off the letter. No photo."

"I'll have to think about that," said Geneva, looking for a way out. But some mad imp inside me would not let it rest. More had to come out.

"You might not want to do that," I said. "It would involve acting."

"You have no concept of the art of acting," said Geneva.

"The *art* of acting? The fucking *art* of acting?" She'd caught me on a pet subject. "Children do what you do. Tatum O'Neil was, what, six years old, she wins an Academy Award for best actress. The highest honor in your profession went to a fucking six-year-old. No six-year-old ever wrote a half-hour comedy, I'll tell you that—despite what the critics think. The *art* of acting."

"Fuck you," riposted Geneva.

"Fuck *you*," I said. "You killed Jerry Cardini!"

She gave this a second's thought, "Who?" she said, genuinely puzzled.

"Jerry Cardini. The hairdresser!"

"Fuck you," she said.

"Fuck you! And you're not here to act. The last thing you want to do is act. You're here to make everyone who comes near you miserable. You're full of self-hate, but you don't have the integrity to drown it out with drugs or alcohol, as any decent, self-respecting person would do. No, you take it out on everyone else—"

"Fuck you," said Geneva.

"—you stay high by bringing pain into everybody else's life—"

"Fuck you!" She stomped away.

"You're a turmoil junkie!" I called after her.

Within ten minutes, Geneva was spotted driving out the Melrose Avenue gate in full makeup, hair, and wardrobe. People standing in line for the show saw her driving down Gower Street, and they waved and applauded as she drove by. That was the last anybody saw of her that night.

Polonia Productions ate the show, at an unexaggerated cost of $600,000. No one was able to reach Geneva by phone. When we gathered the next morning for the reading of the new script, she didn't show. The cast was dismissed and told to wait for further instructions. There were phone calls back and forth all day between our offices, Polonia's offices, and the offices of Triumphant Artists, Geneva's agents. Finally, Polonia's head of production decided to shut down the show for a week. Geneva surfaced about an hour after that decision was made, by means of a conference call to Avery Schine and David Putzman. Apparently, she had saved up all the acting energies she had not expended the night before and used them to plead her case to those boys. In my opinion, a person who walks off a show should be held responsible in some way. But in this case, that was not the opinion that prevailed. Avery Schine and David Putzman tripped over themselves in a frantic race to be the first to kiss Geneva's ass. It was a tie.

A meeting was called for three o'clock Friday afternoon, at

Geneva's request. It was perfect Geneva Holloway timing: We would be meeting at the Polonia offices during the middle of the Polonia Christmas party. Or, Holidays Party, as it was called.

The Thalberg Building, the keystone of the old MGM, where the current emperor always sits, was being renovated and refreshed for the third time in as many years as I drove onto the lot that day. But the Franklin Pangborn Building, where Polonia had its offices, was the same as ever. MGM had sold the lot to Lorimar-Telepictures. Then Warner Brothers bought out Lorimar-Telepictures. Then Coca-Cola sold Columbia Pictures to Sony, and Time, Inc., merged with Warner Brothers. Then Time-Warner traded lots with Sony-Columbia, so all the Lorimar-Telepictures people moved to Burbank and all the Sony-Columbia people moved to Culver City. In the meantime, MGM, which had moved across the street from its old lot, merged with Pathé. But through it all, Polonia kept paying rent and saluting whatever flag was flying over the Thalberg Building.

In the lobby of the Pangborn Building, above the rows of Christmas trees, loomed photographs the size of bay windows of Clark Gable sweeping Vivien Leigh up the stairs, Spencer Tracy fuming at Katharine Hepburn, Judy Garland walking arm in arm with Jack Haley and Ray Bolger, and scenes from many other historic and beloved movies with which Polonia was in no way connected. In the corridors off the lobby hung posters that more accurately reflected Polonia's own contributions to world cinema: *Blood and Mud,* a William Friedkin comedy; *Second Chances,* a romance with Gabe Kaplan and Suzanne Pleshette; *To Die in Blood,* the second picture in William Friedkin's three-picture deal with Polonia; *Coal Mine Moma,* with Dolly Parton and Judd Hirsch (in which he goes topless, but she doesn't); a version of *The Seagull* set in contemporary Carmel, California, produced by Tiffany Schine and Avery Schine, Jr.; and William Friedkin's space adventure, *Blood on the Moon.* These, and several others, stood as a salute to Avery Schine's passion for moviemaking. They represented a cumulative net hit of $230 million to Polonia's bottom line.

I made my way through the Christmas party to the elevators. There was a circus theme to the event, for some reason: Jugglers, white-faced mimes, and an organ grinder with a monkey worked the crowd. The servers behind the catering tables were dressed like clowns. A popcorn vendor in a barker's outfit unwrapped bricks of hydrogenated palm oil. A roving klezmer band played "God Rest Ye Merry Gentlemen." A few people saluted me with plastic glasses of white wine. Our production accountant intercepted me at the elevators with a boozy, sexy look; she wanted me to have my picture taken with her on Santa's lap.

The second floor, the executive lair, was deserted. A thief could dash through the offices and make off with all sorts of loot: purses, computers, ideas for bad movies. Avery Schine's secretary stood at the end of the corridor as if she was waiting for me. Which, in fact, she was. I was on time, but everyone else had arrived early. I was shown into a conference room with a small, open kitchen tucked behind a counter. Neil was already there and, to his credit, saying funny things. Putzman grinned out of all proportion to his understanding of humor. Geneva was there and, to my shock and dismay, Emil Novak was sitting by her side. Avery Schine stood at the head of the table while everyone else sat. The air of jocularity Neil had instilled was dispelled by my entrance, as if everyone were waiting for the bad guy. I took a seat and distributed contained nods all around.

Avery Schine moved behind Geneva's chair and put his hands on the back of it. He spoke directly to me.

"We're extremely lucky to have a Geneva Holloway. She's a very great star," he said, once again keeping rein on his fabled brilliance. "She hasn't been treated well. We're here to correct this. Because we're here to make her happy. *I'm* here to make her happy. So she can continue to do the great job that she does, which all the critics agree on."

Neil followed Avery's words with intent curiosity, as if a docent were explaining the glories of a museum we were about to enter. Geneva worked up a little suppressed hurt, a schoolgirl vindicated by the teacher. I stared impassively, like the recalcitrant lout that I was.

"We've had some discussions with Geneva and we've reached some decisions about it that David will tell you about, because I have to call New York. But the purpose of this meeting is not blame and recrimination. It's to make Geneva happy."

Avery patted Geneva's shoulder and she put her hand over his. Then Avery gave me a look that I think most objective observers would agree was life-threatening, and left the room. This brought David Putzman to life.

"Geneva agrees, we should all start with a clean slate. And what we've come up with is a plan that I think should work out well for everybody. What we're going to do, to assure Geneva's creative interests are being protected, which they are not, is we're going to bring aboard Emil Novak here as an executive producer."

Emil nodded like a panelist being introduced on *Washington Week in Review.*

"Excuse me," I said, "you're making Emil an executive producer on our show?"

"To make Geneva feel protected. So there's a balance."

"Emil, in all due respect," I said, "you're a body trainer."

"He's my manager," said Geneva. She would not have this man's impeccable credentials questioned.

"Since when?" I said.

"I replaced Milo."

"Then he's been your manager for twenty minutes. Emil, really, do you think you're ready to be an executive producer?"

"I took some acting classes in New York," said Emil. "Most of my clients out here have been actors, or in the industry. I've picked up quite a bit."

"Well, great," I said. "I guess that's the way it goes." I stood up. And then I said—I can't believe I'm such a prick—with a perfectly straight face, "I can only wish you good luck. We have—what is it, Neil?—three pretty good first drafts, and maybe three promising story ideas. You're in fair shape. It'll be kind of a crunch to make it to the end of the season, but it always is."

"Where are you going?" said Putzman.

"Look, no hard feelings. We have artistic differences. It happens. Neil and I will bow out gracefully. Geneva's got the creative protection she needs."

"But I don't write," said Emil, with about as dumb a look as a face could have and still be a mammal's.

"It's a good staff. I'm sure they'll help you as much as they can. Let's go, Neil. These people have a lot of work ahead of them."

I started for the door. Putzman called after me, "Come on... come on..." as if I were playing a good-natured joke.

"Jim..." Neil said, and then, as I went out the door, "I'll go talk to him." And Putzman said, "I'm going to talk to him, too. Excuse us for a sec..."

I waited in the outer office and soon Neil and David Putzman came through the door. Putzman made me nervous. He looked almost gleeful, as if he welcomed my misbehavior.

"What exactly do you think you're doing?" said Putzman.

"You have to learn, Avery Schine has to learn, there's more than one ass to be kissed in a situation like this," I said.

"I don't think so. I checked your contract. There's nothing in it about kissing your ass."

"Fine. Have a great show."

"No, you don't get it. You have a contract to produce this show for two seasons."

"Yeah. Well, artistic differences. We're walking."

"No. You have a contract. We're not letting you walk."

"David, what are you going to do? Are you going to stand over us with a gun and make us write?"

"I checked all this out with legal," said Putzman. He was ready to spring his surprise. "If you walk, we suspend and extend your contract. We cut off your pay, and we keep you from working anywhere else. It's all legal. I checked it out with legal."

"Fine. We'll arbitrate."

"I hope you do," said Putzman. "We'll make sure it takes

months. We'll throw all kinds of money into it. It'll cost you a hundred thousand, easy." He was enjoying this thoroughly, getting back at us for all the little jokes and digs he'd endured at our expense. "And I'll tell you something else. You walk, and we'll contest your profit participation."

"You can't," I said. "Our profit deal is based solely on creating the show."

"We'll contest it. And anyhow, maybe there won't be any profits. Amazing things can happen with numbers."

"Jim," said Neil, "I think we should look at this in perspective."

"I have, Neil," I said, "I honest-to-Christ have. And I'm walking. David, I leave you with George Bernard Shaw's remark upon parting from Joseph Conrad: 'Fuck you in the ass.'"

I took the elevator down to the first floor and mingled at the Christmas party. I guess the theory behind this midafternoon fete was that you save money by not having to include spouses. Of course, you also set up a situation where some guy from office services, unaccustomed to strong drink, tosses back a few margaritas and then, insensate, gets behind the wheel of his car while there are still school buses on the road.

Neil came out of nowhere and pulled me away from the quiche squares. "Jimmy, I can't do this," he said.

"Come on. Show some *cajones*."

"They have a contract."

"Let them sue."

"I can't afford it. I can't afford to walk."

The klezmer band returned from its break and broke out into a rendition of "Oh, Holy Night." Neil ushered me into a men's room.

"They don't have a show without us," I said. "They should be kissing *our* ass."

"We already walked once this year," said Neil.

"And it turned out great," I said.

"This is different. Putzman wants to nail us to the wall," said Neil. "I can't afford it psychically, I can't afford it financially."

"Neil, I can't stand her. I can't stand the idea of working with her. I look at her, I want to push her face in."

A mime entered the men's room, merry and gesticulating, and we stopped talking. The mime began performing. If you want to approximate what an eternity on the burning rocks of hell would be like, try spending a few minutes trapped inside a men's room with a mime. I understand that mime bashing is a little passé, but this, truly, was a special agony. First he pretended to wash his hands at an imaginary sink. Neil and I offered token, impatient smiles. Then he pretended to comb his hair before an imaginary mirror. Neil threw him an abated chuckle. When he pushed the button on an imaginary hand dryer and pretended his body had to fight against the gale it produced, I exploded.

"Get the fuck out of here!" I yelled, startling him out of character. "Out! Get out!"

He scrambled from the room like a normal human being.

"I'll talk to Geneva," said Neil.

"About what?" I asked.

"No, I mean, I'll do all the talking to her. I'll deal with her. I'll handle all the readings and the run-throughs. You don't ever have to speak to her."

I thought about this. "I guess I could watch the run-throughs from the director's booth."

"There you go," said Neil.

"You're saying I don't have to talk to Geneva at all?"

"Not if you don't want to. No."

"But you can't stand her, either. And you *hate* working with actors."

"Please, Jim. Just agree to this. Because I cannot afford to walk."

"No greater love than this has any man," I said.

"There you go," said Neil.

And so, a few days before Christmas in 1988, I sacrificed my partner on the altar of Geneva Holloway.

# Chapter
# 16

■ After a disappointing run-through of the *Maude* show, Bob Weiskopf, one of the writer-producers, complained to the director about the performance of the cast.

"The actors were tired," the director explained.

"They're actors," said Weiskopf. "Tell them to act not tired."

◆ ◆ ◆

Geneva's conduct during the remaining seven episodes was, as Gibbon said of Corsica, easier to deplore than to describe. You might think, given Neil Stein's winning nature and gift for compromise, that things would have gone better over on the stage. But Geneva Holloway was unquenchable. Whenever she was given what she wanted, she simply escalated her demands, starting the game all over at a higher level. Neil was no match for her. She required tough old guys named Mort or Sol with skin as thick as belting leather, who had faced down the likes of Eddie Cantor and Red Skelton and Redd Foxx.

I had the lesser burden of Emil Novak. Emil was given an office, a secretary, a parking space, a salary, and the galling title of coexecutive producer. He was not, however, given any increase in native intelligence. He didn't have a clue as to what sort of things a coexecutive producer might be expected to do, and I was careful not to offer any hints. Emil was very secretive about his personal affairs; he kept firing secretaries because he thought they were spying on him. As a result, the bulk of his official duties consisted of interviewing new secretaries.

Neil's trips to the stage took their toll. He started gaining weight, and he took to having his own little in-house cocktail hour every afternoon around five. This sometimes rendered him worse than useless during late-night rewrite session, where he slowed us down with convoluted digressions or pitched long, complicated jokes that didn't pay off.

Out of concern for his safety on Sunset Boulevard, I arranged to have a Teamster drive him from his home and back in a Polonia station wagon. Unfortunately, this Teamster had access to generous quantities of Tylenol with codeine, the very drug that had caused Neil to spend several weeks in a rehabilitation center seven years earlier.


In the midst of the long march to the end of the season, I experienced an interlude of domestic bliss. The occasion was Bennett's ninth birthday. Miranda had arranged a party at an ice rink. For some reason, probably because he was advancing properly in wisdom and grace, Bennett wanted me there instead of the Reverend Emery Dierdorff.

I was never much on the ice, and after twenty minutes or so my insteps felt as if they were balanced over broom handles. My reward was the sight of the long-legged Miranda Erikson in her skating skirt. As the little boys wobbled to hold their balance or thundered into each other and went sprawling, Miranda circled us, lost in her own rhythms, wearing a look of concentration that I always found very attractive. When she changed directions her skirt flew up from the breeze she created and gave me teasing glimpses of her inner thighs, those sweet loaves of flesh I knew so well.

Back at the house in Rustic Canyon, after the last child had screamed good-bye to Bennett from the open window of an expensive foreign car, Miranda invited me in for a drink. Bennett was ordered upstairs to call his grandmother in Santa Rosa and thank her for her birthday present, a certificate for drum lessons. Miranda drank vanilla tea and I had a glass of Chardonnay from a previously opened bottle that had been sitting in the back of her mammoth Sub-Zero a little too long. The late afternoon sun gave the yellows of the "Monet room" their own luminosity.

Miranda asked me about Kiki, but in a straightforward fashion without any subdued meanness. She wanted to know my intentions.

"I'm not sure," I said. "She's really wonderful. It's very comfortable."

"Does she want to get married?"

"She never says. That's what makes it so comfortable."

"Do you want to get married?"

"I don't know. Sometimes I think I do. The problem is, she's not what I thought I wanted."

"Was I what you wanted?" asked Miranda.

"For a long time, I certainly thought you were. But I guess we all keep a secret ideal in our minds that no one in real life measures up to."

"Men do," said Miranda.

"Just men?"

"Yes. When women are unhappy, it's usually because they want something very concrete that they don't have. A house, a relationship, a job. When men are unhappy, it's because they don't know what they want. They have vague, undefined longings. That was true with you."

"Is it true with Emery?"

"To some extent. But he's lucky. He pretty much knows what he wants."

"To help save the world and then take all the credit for it."

"We're not talking like that now," said Miranda. She was in a transcendent mood. "Emery's lucky because what he loves to do he can generally do with decent, fair-minded, even charitable people. What you love to do, you have to do with monsters."

"I love what I do."

"You love to write funny things, that part you like. But look what's happening to Neil . . ." I had told her about Neil's decline. "What other business does that exist in?"

"Slavery."

"That's about right. Admit it, you're in a horrible business."

"It's not much fun right now."

"It's horrible. And that's what's so sad. To do what you love to do, you have to tolerate impossible people and impossible conditions. I don't know how you do it. I couldn't. I don't think I ever appreciated enough what you went through, when we were together."

It was curious, all the gratification those few sentences gave me. Our love had long since died; and yet, more than anything else, I still wanted approval from Miranda Erikson. She had the whammy on me.


The 1988–89 television season, like the Bataan death march, eventually came to an end. Neil and I sponsored an informal wrap party on the stage after the last show: deli trays and wine in plastic cups. Geneva organized something a little more elaborate for the cast and writers, a late supper at Patina, down the street on Melrose where St. Germaine used to be. Neil and I were invited and graciously declined, citing the press of editing duties, in which there was a hint of truth. Instead, we took some wine back up to the office and just sat and chatted, tired and content, reluctant to leave.

"Can you imagine being at an intimate little dinner with Geneva Holloway right now?" I asked Neil. "Why would she even ask us? What was she thinking?"

"It's like the story Jay Burton tells about Jack Carter," said Neil, more sober at this hour than I had seen him for several weeks.

"Don't know it."

"Jay Burton is working with Jack Carter on something, writing something for him, and they're together all day. So it's time to leave, and they're outside the offices, and Jack Carter says, 'Hey, let's have dinner.' And Jay says, no, that's all right, I'm going home. And Jack Carter says, 'Come on. I'll take us to Trader Vic's.' And Jay says, no, he really doesn't feel like it. And Jack Carter says, 'Why not? We're having a lot of fun, aren't we?' And Jay says, 'It may be fun to *be* Jack Carter, but it's not fun to be *with* Jack Carter.'"

I laughed and said, "Exactly," and then decided to capitalize on Neil's reflective mood.

"May I speak frankly?" I said. Neil gave me a nod of assent. "I think you're a candidate for self-referral to one of those little rehab hospitals. There's that one out in Marina del Rey that Lisa Silverman went to. I think she said it was pretty nice."

Neil shook his head.

"Too many actors. It's an actor who drove me to this in the first place."

"What about that one you went to last time, in the Valley?"

"No. I'm sorry. I don't think so. I was with people who were excited to be there because they were getting three meals a day."

"But it worked for you."

"It didn't, Jim. It really didn't. I left two weeks before I was supposed to. I mean, it worked in the sense that I got detoxed, but the *program* didn't work. I basically stopped on my own."

"Well, you have to do something. You're a fucking wreck."

"James, believe me, once the plane lands in Maui, I will have no more need for chemical depressants. By the end of the week, I won't even need Riopan." Neil and Renata were leaving for Maui in two days. I had volunteered to get our final shows network-ready on my own. "I'm not even taking any Xanax with me, except enough for the airplane ride. I can't handle an airplane without Xanax."

Neil hated airplanes. He considered any successful trip by air nothing more than a failed suicide attempt. But he loved Hawaii for its proven restorative powers, and bravely enplaned to expose himself to them. Now, more than ever, he needed the long hours of snorkeling in beautiful Napili Cove, until the backs of his legs were sunburned.

Neil made it to Hawaii on two and a half Xanax and three Bloody Marys and a glass and a half of Trefethen Sauvignon Blanc. I know this because he called me from the airplane to tell me just before they landed in Honolulu. He and Renata then made their connection to Maui and checked in at the Kapalua Bay Hotel in the dark of night. They did some token unpacking and went to sleep.

The next morning, Renata said, "How about a nice, big breakfast, to dispel the memory of airplane food?" But Neil didn't want breakfast. "Honey, you eat," he said. "I just want to get out there and lie on the beach and feel the sun on my body." After particularly upsetting encounters with Geneva during the previous weeks, Neil had tried to calm himself by evoking the sensation of the Hawaiian sun caressing his body. It became his meditation, his prayer. And now the holy moment had at last arrived. Neil slipped on the green-and-white Ralph Lauren swimming trunks Renata had bought for him at Nordstrom's, and the pale blue terrycloth beach jacket Renata had bought for him at Carroll and Company, and the cord-and-rubber beach slaps Renata had bought for him at Aussie Sport. He put on the sunglasses with matte black Italian frames that Renata had picked out for him at L.A. Eyeworks, and rolled up a bamboo beach mat supplied by the hotel and slapped it under his arm like a newspaper. He kissed his wife good-bye solemnly, as if he were being called onto the spaceship at the end of *Close Encounters of the Third Kind,* and emerged from his $750-a-day bungalow out onto the friendly white sands. He unrolled his mat at the ocean's edge, that he might feel the salt water lap against his feet. He slipped off his terrycloth jacket, which was cut like a sport coat for casual lunches in the hotel café, and stretched his olive of a body on the comforting strips of bamboo. He closed his eyes and felt the smiling light of the sun sweep over him. He inhaled it and warmed his very bones with it. For the first time in months, Neil Stein relaxed.

As the young lady who went to bed with the rodeo rider said, "It was the best seventeen seconds of my life." No sooner had Neil's jaw relaxed, no sooner had his breathing established long, comfortable rhythms, than he was jolted by a clammy smoothness against the sole of his right foot. He bolted to an upright position, expecting to encounter a jellyfish or squid or some other unpleasantness. He was certainly not expecting to see the back of a human hand nudging against his instep. The hand was attached to the decomposing body of a Japanese male just about Neil's age and size. The lapping water pushed his hand into Neil's sole as if it were knocking for reentry into the world of the living.

Neil, by his own account, stood up and pointed at the body and screamed, "Ahhh! Ahhh! Ahhh!" just like someone in a bad horror movie. Others on the beach rushed to the water's edge to investigate. Neil picked up his beach mat and terrycloth jacket and stumbled back to his bungalow, numbed with upset. He startled Renata, who was slipping into her bathing suit.

"What—?" she said, but Neil cut her off with a pushing-away motion of his hand. He did not look at her, but stared straight ahead at the bathroom as he plodded forward and disappeared into it. Then Renata heard him as he rifled through his unpacked Italian leather toiletries bag searching for Xanax.

The restful vacation was ruined. Neil refused to return to the sand and water. He played video games in the hotel game room and drank blue drinks at the cabana bar. At first, Renata was understanding. She generally enjoyed a good crisis; it gave her a chance to display her strength. But when Neil scored some marijuana—not a particularly difficult thing to do on Maui—and then found a source for Tylenol with codeine, Renata suddenly cut the vacation short. Three days after they had arrived in Hawaii, Mr. and Mrs. Stein returned home.

# Chapter

## 17

Frank Keenan, the American actor, resisted the urgings of his two daughters and his son-in-law (Ed Wynn) to come and stay with them after the burial of his wife. As he said good-bye to them at the door of his Long Island mansion, they repeated their request. Keenan spoke eloquently:

"No, no. Just because we put a body in the ground today, that doesn't mean I'm alone. Your mother is here in the house with me. I feel her spirit in every wall and lamp and curtain. I'd be lonely for her anywhere else. No, I'll stay right here, where my love abides."

Wynn and his wife and sister-in-law, sobbing, said their good-byes and left for the train station.

Months later, at dinner with his father-in-law, Wynn saluted the old actor for the poise and courage he had displayed throughout the time of his wife's death. "Thank you," said Keenan. "How did you like me at the door?"

◆ ◆ ◆

It was inevitable, I suppose, that *All Rise* would be renewed. We had finished the season with a 14.2 rating and a 22 share, ranked 31st for the year. Neil and I were, as the saying goes, chained to a hit.

The writing staff regrouped in June, half of it sunburned from beach vacations, half of it overfed from European vacations, and applied itself to the new season. In spite of our resentments toward Geneva, we found ourselves coming up with stories that would serve her very well. That's the thing about writers: they're high-minded.

Geneva Holloway spent her hiatus, which is what we in TV call our time off, in Atlanta, where CBN's in-house production company was putting together a Civil War miniseries for the fall season. Geneva played Mary Chestnut. She managed to get Emil Novak attached to the project as an executive consultant, but I understand he spent much of his time over in Florida at the dog races.

During Geneva's sojourn in the South, her agent, Bobby Meyerhoff, at Geneva's request, told Polonia to open up its bank vault if it wanted her back. Geneva demanded a bump in her per-show salary of $15,000, taking her up to $75,000 an episode. She wanted an increase of $7,500 for Emil Novak's executive producing skills, bringing him up to $18,500 an episode. And she thought a 10 percent increase in her share of the adjusted gross profits might be nice. Geneva had signed an iron-clad five-year contract for the series, which she apparently viewed as a springboard for annual salary and compensation discussions.

Bobby Meyerhoff and Polonia's business affairs people, after much head butting, had agreed on the per-show increases by the time Geneva and Emil returned from the South. The redistribution of the profits, however, proved far more problematic.

The first news I had of Geneva's return to Los Angeles was when our runner, Rick Barnes, asked to see Neil and me. Rick, normally an earnest and gentle young man, was agitated. He sat there in his Oberlin sweatshirt and two-tone deck shoes—he looked like Kurt Schmoke on his day off—pushing his glasses back up on his nose as he spoke.

"Geneva called me," he said. "She wants me to do something for her."

It turned out that while Geneva and Emil were in Atlanta, Emil had his two attack rottweilers retrained, so Geneva would allow them on her property in Malibu. The wrangler guaranteed that he would turn these killer dogs into cuddly house pets. When Geneva and Emil returned to Los Angeles, the dogs did, indeed, appear gentle enough, but they hadn't been exposed to strangers. Geneva, fearful of lawsuits, asked Rick, whom she viewed as an all-around servant, to come out for a test run against the dogs. His assignment was to pass through the courtyard where the dogs roamed and see if he made it to the front door alive.

Rick told me the story, and then asked, "Do I have to do this?"

"Fuck them!" I explained. "Of course you don't have to do this. Of course not. Tell her no."

"The thing is," said Rick, holding his glasses to his nose with his index finger, "I told Geneva I didn't want to do it. And she said, 'Well, of course you can refuse, but if you do, I can't speak to your future in the company.'"

"That's bullshit. Why does it have to be you?"

"Because I'm black."

I took this in.

"She didn't say that?"

"Yeah, she did. She said she was worried because the dogs hadn't been exposed to a black person since they were retrained. You know, Malibu. She's worried that some black gas company guy or cable TV guy will come out there someday and—"

"No..."

"Yeah. She had me talk to the dog trainer. He said they shouldn't attack, but if they do, that I should offer them my least important arm and cover my head with the other arm."

Neil, who is slow to anger but impressive when he finally does, jumped up from his chair.

"Stop!" he said, as if he were in pain. "This is the worst thing I ever heard. First of all, I would like to apologize on behalf of everybody in my subgenus. Secondly..." He yelled out the door of the office, "Sharone! Get me Geneva on the phone right now!"

Neil ripped through Geneva like a bullet. It was a wonder to witness, a blaze of righteousness. If Neil had been around at the time, I'm sure Jesus would have said, "Hey, Neil, drive these money changers out of the temple for me. You're better at it." I imagine Geneva just stood there staring at the receiver for five minutes after Neil hung up.

The next news from Geneva came two days later in the form of front-page headlines in both trade papers: "Geneva Holloway to Leave 'All Rise.'" Negotiations had collapsed because of Geneva's demand for 10 percent of the profits. Geneva, coached by a publicist, described the dispute as her fight for a fair share. She framed her argument in terms of creative rights and economic justice, but I think it all rested on the fact that Neil wouldn't let her test out her rottweilers on a black guy.

Initially, the prospect that Geneva might not be coming back electrified the soul. But the glee was quickly shaded by other considerations. Neil and I finally had a hit show on our hands. All we had to do was hack our way through another twenty-two episodes, and we were finished with our contract. Then Polonia could bring in a couple of professional wrestlers to take over for us. The goal was to keep the show on the air for five seasons and make a healthy syndication sale. My fifty million dollars was floating around out there.

Those were my thoughts. Neil Stein was thinking more creatively. "Let's replace Geneva with someone else," he said. "Who?" I asked. "Hannah Cane," he said.

Hannah Cane. These were magic words.

Hannah Cane was the World's Most Perfect Person, for three reasons: (1) her heart-stopping beauty; (2) her refined sense of comedy; (3) the fact that such beauty and such comedy were present in one person. In addition to all this, Hannah was a very pleasant human being to work with. And I'll pay her my highest compliment: Someday, she'll make a great Lady Bracknell.

Neil and I made discreet inquiries of Hannah's agent. Word came back that Hannah would, indeed, be interested in taking over Geneva's roll in *All Rise,* but under two conditions: Geneva had to be out officially before Hannah began any serious discussions

and, more endearingly, Neil and I would have to stay on as producers. This last requirement is a testimony to Hannah's intelligence; she was smart enough to flatter writers. So many stars
seem unaware that a little offhand affection strewn before a writer
will keep him groveling for weeks.

Neil and I relayed our information directly to Avery Schine,
delivering it to him personally in his aerie at Polonia Productions.
He rolled it around before him, clawed at it a little, but did not
bite. He felt it was too risky to change actresses. Instead, he
decided to try the neighborhood thug approach with Geneva, which
had served him so well throughout his career. He issued an ulti-
matum: if Geneva Holloway did not report to work by July 12, as
scheduled, she would be held in breach of contract and sued for
$520 million and all her makeup and underwear. This had a sobering
effect on Geneva. She countered with a new proposal: she would
reduce her demand for a 10-percent increase in her piece of the
adjusted gross profits down to 6 percent.

Polonia found Geneva's new spirit of cooperation refreshing.
They gave her 3 percent, and they took the other three percent
from Neil and me. There was a sneaky little provision in our deal
that said we could be forced to kick back that much "for the creative
services of a third party." The idea behind this was, if Neil and I
left the show, Polonia could offer a little piece of the action to the
next writer-producer to take over. Now they were claiming Geneva and Emil were offering "creative services."

Neil and I screamed and yelled for a while and threatened to go
to court, but eventually we caved in. We had no power. As the
man said, "I talk about pussy, but I eat corned beef."


The thrill of not having Geneva back, the dread of having Geneva
back, the burden of getting scripts under way, the lingering horror
of a bloated dead man brushing against his feet: none of this had
a salutary effect on Neil Stein. He increased his intake of Tylenol
with codeine. Once, under pressure from me and the other pro-

ducers, he admitted that he was taking fifteen tablets a day.

"That's an awful lot of codeine," I told him.

"Fuck," said Don Blatz, "that's an awful lot of *Tylenol.*"

Neil took to coming in late in the morning, citing mysterious doctor's appointments as the cause. His sense of story structure, never his strongest point, collapsed. His great jokes, his wild left turns, disappeared. My reserves of sympathy exhausted themselves. I started yelling at Neil behind closed doors, and soon I was humiliating him in front of everyone else. He accepted this abuse as his due.

A week before production was scheduled to begin, Neil surprised us all by showing up less late than usual, but looking like the dog's breakfast. His skin was the yellow of church candles, and his black eyes were sunk deeply into their sockets like olives at the bottom of a bowl. He had not shaved. There was something false about his brave "hellos" to everyone. As he poured himself coffee, I addressed him in my schoolteacher's voice.

"You have to be here on time tomorrow," I said. "Geneva wants to have a creative meeting. It's in her contract."

"Oh, Christ, she's not going to start interfering with scripts?"

"That's what I was worried about. No. She's got some exciting new ideas about her character's wardrobe to present to us. But you have to be here, you fuck. She's your responsibility."

Neil held out his hand to interrupt me, then directed me into our office with a movement of his head. When we entered, Neil signaled, again with a motion of his head, that the door should be closed.

"Renata kicked me out," he said.

"Oh, perfect, just what I need," I said. "What happened?"

"Apparently I said something horrible to her last night."

"What?"

"I don't know. I was stoned. I don't remember."

"Jesus."

"We were coming home from Greg Paul's house. She was driving. And apparently—"

"You go to Greg Paul's house?" I was hurt.

"Oh, come on. It's this charity thing. Renata and Caroline Paul raise money for the rain forest—"

"But you never said you go over to his house."

"You know about those fund-raisers, that I've been there before."

"But I thought it stopped."

"Excuse me," said Neil, "but my life is in the toilet, I'm out on the fucking streets, and you're acting like I'm cheating on you."

"Where did you stay last night?"

"The Holiday Inn on Sunset at the Four-oh-five."

"Neil, what happened? What did you say to her?"

"I don't know. She says she won't repeat it. She says she wants a divorce."

I considered all this for a moment.

"I'll call her," I said.

"She's at her kundalini yoga class right now."

"I'll call her later."

Renata was a wall. "If I told you what he said to me, you'd tell me to divorce him," she said. "No, you'd tell me to kill him."

"What did he say?"

"I'll never repeat it as long as I live."

She seemed pretty firm on this.

Neil left the office at noon for a doctor's appointment and, for a change, actually went to see a doctor. He came back at two and once again sealed us behind the office door.

"I have to enter a drug treatment program. I just talked to this doctor. There's a pretty good one in Santa Monica. He can get me in."

"Excuse me, Neil," I asked, "but when are you planning to do this?"

"Jim, this is my only chance with Renata. I know her. She'll go for this."

"Yeah, but when are you going to do this?"

"Right now. This doctor says I can get in next Monday."

"For how long?"

"The in-patient part is for eight weeks."

"Eight weeks, Neil? Eight fucking weeks? You're going to be gone for the first two months of the fucking season?"

"I'm not any help this way anyhow."

"Exactly. Why can't you just go into one of those twelve-step programs?"

"I can't detoxify like that. And Renata should see me in a hospital. I know her. She'll see me in a hospital and I'll have a chance. She respects science."

"And I just produce the whole fucking show alone?"

"Jimmy, I've never seen her like this. Never before."

"The time to do this was on hiatus, when I told you, not now."

"I'm going to lose her."

"You're going to lose me! I'm supposed to work for, what, half a season, carrying you? And I face Geneva Holloway alone? Fuck that, buddy. Fuck that in the fucking ass."

I walked out and slammed the door behind me. I had no more contact with him for the rest of the day. When I left, he was hunched over the computer, trying to show me how hard he was working.

That evening I went to see Kiki and found her crying. Her twin sister had sent her a newspaper clipping from Tyler, Texas: an elderly man confined to a wheelchair had been given a puppy by neighbors, to cheer him up. The puppy chewed off the man's left foot, but the old gent, because he had no feeling in his legs, was unaware of the problem until a visiting social worker discovered it. (What would a social worker say in a case like that? "Excuse me, sir, is this yours?")

"It's very sad," I told Kiki. "But, apparently, the old guy's all right now. And you didn't actually know him or anything, did you?'

"I don't give a fuck about him," said Kiki. "Hell, I thought it was funny. The dog chewed off his foot, and he didn't even know it."

"Then why are you crying?"

"Because the story makes me so homesick for Texas."

I took her to Gilliland's in Santa Monica for comfort food; she favored their Irish stew with champ. Her hair was cut boyishly short for a part in a play that never opened. (The Curtain Call Dinner Theater in Tustin, California, had planned, then canceled, a production of *The Wild Duck,* to be complemented by an all-duck menu.) Her blue eyes were even prettier for being sad and wet. She told me about a dream she had in which she looked in a mirror and saw a list of everything she had ever eaten written on her teeth. I asked her what it meant. She said it meant that Los Angeles is evil. Lately, everything tended to mean that Los Angeles was evil.

"It's a terrible city," she said. "I can't even afford health care."

"Are you sick?"

"No, for my tortoise. I can't afford a veterinarian."

"What's wrong?"

"She seems sluggish."

"Kiki," I said, "she's a tortoise. She's supposed to be sluggish." She ignored me.

"I hate Los Angeles," she said. "It's my own fault. I should have never come here. I came for the wrong reason."

"I thought you came to further your acting career."

"Not really. I came to get away from a guy in New York."

"You never told me that. You're not much on personal information."

"I think I'm going to have to go away soon," she said.

"Kiki," I said, "you've been going away since the first day I met you."

"I know," she said. "That's what I'm like."

The next morning as I came into the outer office Sharone held up her hand to stop me and quickly scooted up from behind her desk. She was wearing a belt the width of a highway stripe; it crossed over itself to form a triangle in the area of her pubis. "What dey don't show, dey points to," as the old black lady said.

"Neil spent the night here," said Sharone in a respectful level just above a whisper. "He's asleep on the sofa."

I nodded with equally respectful understanding. I crossed over to the office and cracked the door a little. Neil was asleep facedown, his arm lying hand-up at his side, his rump slightly elevated, like a toddler. An open copy of *Everything That Rises Must Converge* lay on the carpet beside him. I closed the door cautiously, and then felt a wave of ire flush through me. I went back in and started yelling.

"Neil! Come on, Neil, wake up. You have to face Geneva with me." I pushed on his shoulders, but he merely reslumped. "Neil!"

Sharone entered. "He left something on his computer," she said, and handed me the printout. There were two spare lines: "Nothing in his life became him like the leaving it . . . except for that Armani suit he bought in 1986."

"This is not good," I said. I tried harder to rouse him. "Neil!" I yelled. "Neil!" I accidentally kicked aside the Flannery O'Connor and revealed an amber vial on the carpet. It was Elavil, and it was empty. On the label, below the instructions, was the message "Have a Nice Day!" with a little yellow smile face. Don Monahan and Don Blatz entered the office. Don Blatz opened the blinds.

"Neil," I called again, shaking him. "Neil! Hey!"

"This is big-time," said Don Monahan.

The paramedics were boyish and sincere. One sported a blond moustache that, in its ungenerosity, underscored his youthfulness. The other was tense-jawed and athletic and wore glasses with very fine wire frames. Their absolute focus on the task at hand inspired a confidence that their years could not. The one with the moustache applied himself to Neil while his partner set up the EKG monitor, established radio contact with a doctor at Cedars-Sinai, and asked us the questions that needed to be asked.

"How many pills were in here, do you know?" he said, holding up the brown vial.

"I have no idea," I said, and then Sharone surprised me by answering, "At least twenty. It was full yesterday. They were red, I think one hundred milligrams."

The paramedic then talked into his radio and received responses in a squawky crackle from the physician on the other end, a woman, who responded matter-of-factly, as if this were just another part of her day. It bothered me that my partner's attempted suicide could not coax a little tension into her voice. She sounded boyish, just like the paramedics. I overheard words like "stupor" and "dilated pupils" and "cardiac arrhythmia," and "neostigmine."

The paramedic with the blond moustache, who was down on both knees at the side of the sofa, gave Neil an injection. His partner explained, "We have to stabilize him before we can move him." For the first time I saw the awful bisque color of Neil's face and the chalky blue of his lips.

"What's his name?" asked the paramedic at Neil's side.

"Neil Stein," I said, thinking the paramedic was about to fill out a form. But that's not why he wanted the information. He moved his mouth to Neil's ear and spoke in a firm voice.

"Neil. Come back, Neil," he said. "Come back, Neil. We want you back here, now."

There was a faint, promising response from Neil, a slight movement of the head.

"Neil. Come on, guy."

Sharone tugged at the back of my shirt. At first I thought it was from anxiety. But then she whispered, "Geneva's at the door."

I went to the door of our office suite, which Rick Barnes was guarding. He opened it enough to let me slip into the hall, where Geneva waited. Her hair was in a snood for some reason, which emphasized the apprehension in her eyes. Lingering a respectful distance beyond Geneva were a handful of people from other offices who had heard about the drama and came to show concern.

"How is he?" asked Geneva, and with such straightforward sincerity that I felt that for the first time we might talk simply as human beings.

"He's taken an overdose of Elavil, but we're not sure how much," I said, darting my eyes down the hall to include the others and then bringing them directly back to Geneva. "The paramedics are working on him right now. They have to stabilize him before they can get him over to Cedars and get his stomach pumped. Frankly, it's touch and go."

Geneva took this in and pursed her lips. She looked as if she needed to be comforted. I was about to say, "Don't worry. He'll pull through. He's a very tough little guy." But Geneva spoke first.

"I guess, under the circumstances, we should hold the meeting down in Emil's office."

If this had been a macabre joke, it would have gone a long way to break the tension. But I did not see the barest suggestion of irony on Geneva's face.

I replied in measured tones, as if I were explaining something important to a child. Which, in fact, I was.

"Geneva, Neil's my partner. He may be dying. I don't think I could do your wardrobe the concentration it deserves right now."

Geneva nodded. She understood.

"Okay," she said, "but I don't have any other openings until Friday."


I reported this to Neil a week and a half later, and got my first big laugh out of him. He was out of Cedars-Sinai by then and in a drug-rehab clinic in Santa Monica. It was our first visit. We sat in a little visitors area at the end of a corridor. Neil was in powder blue Nordstrom's pajamas, a black-and-green Ralph Lauren bathrobe with wide, Japanese-style sleeves, and blue Nubuck slippers from Eddie Bauer. It was apparent from all this that Renata had come back into his life.

Kiki was with me. She had brought along a coloring book and a box of state-of-the-art Crayolas as a gift for Neil, and she sat with her legs crossed on a lounge chair, coloring for all she was worth while Neil and I chatted.

Our conversation had been a little too reverent until that first big laugh. After that, I felt better about telling Neil what an asshole he'd been, and getting him to laugh some more. I accused him of writing the most pretentious suicide note ever put onto a computer.

"It was supposed to be funny," he said.

"You could have at least worked the word 'farewell' into it somewhere," I said.

"Listen to this schmuck," Neil called over to Kiki. "He's rewriting my *suicide* note."

She looked up and smiled, and brushed crayon leavings from her coloring book.

"So," said Neil, "you know what it is I told Renata that night, that got her so upset with me? This horrible thing I said?"

"Did you remember it?"

"No. But we had this therapy session together. Renata admitted it in front of the therapist. It took all her courage."

"What did you say?"

"We're driving home, and I'm drunk, right?"

"Right."

"I told her, 'Let's go get our cocks sucked.' "

Neil laughed so hard that at first I thought it might do him some harm. But as I looked at him, I'd have to say I'd never seen him happier.

# Chapter

# *18*

The producer Mike Todd, on the brink of bankruptcy, irritated his lawyer by continuing to smoke expensive Cuban cigars.

"Jesus, Mike," said the lawyer, "look at your debts. And here you are, smoking five-dollar cigars."

"I owe forty-eight million dollars," said Todd. "You want me to give up cigars?"

◆ ◆ ◆

The key to being a prick in the entertainment industry is to only be a prick to those below you on the food chain. Geneva Holloway forgot this; she made the mistake of taking on Avery Schine.

Geneva was stung that Avery Schine had played rough in getting her back to the bargaining table. She was mortified to have been served a subpoena while entertaining friends in the privacy of her lanai, while two stupid-ass rottweilers looked up at the process server for approval, never once thinking of tearing off large sections of his body. Geneva panicked and ranted and cried when she read the subpoena, making a fool of herself in front of her friends. Somehow, this information found its way into the Calendar section of the *Sunday Los Angeles Times,* embarrassing Geneva further. Geneva saw Avery's action as a brutal betrayal. She was forced to shed the illusion that there was a higher power looking out for her best interests, from whom all fairness flowed.

Avery Schine at sixty-one had reached a level of prosperity that enabled him to arrange public tributes for himself: the Friends of Hebrew University Man of the Year Award, recipient of the Golden Cup from St. John's Medical Center, the Foresight Award from the Alhambra Rape Crisis Treatment Center. These were the rich man's equivalent of stars in the Hollywood Walk of Fame. (Those, once you reach a bare modicum of celebrity, cost a mere five thousand dollars, which you donate to the Hollywood Chamber of Commerce in advance.)

In July of 1989, Avery had the rare good fortune to be chosen for the Lifetime Achievement Award by the Max and Ruthie Schine Charitable Trust, a foundation he had organized and named after his parents. The award was to be presented at a ten-thousand-dollar-a-table dinner dance on the sound stage at the Paramount lot where *All Rise* was filmed.

Avery Schine stood to be acutely embarrassed by Geneva's contract dispute. The invitations to his award banquet had been mailed and arms were already being twisted to assure a sellout. Geneva was named in the invitations as a presiding celebrity. It was in Avery's interest to resolve things as quickly as possible. That's why he resorted to the lawsuit, thereby inadvertently causing Geneva to be humiliated in front of her friends.

It's difficult to know if Geneva planned her little prank ahead of time, or if it occurred to her in the flow of events. I think the latter, with the understanding that mean-spiritedness favors the prepared mind.

We had been asked by Avery Schine's office to be off the set of *All Rise* by 5:30 P.M. on the Friday of the gala, so the caterers could set up. We scheduled our run-through early, to accommodate the request. After the run-through, Geneva asked Don Lasker and Joseph Landry and the director, Jonathan Metzger, to stay a little longer and work out the mechanics of a scene in the kitchen that involved juggling vegetables back and forth. Geneva was weak on physical comedy and needed practice. In addition, she had nowhere else to go; she was staying on the lot and changing in her trailer, and then making her appearance at the tribute to Avery Schine.

That was at 5:15. At 5:30, the building services people from Polonia started hauling in potted palms while the caterers rolled in their steam tables. At 5:45, one of the catering drones dropped a milk crate full of chinaware on the floor, to nerve-shattering effect.

Geneva went nuts. She advanced on the workers with a mad glare in her eye and launched into a stream of expletives so profane that "ass fuckers" is the only word it doesn't embarrass me to put into print. Caterers and workmen all cowered in the face of her wrath and left the building. Geneva ordered the unit production manager to bolt the sound lock and to bring down the immense corrugated shutter that was the main entrance to the stage. Then she continued to rehearse her scene with her shaken companions amid the garlicky vapors of the steam tables.

After half an hour—shortly after security started calling through the door with an electronic bullhorn—Jonathan Metzger begged Geneva to reconsider. "We've proven our point, Geneva," he said, wisely aligning himself with the star even as he coaxed her away from her folly.

When the gang of four emerged from the stage into the crowd of caterers and early arriving guests and the swirl of orange lights from the tops of the electric carts the security people used, Avery Schine was waiting for them. He had escorted his mother to the lot, where a comfortable trailer had been requisitioned for her, so she could relax and watch *Entertainment Tonight* until the gala began. Avery was in most of his tuxedo already, except for the jacket and tie. Mrs. Schine, eighty-two years young, stood at the steps to her trailer, adorned in party finery, supported by a multifooted cane.

Avery, cold and angry, approached Geneva, who said, "It's all yours," and brushed by him. Avery reverted to his early days in the pinball distribution business and grabbed Geneva's arm, yanking her back toward him. Geneva turned on him with a fury, flailing at him with her free arm.

"Let me go, you Jewish gangster!" she screamed.

"Apologize," said Avery.

"You larval monster!"

"Apologize, in front of all these people."

"You needle-dicked bug fucker!" At this, Geneva started kicking. Avery let her arm go to protect his groin. Geneva darted backward.

"He assaulted me! Arrest him!" Geneva said to the security guards, who looked on awkwardly. Then she turned back to Avery. "I quit! I'm off the show!" she said.

Geneva turned dramatically to start away and was nearly cross-body blocked by the elderly Mrs. Schine, who had hobbled several yards to get a good look at this famous star. Surely Mrs. Schine had seen this struggle, and heard Geneva call her son a needle-dicked bug fucker, but such is the siren call of celebrity that she chose to ignore it. Instead, she said, "I watched you every week when you were Chelsea on *Bel Air Terrace*. I just loved you."

Geneva transformed herself instantly and took both of Mrs. Schine's hands in hers and said, "That is so very *sweet*."

Putting Avery Schine in a bad light was one of the sins Avery Schine could not forgive. He spent a few hours over the weekend setting a trap for Geneva. He consulted with lawyers. He telephoned Joe Danko of CBN and told him Geneva had walked. Danko, furious after just stepping up to the extra fifteen thousand dollars an episode Geneva had demanded, said, "Let's cut her balls off." He agreed to go on with *All Rise* by recasting the leading role. Avery Schine suggested Hannah Cane as a replacement. Joe Danko liked this idea, because CBN already had an overall deal with Hannah. Avery called Hannah Cane's agent, who said he would not enter negotiations until Geneva Holloway was formally fired, but he indicated that a deal could be made without undue throat cutting. By four-thirty on Saturday afternoon, everything that could be known was known. Avery Schine had now only to wait until nine-thirty Monday morning to see if Geneva showed up for work.

She didn't. At ten o'clock the proper legal papers were messengered to Geneva's agent, notifying him that Geneva Holloway was in breach of contract and therefore dismissed from the show. At this point, a Polonia lawyer called and told me what was going on. It was then my duty to go over to the stage and tell everyone that we were shut down until further notice.

I came back from the stage and phoned Neil at the rehab clinic; they were reluctant to call him out of his group therapy session, but I assured them that what I had to say was more beneficial than any therapy. "Geneva's out," I told him, almost whispering. "Avery Schine fired her." Neil and I were silent for a moment. "This is more than I ever dared to hope," said Neil. "It's over, buddy" I said. "No matter what happens now, the nightmare part is over."

After another beat of silence, we both started laughing. As the laughter mounted, Geneva Holloway suddenly appeared at my office door. Her attorneys had got word to her that Polonia was playing for keeps, and urged her to hurry over to the studio to try to salvage the situation.

"There's nobody over on the stage," she said disingenuously. "What's going on?"

I got to tell her.


We hammered out a deal with Hannah Cane in a New York minute. But then we wasted the better part of a week trying to figure out how to introduce her on the show. Do we say the "Geneva" character is away? Dead? Do we make Hannah Cane a sister to the "Jack Mullins" character, who's there to help out while "Geneva" is away? Do we make her his new wife, because "Geneva" is dead? It was Neil Stein, from his bed of addiction, who solved the dilemma.

"Just make her Geneva," he said during a conference call. "She's

Geneva Mullin. One actress left the show; now there's a new one."

"Won't people find that a little jarring?" I said.

"People don't give a fuck, if they like who it is. There's been more than one Lady Macbeth, you know."

"It's a tempting idea. We wouldn't have to change the scripts."

"*Bewitched* had two Darrins," said Neil, clinching the argument.

Hannah stepped in and learned her part for the first show in less than a day. The season's production got under way only a week and a half late.

When I watched Hannah Cane work in that first show, I had a gnawing feeling that something was missing. I finally identified it: Dread. Somehow, Hannah did not provoke in me the roiling dread I had come to expect from Geneva. I realized that I would now have to content myself with the routine nightmares, horrors, and impossibilities that accompany every weekly television series. I could no longer depend on Geneva Holloway for that extra measure of misery and abuse. I once read of a man who lived with a railroad spike embedded four inches into his skull. When they took it out, I suppose he missed it for a while.

Neil came back to work, drug free and, to his own surprise, happily separated from Renata. He had learned in therapy that he took drugs primarily to provoke Renata into leaving him; he'd gotten what he wanted. He found a pleasant apartment in Beverly Hills, just behind Neiman Marcus, that was furnished all the way to the point of bed linens and coffee filters. I worried about his lonely hours there, but he assured me he was very happy. He spent long, rapturous evenings writing short stories. At the office, his old fervor and wit had returned.

The series, after Geneva, did better than it had done before. This was gratifying to everyone involved except Geneva. People liked Hannah Cane, and Joseph Landry's "Louis" character had "broken out," as they say in network programming meetings. We won our Monday night time slot by three or four share points every week, unless there was a very good Monday Night Football game against us.

Geneva was reduced to hauling Emil Novak around the country appearing on television talk shows, griping about her mistreatment at the hands of Hollywood moguls. She introduced Emil as her fiancé and partner. They presented themselves as a nurturing, creative team whose "baby" had been ruthlessly snatched from them.

In September, Geneva filed suit for wrongful dismissal and breach of contract, asking for $90 million in damages from the Continental Broadcasting Network, $90 million in damages from Polonia Productions, and $90 million in damages from James E. Hoy and Neil F. Stein, d.b.a. Mirthmakers, Inc.

I worried about how Neil would take this news. It was the sort of thing that would have sent him over the edge in the past. But he just looked over the suit and said, "Fuck 'em, let's pay it!"

I think it speaks to our grandeur as a nation that a country saddled with a recession, a mounting deficit, breathtaking financial scandals and uncounted homeless still found time to take thorough note of every single fillip in Geneva Holloway's dispute with Polonia Productions. It was big news in the entertainment industry, which meant it was big news on local television news broadcasts all across the land. And the public prints could not be accused of underplaying this little spat, either. I developed a stock response to reporters who called me from all over the hemisphere, wanting to know what really happened: "Geneva Holloway left because of creative differences; she thought she was creative, and we differed."

The juicy headlines generated by Geneva served to obscure the more significant news that Polonia Productions was going broke. Finally, Avery Schine's overwhelming drive to be a movie mogul had splatted against an inconvenient fact: He had no talent. Polonia's film division was hemorrhaging money. Leo Becker was no longer around to generate new television revenues to compensate for Avery's money-losing films. It fell to David Putzman to play the little Dutch boy coming to the rescue. But instead of putting his finger in the dike, Putzman had been walking around with it up his ass. By the end of fiscal 1989, Polonia was losing $28 million a quarter. The company's big Christmas release, a horror fantasy called *Rodent,* starring Sean Young and Andrew McCarthy, functioned as the coup de grace.

Harry Ward of Massillon Pictures "came to the rescue." The press releases tried to make it all sound like a happy merger, but it was a total buyout by Harry. And suddenly, we were all working for a new outfit called Massillon-Polonia. It sounded like an exit on the Ohio Turnpike.

The merger went largely unnoticed on the *All Rise* set. In mid-March, we ended our second season with an average 15.3 rating, 24 share, the 18th ranked show of the year. In a few weeks, *Holloway* v. *Polonia et al.* was scheduled to go to trial. Neil and I deferred our vacations until it was our turn to go to court out in Santa Monica. We went into the office every day and worked on stories for next season. Finally, it was our turn to testify. I think the resultant headlines accurately captured the spirit of our remarks:

FURY, HYSTERIA, PARANOIA ON THE SET OF 'ALL RISE'
—*Daily Variety,* April 2, 1990

PRODUCERS TELL OF HOLLOWAY'S 'BORDERLINE' BEHAVIOR
—*Hollywood Reporter,* April 2, 1990

'GENEVA IS NUTS' PRODUCERS TELL COURT
—*Star,* April 4, 1990

After our day in court, Neil left for some sort of writers colony in Vermont. He told me it was to be very small and intense. "It's like having a personal trainer for short story writing," he said.

I wanted to take the lovely Kiki Burmeister to Paris, and then possibly to London, for a spring holiday. But Kiki's bedmate Leroy Butley was getting married, and Kiki had volunteered to organize the reception. I agreed to stay in Los Angeles with Kiki until after the wedding, and then we would both go to the Mauna Kea in Hawaii for Easter.

Leroy's fiancée was a lovely young French Canadian named Sabine Duroq, who had come to the United States to be with her lover, Clovis Baines, an assistant casting director at Big Creek Productions, and also a woman. Clovis was a friend of long standing to Leroy, and imposed upon him to enter into holy matrimony so Sabine could get a green card. Leroy didn't mind.

Kiki's identical twin sister Jonquil, who at one time was practically engaged to Leroy Butley back in Tyler, Texas, flew in for the wedding. The twins didn't look very identical. Kiki had been losing weight and was almost gaunt; Jonquil was flush and had twenty pounds on her sister. Kiki's hair was chestnut and close-cropped; Jonquil's was red and full. But their voices were identical. I couldn't tell which one was speaking unless I was looking directly at them.

The wedding and reception took place at Leroy's stucco bungalow in Hollywood. Kiki had arranged for a big tent in the backyard; she'd borrowed it from a New Age funeral parlor on Melrose called Remains to Be Seen. The vows were administered by a free-lance psychic nutritionist who also worked at Fred Segal. Then came an energetic performance by a female stripper. Kiki said that since most of the guests would be either men or lesbians, she figured the stripper would be a crowd pleaser.

The champagne flowed, especially into Jonquil Burmeister, who led a select group in a version of the dirty boogie. She was obviously enjoying this little break from the domestic bliss of husband and children back in Tyler. The music was provided by a fortyish woman in a net formal at an electronic keyboard. During a break I found myself standing next to her, and said, just to make conversation, "Hi. Are you a lesbian?"

"Oh, no, I'm a man," she said.

"Well, you're a very lovely man," I said.

"Thank you," she said. "Actually, I'm in the middle of a sex change operation. I've had my breasts done. Now I'm saving up money for a vagina. Vaginas are very expensive."

"Tell me about it," I said.

When it came time to leave, Kiki looked all over for Leroy, to say good-bye, but couldn't find him. She questioned the bride, who interrupted a languorous cheek-to-cheek dance with her girlfriend to say that she had no idea where her husband might be. Then we looked for Jonquil, who was coming with us to my house, and there was no sign of her, either. Kiki tried the door of the bedroom she shared with Leroy, and it was locked.

"Leroy?" she said. "Are you in there? I need my contact lens solution."

There was no answer.

"Leroy?"

"Just a second," said Leroy, faintly.

A pair of feet padded across the floor and the door opened the barest crack. It was Jonquil. She handed out a bottle of contact lens solution. She was naked. Her left breast, which was all I could see, was, indeed, identical to Kiki's.

"I'm staying here tonight," said Jonquil. "Okay?" Her eyes were a plea for understanding.

Kiki and I gave the bride and her girlfriend a lift to their place near Fountain and Sweetzer. They lived in an apartment building excessively named The La Ronda. On the drive home from there, Kiki gave vent to her upset about the conduct of Leroy and her sister. I tended toward leniency. I figured, here was Leroy with a bedmate who wouldn't have sex with him, and a wife who wouldn't have sex with him. I was glad to see him finally get laid.

"Watch Jonquil's husband find out, and then I'll get blamed," said Kiki. "It's this city. It's no good. I wish I could afford to live in New York."

"I wish you could afford to live somewhere," I said.

"That's my whole problem right there, isn't it? I can't afford to live anywhere."

We went home and went to bed. I awoke at four in the morning and found Kiki crying on the floor of the bathroom. She was naked, and her body was covered with horrible red welts, as if from an allergic reaction. They looked like little Indian burial mounds.

"I can't stay in Los Angeles," she cried.

I took her to the emergency room at Santa Monica Hospital. They gave her Prozac and said she'd better stay in the hospital for a couple of days. I waited until seven-thirty and called Jonquil over at Leroy's house. She got to the hospital by nine. Jonquil examined her sister and then, brooking no debate, announced that she was taking Kiki back to Tyler.

"I just can't stay in Los Angeles," said Kiki. "I know you don't believe me, but it's evil."

"I believe you now," I said.

And that's how my relationship with Kiki Burmeister ended. I was left stranded, without a lover, during my scarce and valuable vacation days. I moped for half a week. I considered going to Hawaii by myself, but I dreaded being seen alone at the hotel on Easter Sunday. That struck me as particularly embarrassing and pitiable. I actually went as far as to concoct an insane plan: I could go to Hawaii, and then, on Easter Sunday, just stay in my room all day. I'd order two dinners from room service; when the waiter came, I'd have the shower running, and tell him to go ahead and leave everything, my girlfriend would be out in a minute.

I was interrupted from these loopy reveries by the ringing of my telephone. It was my ex-wife calling from San Luis Obispo. She was in jail. Emery Dierdorff had brought her up there to take part in an Easter week demonstration against the San Onofre nuclear power plant. In the midst of the march, Miranda had been swept along, against her will, by a group of activist nuns who were intent on trespassing. The nuns and Miranda were arrested. She'd spent the night in jail.

"I've thought about it," she told me on the phone, "and you're the only person I'd let get me out of jail."

"Where's Emery?"

"He went back to L.A. He didn't want to miss this big party for Robert Blake at Martin Sheen's house."

"And he just left you in jail?"

"Well, there was some guy in charge of bailing people out. But the nuns didn't want to be bailed out. They want to call attention to their plight. So, I got overlooked. Jimmy, can you come get me?"

"Miranda, I'll tell you the truth, I'm glad for the distraction."

It's about a five-hour drive up to San Luis Obispo. I played audio tapes of Max Von Sydow reading *The Magic Mountain,* which my partner foisted on me for my birthday. Yeah, that would make a real good movie. When I got to the jail, Miranda was unaccountably serene. She appeared in the reception area outside the lockup with a deep-set, satisfied smile, as if I were picking her up from yoga class or a music lesson. The way she said good-bye to her jailers you'd think she was leaving summer camp.

"What is this place, a spa?" I asked her in the car. "You look great."

"I look great because I have no more worries," said Miranda. "I've had all these months of tension about Emery, trying to find out where we stood with each other, and now I know. We stand nowhere. He left me in jail while he went down to L.A. to star fuck. And I feel enormously relieved. The question is settled. He's out of my life forever—look, there are those windmill things that generate power—so everything is resolved. You know he was fucking around on me."

"No. How would I know?"

"Well, for one thing, it was in the newspapers, James. You didn't read about that 'service' he organized? 'Naked Before the Lord'? He had everybody taking off their clothes in church."

"Jesus, Miranda. How could you tolerate that?"

"Apparently, not well. That's why I feel so good right now. Could we possibly get something to eat? All they had in jail was this health food crap. The nuns wanted it."

We ate at a Mexican steakhouse among Latinos in straw cowboy hats. I told Miranda about Kiki.

"Poor Jimbo. How do you feel?"

"Relieved, too, in a way," I said. "Miranda, where's Bennett?"

"With my mother. Which is another thing that pisses me off. This was supposed to be my vacation, and I've wasted it demonstrating against nuclear power. Do you want to know the truth? In my heart, I think we might *need* nuclear power."

"The reason I asked is, then you don't have to get back down to L.A. tonight."

"I have no pressing reason."

"We could spend the night together."

I just set the idea down on the table, and she did not bat it away. In fact, after some deliberation, she said, "Well, yes, we could."

It was difficult to find a motel room because of some famous Easter pageant in the area. I convinced the desk clerk at a place with "Paradise" in its name to rent us the motel's meeting room for the night. "This woman has a metal plate in her head," I said, pulling Miranda close to me. "We *must* find her shelter." He told us we'd have to check out by nine o'clock, because they used the room for church services on Sunday mornings.

The room was a small auditorium, with a stage, stacks of metal folding chairs, and a kitchen unit. A queen-sized bed and two night tables rested under a basketball hoop.

We made love, but it didn't go very well. When it came time for me to enter Miranda she was dry and raspy.

"I'm thinking too much," she said. "I'm sorry."

"It's just nice to be with you again," I said. We snuggled together like nested chairs and went to sleep.

We were awakened too early on Sunday morning by the sun

coming through a skylight. We made love again, with much more success. The anxieties of the previous night had vanished in our dreams. Miranda made a woeful little gushing sound as she came. I felt wholly reconnected with her. As we lay together in gummy bliss, someone unlocked the door and tested it against the chain. The door was reclosed, and a loud knocking began. I scampered over the chilly tiles and cracked the door wide enough to see three ladies in late middle age, each of them a dumpling.

"We have to set up the chairs for church," said one of these three fates.

"It's only a quarter to eight," I said.

"No, it's a quarter to nine. The time changed last night."

"Spring forward," said one of her companions.

"Jesus," I said. "Give us five minutes."

Miranda and I gathered our clothes and scrambled into the bathroom—rows of urinals across from rows of sinks—to put them on. Twenty minutes later, slightly disoriented, we stood at the window of a Dairy Queen drinking coffee from large Styrofoam cups. Miranda gave me a very odd smile.

"What?" I asked.

"Nothing," she said, and then laughed.

"What?"

"I'm standing here unwashed, my hair's a mess, and now there's come dribbling down my leg."

We got into the car and started driving toward Los Angeles. We fell into our private thoughts as we drove, lulled by the slap of the tires over bands in the asphalt.

"So," I said eventually, meaning my question to be taken broadly, "now what?"

"Well," said Miranda, "you're the boy. I guess I have to wait and see if you call me again."

After a few hours, Miranda said, "Music?" and punched on the radio. We came in on a syndicated gossip show, *The Hollywood Report* or something like that, in time to hear an overexcited reporter say, "Is Geneva Holloway happy with her ten-million-dollar victory over Polonia Productions? Just ask her." And then there was an intercut of Geneva, nearly incomprehensible with joy: "It was painful... the biggest powers in the industry were aligned against me... but truth was on my side."

# Chapter

# *19*

Sam Speigel, the producer of *Lawrence of Arabia,* stayed on his yacht in neutral waters during filming, reluctant, as a Jew, to set foot on hostile Arab land. Protocol, however, demanded that he receive King Hussein as a visitor one day. Speigel offered the king lunch.

"No. I'm sorry," said the king, "but it is Ramadan, a time of fasting and spiritual reflection for us."

"Ah," said Speigel, "like our Lent."

◆ ◆ ◆

Geneva's basic posture at her trial was "I didn't quit, I was fired." Of enormous value to the plaintiff was her ability to stay in the character of Chelsea Huntington, the poor little rich girl of *Bel Air Terrace,* throughout the ten days of the trial. This was how she was best known to the American people and, more important, to the twelve members of the jury. So she sat there just like Chelsea, as sweet to look at as a rose geranium.

It worked. Certain uncomfortable facts—say, eight or ten people testifying one way and only Geneva testifying the other—created no appreciable cognitive dissonance among the jurors. Shortly after the verdict was read and the court was dismissed, they all swirled around Geneva for autographs. The jury foreman, a retired postal employee, expressed their sentiments best: "We felt all along, guilty or innocent, she was innocent."

And what did Geneva gain from all this? The reports in the popular press kept referring to a "$10-million-dollar settlement." If you believe that, I have some desert property I'd like to interest you in. In the bright light of day, Geneva walked away with the remainder of her year's salary: $1.6 million American dollars . . . about $500,000 less than Polonia had offered her to settle out of court weeks before the trial began. The "$10 million" was Geneva's lawyer's projection of what her profits might be if the show were as profitable in syndication as *I Love Lucy.*

While the jury believed Geneva, no one else in Hollywood did. A letter to the editor in the Sunday Calendar section of the *Los Angeles Times* raised the question, Will Geneva Holloway ever work again? A naive question. Celebrity is a scarce commodity, and commodities tend not to be penalized. No one stopped using oil because of the mess it had made of Prince William Sound. The fact that Geneva would soon work again was no surprise. The surprise lay in who hired her: Two days after the trial, the Continental Broadcasting Network announced that Geneva Holloway would star in a major movie of the week, with production slated to begin immediately.

When Geneva walked off *All Rise,* Joe Danko was widely quoted as saying, "As a career move, this will rank with McLean Stevenson's departure from *M\*A\*S\*H*" and "If Geneva calls me, I'll give her directions to Pernell Roberts' house." But that was then and this was now. As the trial began, Joe looked closely at the intense press coverage that positioned Geneva Holloway as an endearing victim. He quickly understood that her TV-Q—the systematic determination of how likable and well known any given television performer is at any given moment—was likely to rise after the trial. By offering Geneva a movie of the week, he could capitalize on her new level of fame. Geneva, who saw a job offer by CBN as a further public vindication, accepted without undue reflection. And thus Joe Danko exacted a revenge of a sort: the project meant that Geneva would be spending over six weeks in the arid wastes of Djibouti.

* * *

Anyone with an interest in stories about horrible tragedies afflicting beautiful and famous people is already aware of what happened to Geneva Holloway on that trip to North Africa. The news, when it was finally made known, could not have been more widely circulated. Certainly, no one would have wished it upon her, except perhaps for Avery Schine. But what has generally been reported is not, in fact, what actually happened. What follows is the true account, relayed to me over several Kir Royales at the bar of the Bel Air Hotel by Francis Rooney, the unit publicist, who was there to see it all.

The CBN movie, *The Ordeal of Maggie Dolan,* was "based," as they like to say, on a true story. It told of a young American woman who followed her husband, a geologist, to an unnamed Gulf state, where he had been hired to do something with or about uranium. Maggie adjusts to life in this Gulf state's small European community until her husband mysteriously disappears. It's then up to her, in a society where women are severely restricted, to find him. It's the sort of thing you usually get Marlo Thomas to do. It's also the sort of thing you usually film in the amply arid wastes of California or Nevada.

*The Ordeal of Maggie Dolan* was a coproduction between Landmark Films, a smallish movie-of-the-week outfit in Burbank with Denver shopping mall money behind it, and Merrile et Cie, a French production company linked to Channel Cinq. The French connection explains why Djibouti, a French protectorate, was chosen over California or Nevada. Also, there are certain economies inherent in shooting a "cast of thousands" movie in a country where the per capita income is four hundred dollars a year.

The film crew, largely French, was efficient and professional, according to Francis Rooney. The director, David Mace, who fancied himself in the John Huston mold, thrived on the technical challenges the location presented. He looked upon actors as the things that got in the way of his having fun with the lighting and tracking shots and explosives. As a result, he did not have the one, simple qualification Geneva Holloway required of a director: that he continuously remind her that she is the most beautiful, talented, and desirable actress that the human mind, in its present state of evolution, could conjure.

To add to her burden, Geneva was forced to endure what she felt were unlivable conditions: pervasive sand, strange food, tentative plumbing, intimidating insects, and poor people. As shooting progressed, Geneva's mood deteriorated. But this proved not to be a disadvantage to the film; Geneva's downward spiral corresponded with the deterioration of Maggie Dolan in the script. *The Ordeal of Maggie Dolan* did not suffer; Emil Novak did.

In the flurry of negotiations, Geneva was unable to attach Emil to this project as any sort of a producer. The best she could do for him in the contract was an airplane ticket and a modest per diem. With no official production duties to avoid, Emil was at a loss. He had himself listed on the staff sheet as Geneva's manager. This put him a few ranks above his obvious and true title, "star's boyfriend," and made him feel a little better about such duties as lugging around the Banana Republic flight bag in which Geneva kept her bottled water and vitamins and herbal tea. It did not, however, ease his burdens back in the privacy of their hotel room, where Geneva Holloway's manager found his client increasingly unmanageable.

In my observation, Geneva had one overriding ambition in life: to find someone to blame. Her motto was, I'm unhappy, and it's your fault. The days on *All Rise* were ideal for this disposition, because they were rich with enemies: producers, writers, production company executives. Geneva's bond with Emil Novak strengthened and grew over those months in direct relation to the forces pitted against her. The more people there were to blame, the more room there was in her life for someone who could help her blame them. But this problem-ridden shoot in the North African desert offered no satisfying target for her venom. The two producers were almost annoying in their efforts to make Geneva comfortable within the context of these difficult conditions. They had brought along a supply of gifts to dole out to her once or twice a week: a sterling silver Elsa Paretti heart from Tiffany's, a Lalique porcupine, a carriage clock inscribed TO GENEVA, WORKING WITH YOU IS A DREAM, NELS AND R. J., DJIBOUTI, AUG. '90. The director, David Mace, the most likely object of Geneva's wrath, proved all too accommodating when Geneva complained about specifics. Because she could not voice her true objection—that David did not properly adore her—Geneva could not hold him accountable.

Emil Novak was the only one left to blame. And blamed he was, for the sand, for the heat, for the ugliness of the natives, for the rain, for the lack of rain. Emil submitted to Geneva's attacks, according to Francis Rooney, but there was always in his eyes the hurt look of a dog that doesn't understand why it's being beaten.

As the production wound down, so did Geneva's limited stores of goodwill. She refused to come out of her trailer for a crowd scene one afternoon. She denounced her Djibouti coworkers as "filthy and smelly, and I can't stand those stupid grins because of their horrible teeth, and look at their faces. For Christ's sake, they look like fucking monkeys." Later that evening, at a banquet arranged by local businessmen and government officials as an expression of thanks for the commerce the production had brought their way, Geneva was called upon by her Djibouti hosts to say a few words—a singular honor for a woman in an Islamic culture. Geneva rose, all smiles and modest blushes, clearly moved. Her eyes brimmed with gratitude.

"I'm afraid I don't know what to say," she said.

Francis Rooney leaned in her direction and suggested, not in a whisper, "Geneva, why don't you mention a few of the things you were telling us in your trailer this afternoon?"

Shortly after the film crew had arrived in North Africa, Iraq invaded Kuwait, which proved to be of no particular moment in Djibouti. In the final days of the shoot, however, the United States sent its first forces to Saudi Arabia. The reports of rioting in Arab capitals that she listened to on her shortwave radio put Geneva on edge. Diverting the flow of history in her own direction, she suddenly began to see herself as the probable focus of fundamentalist conspiracies, although the Muslims she came into contact with continued to display the utmost kindness and respect toward her. An unlikely incident confirmed her worst fears, however. On a stroll away from the location set one lunch hour, as Geneva was offering Emil Novak elaborately detailed proof that he was nothing more than a worthless piece of zoo meat, they were approached by a young man in paramilitary garb. Something about Geneva agitated him; he pointed at her and spoke harshly in Arabic. As Emil stepped forward as a buffer, the young man slipped around him and wrenched Geneva's Banana Republic flight bag from her shoulder. He threw it into the pathetic little stream nearby, screaming, *"Mish bah-hib! Mish bah-hib!"* (which Geneva took to mean, "Death to the American bitch," but in fact meant "I don't like it.") Then the young man ran off down the road.

What had incensed the youth was the stylized red eagle embroidered on the flap of the bag. In fact, the Banana Republic, in its point-of-sale display, had correctly described the product as an Israeli paratrooper's flight bag. The reaction of this politically fervent young man, in a country where mention of the word "Israel" was forbidden, was hardly astonishing. But Geneva took the incident far more personally. After Emil had retrieved the bag from the mucky stream, she announced that they were leaving the country the next day.

The producers implored Geneva to stay on at least two days more; they needed that much time to finish a key scene of Geneva searching through the bazaar, which could not be duplicated back in the States. Reluctantly, Geneva consented, but she ordered Emil to have the luggage packed and ready, and she carried her passport with her on the set.

Shortly after Emil finished the packing, he collapsed with a fever. He was unable to join Geneva at the shoot, which heightened her sense of unease. Emil had been laid low by a parasitic illness called bilharzia, brought on by his little dip in the stream to retrieve Geneva's flight bag. Had he been aware of bilharzia, Emil would have plunged into dirty water much sooner; for the first time in forty days, as he lay in the rickety hotel bed, he was free from Geneva's continuous hectoring. In contrast, he found the debilitating fever and rat tooth pain in the intestines relaxing.

It then fell to Francis Rooney to secure the airplane tickets and in general act as Geneva's caddy. Given the paucity of international flights out of Djibouti, Rooney chose a short hop down to friendly Nairobi, where they could catch their breath and then book a flight back to the United States via London. This was a sensible plan, and if Geneva had not caused a disturbance at the Djibouti airport, the world would never have known she left the production early. (Sharp-eyed cineastes, of course, might note that in the final scene of *The Ordeal of Maggie Dolan,* the Maggie who rushes forward and embraces her husband as he steps off the bus is, in fact, a diminutive Arab male in a blond wig.)

It's hard to know why Geneva did what she did at the airport. Certainly, her nerves were frayed. And certainly, she felt foolish to have her protector, Emil Novak, being rolled along beside her on an upright dolly, pasty and wet-eyed. But that Geneva Holloway, at a moment when she was in fear for her life, should slip into a torrent of insults at a routine frustration, risking arrest, is a tribute to the force of habit.

The focus of Geneva's animus was a well-spoken Air Djibouti clerk whose duty it was to inform Geneva that each of the three travelers in her party was required to pay an exit tax of six thousand francs. Coming as this did to a total of seventy-five dollars, it should have presented no hardship to a television star who had just won a handsome court settlement. But Geneva had already cashed out most of her francs for Kenya shillings, and something about the clerk's good manners and command of English irked her. In addition, she was convinced that the whole thing was thievery, an invention of the clerk's.

"I won't pay," said Geneva.

"But, madam, you must pay. It is a tax," said the clerk, almost hurt by her adamance.

"You're trying to gouge me. The price of a ticket is the price of a ticket. I'll have our State Department investigate your airline."

"But madam, it is not the airline."

"Bullshit!" said Geneva. The clerk's jaw dropped and his eyes turned steely at this vulgarity. "I'm not paying."

"Then, madam, you cannot leave the country."

Francis Rooney, who was supporting the dolly that held Emil Novak, said, "Emil wants to say something." Emil was holding up his hand.

Geneva, annoyed, moved close to Emil, who whispered to her like a pope saying his last words. "Pay it."

"Oh, right," said Geneva. "You're such a goddamn help."

"Madam, you must guard your speech," said the clerk.

"Get me a responsible official of this airline," said Geneva. "I'm going to blow the whistle on you."

"It is not an airline matter," said the clerk. "It is a tax. You must pay to exit the country. It is for the Republic of Djibouti."

"Well," said Geneva, "the Republic of Djibouti can suck my dick!"

This was not the best thing to yell at a pious Muslim in a position of some authority. The clerk took a breath. "Madam, I must report you," he said, and walked away from his station.

This led to a certain amount of speculation between Geneva and Francis Rooney as to what might be in store for them. Rooney, partly out of concern but partly for the sheer joy of it, reminded Geneva that they were in a culture where profanity and obscenity were often punished by public whipping.

"But we're Americans," said Geneva, suddenly including her partners in her crime.

"I don't think they especially care," said Rooney.

He suggested they leave the scene. Geneva led the way, struggling with all the carry-on luggage that was not sharing space with

Emil on the upright dolly. She clattered down the concourse and around the corner of the café, where they saw a flight on a carrier called Al-Yemeda boarding at an out-of-the-way gate. Rooney inquired and found that it was a flight to Aden, the capital of South Yemen, a short hop over the lower tip of the Red Sea. Passage could be booked. Rooney huddled with Geneva, and they decided to get on the flight and then work their way down to Nairobi from Aden later. Rooney purchased the tickets, and when the clerk assessed the exit tax, he turned to Geneva and asked, "What do you think? Should I pay it?" Rooney unstrapped Emil from the dolly and then supported him onto the tarmac and up the steps of the plane. Geneva followed, banging the carry-on luggage against the rails of the stairs. And so, without undue formality, the three found themselves on a forty-five minute flight from the frying pan into the fire.

The People's Democratic Republic of Yemen embraced the three Americans with all the enthusiasm and hospitality you might expect from the only Marxist-Muslim police state in the world. They were granted transit visas of seventy-two hours and required to purchase their tickets to Nairobi (including the departure tax of 1,450 Yemeni dinars) before they left the airport. They were then escorted by jeep to the 26 September Hotel, named, Rooney speculated, for the day each autumn when the sheets are changed. The young man who dropped them there, a representative of Felix Arabia Tourist, the official state tourist office, alerted them that they must not leave the hotel except under his escort.

Geneva ordered up an English-speaking doctor who suggested more of the medicine Emil had been given in Djibouti, and informed them that a prescription wasn't required in the local pharmacies. An aged houseboy, responding to a call for refreshments, brought up a tray of sweetened bread, ginger-flavored mocha coffee, and bottles of Canada Dry club soda. He then irritated Geneva by fussing about the room, tidying up and smiling in her direction. His missing teeth were not points in his favor. Finally, Geneva told him to leave. He stunned her by bowing gracefully and saying,

*"Buona fortuna, e buona mangere a tutti."* When the old man left, the doctor explained that many Italians had immigrated to Yemen from Ethiopia after World War II. The old man was showing off. Older people often assumed all non-Arabs spoke Italian. The doctor suggested that Emil rest at least another day before he was put on an airplane.

The following day, Geneva and Rooney took a tour of the various little cities that make up Aden, while Emil was left alone in his misery back at the hotel. Rooney described Geneva's tourist mode as "aggressive." She made borderline comments throughout the day, testing the solemn-faced Felix Arabia guide. "Is it true that it's illegal to say the word 'Israel' in this country?" she would ask, or "Now, do all those women wear those robes for religious reasons, or is it because their tits are sagging?"

"Geneva," Rooney told her at one point, "if we're arrested because of something you say, I'm going to testify against you."

"Fine," said Geneva. And then, as they passed a café where a delivery was being made, she asked the guide, "Tell me, do the people of Aden worship Canada Dry club soda? Is it a sacred object? I've never seen so much of it in my life."

"Very popular when the men chew gat," said the guide. "They chew gat and drink the Canada Dry club soda."

"And what does gat do?" asked Geneva.

"It makes you very pleased," said the guide.

"Something like coca leaves, I think," said Rooney.

Geneva leaned over to the guide to be heard more clearly. "I'm very glad you have gat," she said. "I'd hate to think that people had to live in this shithole without being loaded."

"Geneva, I disassociate myself from you," said Rooney.

"Fine," said Geneva. "Live in fear."

Back at the hotel, Rooney made an excuse to rush up to his room, while Geneva stayed in the lobby to register a series of complaints to the manager, who had been unavailable earlier in the day. Then Geneva climbed the stairs to her room, exhausted, feeling the dust of the day in her nostrils, disgusted by the prospect of opening a door to the ailing Emil Novak, whom she had no inclination to nurse. As she started down the passageway of her floor, she saw the aged, gap-toothed houseboy swing out of her room and close the door rather deftly. He started down the hall in the opposite direction at almost a sprint. "Hey!" Geneva called after him, but either he did not hear her or chose to ignore her. Geneva entered the room, suspicious. Emil lay planked out on the bed like Ophelia floating.

"What did that waiter want?" asked Geneva.

"Nnnnh," said Emil.

Geneva checked the position of her Bottega Veneta overnight case. It seemed not to have been moved. But the hasp was un-snapped. Geneva could not remember if she had left it that way or not. She opened it and sent her hand carefully to the bottom, feeling beneath the layers of silky underthings, until she came to the gray flannel sack in which she kept her eighteen-thousand-dollar gold-and-diamond Oyster Rolex. The sack was empty.

If there is any resource abundant in a police state, it is police. After Geneva rushed downstairs and caused a scene, five or six of them were swarming through the lobby in no time. They were not there at the invitation of the hotel manager; he had been confused by Geneva's raving. ("My watch has been stolen," she shrieked at him, pointing to her bare wrist. "My watch! My watch!" "Ah, yes, madam," said the manager. "It is now five-thirty. Soon, time for prayers.") Instead, the police had been summoned by the dour young Felix Arabia guide, who seemed to live in the lobby. He ushered them in and served as translator. Geneva was forth-right in her charges, finding no use at all for wishy-washy phrases like "I think" or "I suspect." And soon the old waiter was roused from a gat-smoking session, and all the interested parties were assembled before a Qadi, or religious judge, who handled matters of this sort. Rooney, who had been brought into it by now, said the whole episode was like the last scene of a thirties screwball comedy, where disparate elements are brought into a court yelling and accusing while a comical judge tries to keep order. Except the Qadi was in no sense comical. His visage remained as stern as a poster of the Ayatollah, and when he spoke, it was in thundering Arabian expletives. Geneva repeated her charges, adding in this version that she saw the watch in the old man's hand as he ran down the hall. The old man wailed disconsolately, and in rather a short time, the Qadi barked out his decision in the defendant's disfavor.

"What will they do to him?" Geneva asked the guide on the return to the hotel, almost with a bystander's curiosity.

"He goes to the Al-Mansura prison," said the guide.

"For how long?"

"Perhaps not for long."

"My concern, of course, is for my watch. We'll only be here another day."

"Yes," said the guide. "They will ask him now about the watch at the prison."

Geneva gave Rooney a knowing nod at this, a woman who had come to find some practical value in the seemingly harsh ways of a theocratic police state.

Emil was sitting up in bed when Geneva got back to the room.

"You're a big fucking help," said Geneva. "The waiter stole my Rolex."

"The old guy?" asked Emil in a not very strong or sure voice.

"Yes! He came right in here while you were asleep. I had to go to the police station and everything." Geneva rifled through her makeup bag. "How are you feeling?" she asked without looking at Emil. He had become a disappointment to her.

"A little better, really. He brought me some kind of medicinal tea."

"Who? The waiter?'

"Yeah. He kept popping in to check on me."

"He was waiting for his chance," said Geneva, carefully tracking a line of hot pink lipstick across her upper lip. She was decorating herself purely for her own amusement, having been emphatically discouraged by the guide from wearing makeup in public. "He probably put something in the tea."

She swept a bit of blush across her cheeks, opening her eyes wide, reflexively, as she followed her actions in the mirror.

"Are you well enough to travel tomorrow? Well, whether you are or aren't, we have to leave. I certainly have to leave. Not another day, not another minute. These people deserve their culture. They deserve this filth. I better shut up, the rooms are probably bugged, like Russia. Listen, have you been eating anything? We had this stuff for lunch, I have no idea if it was from an animal or some kind of plant—"

Geneva broke off her speech abruptly and hunched over her makeup bag.

"Oh, my God, this is so embarrassing," she said, almost laughing. She turned toward Emil and displayed the pristine and dazzling Rolex, rocking on her index finger.

Rooney, hoping he had heard the last of Geneva's insistent voice for that day, instead found himself once more accompanying her to the municipal building where they had seen justice served scarcely an hour earlier, escorted, inevitably, by the stern young guide.

Geneva explained, to the very same, fierce Qadi, and to a few uniformed officials that had been summoned, that the watch had been found. She did not apologize as she said this, but instead took on an irritated tone, claiming that the misunderstanding would have never occurred if the old man hadn't been in the room without permission.

A commotion ensued all out of proportion to the rather minor inconvenience she had occasioned, Geneva thought. The officials ranted in Arabic for several seconds.

"There has been a misappropriation of justice," the guide explained.

"Well, come on, he's only been in jail for an hour and a half. I'll give him some money. I'll apologize."

It was at this point that the seriousness of the situation was explained to Geneva. The old man's left hand, in a swift and literal application of the requirements of the Islamic Shi‘a, somewhat rare in the Arab world these days but still practiced in Aden, had been cut off.

Geneva was arrested and remanded to the Al-Mansura prison, where violent revolutionaries and traffic violators were held together without distinction. Francis Rooney searched frantically for some sort of American official who might intervene, but the United States had no relations with the Peoples Democratic Republic of Yemen. He managed to rouse an English-speaking lawyer, who only underscored the hopelessness of the case. He spent the night in a powerless vigil with Emil Novak, who lapsed in and out of sleep.

The next morning at 9:00 A.M., shortly after prayers were observed by the jailers and inmates alike, Geneva Holloway had her left hand severed at the wrist by a regulation scimitar, a smaller version of which is worn ritually by many Yemeni males. The English-speaking doctor who had treated Emil's bilharzia was called on to be in attendance at the official amputation. In traumatic accidents like that, where an artery is severed, a person can bleed to death within minutes unless immediately tended to.

The doctor later told Rooney and Emil—as if he were a surgeon letting the family know how the operation went—that Geneva faced her fate more in disbelief than terror. And when the actual blow fell, quite amazingly, she did not bleed. The doctor explained that in certain rare cases the victim's imagination, through sheer power of will, overrides the blunt facts of physical reality. Geneva's was such a case. She staved off the flow of blood with the force of her personality.

# Chapter

# *20*

### *Epilogue*

■   The producer Sam Zimbalist approached Graham Greene
to revise the last part of the script for *Ben-Hur*.
"You see, Graham," he said, "after the Crucifixion, we feel that
it gets a little anticlimactical."

◆ ◆ ◆

We closed out year three of *All Rise* an authentic hit, with an
average 16.9 rating and a 26 share, with particular demographic
strength among women eighteen to forty-nine (a 31 share). On
any given Monday night, twenty million people settled down to
see us. We were the 13th most watched show on television. Now,
as we begin our fourth season, the ratings are a bit erratic, depending on how attractive the Monday Night Football game we're
up against is. But on the West Coast, where football isn't a factor,
we're doing about a half rating point better than last year.

All of this success is surely heartwarming to the shareholders
of the Denatsu-Amagi Corporation in Tokyo, who have become
the owners of *All Rise*. In the summer of 1990, barely months
after Massillon bailed out Avery Schine, Denatsu-Amagi made an
offer for the combined company that Harry Ward, the Massillon
chairman, described as "generous in the extreme." He got that
right. He, personally, came out of it with about seven hundred

million dollars, plus a company car. Avery Schine was shunted off into his own venture capital company under the Massillon banner. And to the great relief of creative people everywhere, the David Putzman joke is over. Harry Ward kicked him off the lot. David, I rejoice to report, has finally found work appropriate to his talents: I read in last week's trades that he's "prepping" a syndicated game show involving a mouse that goes through a hole to pick out the right answer.

Harry Ward, in need of a new czar to head up the television divisions of both Polonia and Massillon, saw fit to bring in Leo Becker. And so the paprika red face of Mr. Becker can once again be seen puffing through the halls of a major production company, terrorizing ass-kissers and offending all the young women. And Avery Schine and Leo Becker once again have very important parking spaces right next to each other, this time on the Massillon lot over in Burbank. On their rare encounters, it is said, they acknowledge each other like dowagers who each thinks the other is lower on the social scale.

Andre Broz, having run through all of Malcolm Dant's money, is in prison in Nevada for attacking a tennis instructor with a linoleum knife. I understand that as a result of persuasive arguments put forward by his African-American prison mates, he has agreed to stop referring to himself as black. I last saw Malcolm Dant playing an eye-rolling buffoon in a small role in Eddie Murphy's recent film, *Ribs of the Gods,* where Eddie, as Jesus Christ, is sent back to earth to work in a barbeque shop.

Milo Lally has retired from the entertainment industry. His young wife, Ashley, has found success painting oil portraits of family pets in the photorealism style. Milo is "managing" her career. It was his idea that she limit herself to mammals.


I was interviewed by *The Washington Post* recently and asked whether, as a producer and writer, I had felt the effects of Japanese ownership at Massillon-Polonia. I answered that, frankly, I had, quite vividly. In what way? the reporter asked. In the employee store, I replied. The employee store is much better now, under Japanese ownership. Instead of sweatshirts with logos and videos of bad Avery Schine movies, we are offered Denatsu-Amagi CD players and VCRs and stereo television sets and personal computers, all at discounts of up to 40 percent. I recommended to all readers of *The Washington Post* who were being courted by Japanese consumer electronics manufacturers to seriously entertain the offers, if only for the purpose of upgrading their employee stores.

As far as *All Rise* goes, however, I can cite no Japanese influence at all. Our little show sails along unbuffeted by the winds of international trade. We haven't brought up Pearl Harbor a lot in the scripts, I admit. But in a recent episode we had Don Lasker, on his first trip to a sushi bar, ask for a Kirusawa, under the impression that he was ordering a beer. We didn't get any angry phone calls from our Japanese bosses about that. (We didn't get any laughs from the American people, either.)

The show is going very well. There's an easy, satisfying rhythm to it, and we haven't yet come to a point where we have to overreach for new stories. Hannah Cane, that wonder of wonders, that beauty of beauties, was up for a best actress Emmy last year, and lost out to Candice Bergen. Joseph Landry, on the other hand, took the best supporting actor prize. He also costarred in a movie with Mel Gibson which is currently taking in all the discretionary income in the free world. To date, however, he shows no signs of incipient monstrosity.

Neil Stein has notified me that this is to be the last year of our partnership. "I've been carrying you long enough," he said. He's been writing his short stories all along, and getting encouragement from the editors of these literary magazines he thinks so highly of. And last spring *The Antioch Review* accepted one for publication, and that crystalized Neil's thinking. He's going to take a couple of years off and write seriously. He spends idle moments concocting fantasy reviews for the book of stories he hopes to eventually see published: "Breathtaking, heartbreaking. . . full of ironies that inform and touch the heart," he'll say to me, out of the blue.

(Neil's story for *The Antioch Review* is quite good. He based it on something that happened to him when he was—surprise—a young boy. A Jewish kid gets sent to a Catholic boys camp one summer, because it's close to home, and all the kids pick on him because he's Jewish. The next summer, his parents send him to a YMCA camp, and, again, the kids pick on him because he's Jewish. Finally, the following summer, his parents manage to send him to a Jewish camp, far away. And all the kids pick on him. And the kid finally figures it out: he's a schmuck.)

Neil's found out that it's dangerous to tell people in Hollywood that you're quitting the business to write short stories. They tend to be stunned and appalled. If they have any sort of financial stake in you—agents, managers, production executives—they get outright hostile. Our agent was almost violent in his contempt for this idea of writing short stories. Finally, as a joke, Neil told him the real reason he was dropping out of the business was because he has AIDS. "Oh," said the agent. "That makes me feel better."

The remarkable thing about all this to me is Neil's sudden indifference to money. He said that sitting through negotiations for a property settlement with Renata had forced him to see that the thousands of possessions that, up until that moment, he had been terrified of losing, were nothing more than a pile of crap. This is all a little too Zen for my tastes, but Neil says it has freed him up greatly.

Of course, it helps to have a rich girlfriend. Neil and Hannah Cane, the world's most perfect woman, have moved in with each other. This is all very hush-hush at present, to avoid problems of jealousy and resentment over on the set, but will probably become known to the wider world next spring, when Neil officially retires to his atelier.

It's difficult for me to understand Hannah Cane's attraction to my partner. He's lost some weight, but he remains pear-shaped and short. He's very funny, of course, but he's still basically fearful and crisis prone. I'm at a loss to understand his appeal to her. Hannah Cane, I would think, should be attracted to someone like, oh, I don't know—me.

But I'm spoken for. Miranda and I are trying it again. Miranda thinks her new standing in relationship to me has a great deal to do with the success of our reunion. She says her years of independence from me, and her new sense of entitlement to the house I have moved back into, give her a fresh footing psychologically. For my part, I think things are going well because she has the whammy on me. She always did. And you shouldn't break up with a woman who has the whammy on you, because it means you're still in love with her.

Bennett is in the seventh grade now, at Lincoln Junior High in Santa Monica. I've offered to spring for Crossroads or one of the other private schools, but Bennett says he doesn't like "the element" private schools attract. "You get that many upper-middle-class white people in one place, there's no telling what they might do," he says. The kid has turned into a wit, which, to my utter astonishment, makes me look forward to being around him. When he's not at home for dinner, for example, I feel an actual twinge of disappointment.

I sometimes bring up the subject of remarriage to Miranda, and when I do she wrinkles her face as if she's waiting for a fright to pass. "Why tamper with prosperity?" she says. I've told her one of my reasons for formalizing this situation is that it might be nice for the two of us to have a child of our own. A totally new thought for me, believe me. She says we can have a baby without getting married. So I guess for now we maintain things as they are. Neither of us is going anywhere.


After Yemen, Geneva Holloway spent two weeks at a hospital in Munich and then returned to the United States and plunged into deep seclusion. The public's interest in her had ebbed during her absence, and no one gave her much thought. Who knows what torments and agonies of the spirit she endured during her winter of silence? Finally, seven months later, she emerged. I'd like to think it was just a coincidence that she went public with her tragedy three weeks before *The Ordeal of Maggie Dolan* was scheduled to air. I'd like to think that but, knowing Geneva, I'm sure she chose to exploit her personal misfortune for the benefit of her career. And that's not necessarily meant as a rap; there was a certain personal integrity involved in her decision.

I understand that Geneva gave long consideration to never mentioning the incident in Yemen, and going on with her life as if it had never happened. But she came to realize that if you're doing a love scene with some guy, and you don't have a left hand, it's one of the things people tend to notice. So, taking George S. Kaufman's advice, she decided to put a lantern on her flaw.

She went public with a vengeance. She was on Oprah, she was on Donahue, she was on Joan Rivers, she was on *Today,* she was on *Good Morning America,* Barbara Walters interviewed her personally for *20/20.* She was on the cover of *People,* bumping Sandra Dee's comeback story a week. With the help of Mahaffey and Wasserman Public Relations, she positioned herself perfectly. The nation was wrapping itself in glory after Operation Desert Storm. Geneva was put forward as a patriot who had been cruelly mutilated by Muslim fundamentalists simply because she was an American citizen. Geneva's message to the public was, "I've been horribly wronged, but that's all behind me; what I want to do now is help others." She said the purpose of her coming forward after all these months was to raise money for and focus attention on the victims of traumatic amputation. She formed an organization called Single-Handed. She managed to say somewhere in each public appearance, "My only real regret is that I no longer have two hands with which to applaud my fellow performers."

So, now we finally know what the sound of one hand clapping is.

You have to be careful, as a writer, giving an actor a limp or a twitch or some other physical handicap. Even the most talented

among them seem to lose their perspective under such circumstances. I cite, for example, Vanessa Redgrave in the movie *Julia,*
when she enters a restaurant at mid-film and Jane Fonda and the
audience discover for the first time that her character now has a
wooden leg. Giving Ms. Redgrave a wooden leg, it turns out, was
like offering whiskey to a man on the way to his first AA meeting.
Suddenly, *Julia* became a movie about a wooden leg. But Geneva
Holloway handled her prosthetic hand with edifying restraint.
Maybe when something's real, it makes a difference. And she
always wore matching gloves of a color that complemented her
ensemble, which seemed to be a way of acknowledging her handicap without attracting undue attention to it.

At Geneva's side through all her interviews was Dr. Arthur E.
Sherman, an orthopedic surgeon of substantial independent means,
whose role was to testify to Geneva's incredible bravery throughout her ordeal, and to look at her with adoring eyes when he wasn't
so testifying. Geneva had dropped Emil Novak as soon as they
got to Munich. (Emil's been going around town trying to stir up
interest in himself as a martial arts movie hero along the lines of
Steven Seagal or Jean-Claude Van Damme.)

Geneva told the story of what happened to her forthrightly and
well during her interviews, moving listeners to tears by the very
lack of drama and tears in her telling. She told it over and over,
and always to great effect. And each time she told it, she lied. In
Geneva's version, she discovers her Rolex missing and reports it
to the hotel manager. Only later, when the watch was found, she
now says, did she realize that someone had been arrested. She
does not say she falsely accused an old man and altered the course
of his few remaining years. Perhaps there is no place in her memory for that deed. Perhaps, considering the consequence she has
brought upon herself, she should be allowed to tell the story however she wants. The war is over, after all; let the victors write
the history.

\*    \*    \*

A month ago, as we were gearing up for production of our fourth season of *All Rise,* Neil and I took time for a nice lunch at the Columbia Bar and Grill. On the way out of the restaurant, we waved to Norman Lear, who was having lunch with one of his daughters. We waved to Gary Cosay, the big writers' agent, who I'm sure would love to have us as clients. We waved to Frank Price, who had just been bought out of the presidency of Columbia Pictures. We waved to Bea Arthur, of *The Golden Girls,* who was having lunch with Rod Parker and Hal Cooper, the producer and director who worked with her on *Maude.* Neil excused himself to stop in the men's room, and I went out to the reception area where a few clusters of people were waiting for tables. As I made my way through the crowd, the door opened and Geneva Holloway entered, backlit by the brilliant afternoon light, as if she were appearing in a nimbus. Her hair, still very blond, was growing long again. She was wearing her trademark white, but in a tailored suit with a jacket that ended at the waist. She wore white gloves on both hands. She saw me—far better than I was able to see her, given the advantage of the light—and we both stopped and took each other in. And then she threw out her arms and advanced on me with a determined gait.

I heard an old man tell a story once: He was a student in Germany in the 1930s, an ardent anti-Nazi. But when Hitler spoke in his town, his school was ordered to make an appearance. And this man said that such was the power of ritual that, as he stood there among the throngs of enraptured people, he had all he could do to resist throwing his arm into the air and shouting, *"Zeig heil!"*

I appreciate his dilemma. If I were in his place, I think I might have caved in. Because I opened my arms and moved forward to meet Geneva, and we embraced and kissed, and she teared up. And I actually felt sincere as I participated in this reunion. I like to think that Geneva's hideous misfortune prompted my reaction. But I'm afraid that even if Geneva were not standing before me with a tragic deficit in one limb, I would have still succumbed to her embrace, denying, or at least putting aside, my conscious, true, waking sentiments in order to put on this big display of affection in the lobby of the Columbia Bar and Grill. It was not a pleasant thing to discover after all these years that deep inside me there is a star-fucking monster yearning to get out.

Geneva Holloway and the very well-to-do Dr. Arthur E. Sherman are engaged to be married. The doctor has given her a diamond the size of a cough drop; she doesn't want to wear it on her prosthetic left hand, and she feels it would be bad luck to wear it on her right hand, so she wears it on a platinum chain around her neck. Geneva has a book coming out in time for Christmas. She coauthored it with Dr. Sherman (and, of course, a third party, who actually did all the writing). It's an autobiography, focusing on her ordeal in Yemen and her subsequent struggles. It's called *On the Other Hand.*

Geneva's career has cooled. I suppose producers are made uncomfortable by her handicap; things might be quiet for her for a few years, until it's time to do *The Geneva Holloway Story.* Dr. Sherman is rich and respected and, being a doctor, not about to jump through hoops for anybody. So I was thinking just last night that maybe Geneva Holloway has already caused all the serious damage it was allotted to her to cause in this lifetime. There are no new victims stepping forward, I thought. But then I read in *Variety* this morning that she's pregnant.

Over the past year, I have come to discover my real pleasure in life: doing work I enjoy, with people who are generally decent. Apparently, this is what I have been after all these years. The lure of very big money is not so important anymore; it's what you get up every day and do, and the people with whom you do it, that's important. If you manage to put enough good days together, then that adds up to a happy life. This is my conviction now, my philosophy, and I hope never to swerve from it. However, if several millions were to come my way, I would have to bow before the superior intelligence of the universe. The prospect is not totally unlikely. If we get picked up for our fifth year next season, we'll have enough shows to sell into syndication, where vast treasures, theoretically, await us. As our agent says, "They can't hide that much money."

Of course they can.